# B&Bers Beh

## at a Devon seas

OCTOBER HOUSE BOOKS

Illustration © John Gillo
River at Kingswear
www.johngillo-gallery.co.uk

B&Bers Behaving Madly at a Devon Seaside Guesthouse can be read as a standalone novel or as the sequel to Bedlam & Breakfast at a Devon Seaside Guesthouse.

ISBN: 9781653201433

# Chapter 1

A BLUE ESTATE CAR PULLED UP across the road and a man in a dark suit jumped out. He glanced furtively up and down the street, before hotfooting it round to the back of the car where he dragged a step ladder from the boot. After placing it in a variety of locations – each time looking up at the cottage wall – he perched it by the front door. Rubbing his hands together, he stepped back to gaze at the cottage until, as if struck by inspiration, he lifted one finger in the air and shot back to the car to pull out a long strip of board.

I chuckled to myself and settled to watch the real-life Mr Bean. That is, until water splashed my feet. I'd been so absorbed in the man opposite, I'd forgotten I held a now-empty watering can. Sodden soil dripped from the edge of the hanging basket, splatting onto the paving slabs below. At least I wouldn't need to water the winter-flowering pansies for a few days now, especially since rain was forecast for tomorrow.

The man climbed gingerly up the step ladder, clutching a board in one hand, a screwdriver clamped between his teeth. Even from where I stood, I could tell he'd sited the step ladder too close to the cottage, where stubby clumps of grass broke through the uneven tarmac. Just then a huge fish-quay lorry lumbered past, obscuring my view. It trundled away, leaving me with the stench of diesel fumes. The man and his ladder had vanished.

I headed across the road to find him sprawled across the pavement, the step ladder embedded in the door of his car.

"Are you okay?"

Grimacing, he shifted around and brushed the knees of his trousers. "Not really."

He took my extended hand, almost pulling me over as he got to his feet. Like a child he stared at his grazed palms, wincing as he brushed away the grit. "I don't think I'm cut out for this."

"New job?"

Nodding, he picked a twig from his suit sleeve. "Started yesterday."

He had my sympathy. It wasn't long since I'd felt out of my depth after we'd moved several hundred miles, leaving our homes and jobs to run a guesthouse in Torringham. My husband, Jason, and I had survived our first season, but it had been more challenging than I had imagined, especially from the end of April to the start of October when we didn't have a day off. Even now, my stomach churned at the thought of another season but, at least this year, Jason and I knew what we were letting ourselves in for and, more importantly, we would support each other when the going got tough. Which it would.

"It'll get better," I told him. "Why don't I hold the ladder for you."

He smiled, until he spotted the ladder planted in the car door. "I had to borrow the boss's car as the ladder wouldn't fit in mine. I'm not looking forward to explaining this."

Poor man. Jason and I had days where things went from bad to worse but the only people who could sack us were ourselves. Technically, the bank manager could if we got into financial trouble, but I prayed that wouldn't happen.

With the step ladder in position, I kept it steady while he

4

scrambled up. When I handed him the rectangle of board, I spotted the word *Let*. The cottage had been empty for as long as we'd lived here. Last September a homeless man had tried to make it his home but he'd been injured breaking in. Shona, who ran the B&B adjoining ours, and I had heard his cries and we'd called for help. The flaking paintwork on the front door and the heavy knocker shaped like a dog hadn't changed from last year. Even the net curtains were the same grubby grey. I didn't envy the new occupants, unless the house was being spruced up before they moved in.

"It's been rented? Who to?"

He shrugged. "I don't know."

He couldn't be the letting agent, or else he'd know. But why would he wear a suit to install signs? As he stretched upwards, the hem of his trousers lifted to reveal a pair of Spiderman socks. What a shame he didn't have his hero's ability to cling to walls. That would have come in handy earlier.

I hid my smile. "So, they don't tell the sign man trade secrets?"

Flushing, he turned away, biting his lip while he positioned the strip of board over the *To Let* on the sign. He took an age. Would he be offended if I offered to do it myself? As I went to speak, the board slipped and a screw fell to the pavement, rolling off the kerb.

"Sorry!" he called.

"I'll get it if you promise not to fall off when I let go."

I picked up the screw from the gutter and handed it to him. "Do you want me to have a go?"

"I've got it under control now."

He kept his word, gritting his teeth as he tightened the screws.

When he clambered down, he said, "Look, I am the lettings agent. I just don't know if I'm allowed to say. Client confidentiality and all that." Then he caught sight of the car door. "Or I was the lettings agent. Who knows what I'll be tomorrow?"

◆

A few days later, as I headed out for milk, Shona opened one of Jetsam Cottage B&B's upstairs window and leaned out. The net curtain perched on top of her spiky hair like a bride's veil. Not that I could ever imagine Shona being married, no matter what Kim wanted.

"Hold on!" she shouted and disappeared.

I tilted my umbrella to protect my back from the stair-rod rain and wandered across the drive to her front door. Gravel crunched beneath my feet and lumps of brown moss littered the ground by her doorstep. We had the same by our porch. The birds must be dropping moss from the roof as they collected it for their nests. Like them, I'd been tricked by the recent spell of sunshine. They didn't call it a fool's spring for nothing. A gust of wind lifted the umbrella and rain spattered my face. I swiped my eye with my sleeve. Roll on summer. At least then it would be warm rain.

Red-faced and panting, Shona opened the door and ushered me inside. "Gotta minute? I'd ask your Jason but I saw him go out."

"I'm just off to get milk."

"I'll give you some if you help me."

Contra-deals never worked in my favour when it came to Shona. I'd learned the hard way to check what I was signing up to before going ahead.

"What do you need doing?"

"Just moving a wardrobe to the other side of the room. Kim's out and I can't get it to budge on my own."

"She knows you're doing it though?"

Shona shrugged. "Don't worry. When it's done, she'll love it." Ignoring my sigh, she shot back up the stairs.

I followed the sound of her voice and found her standing in a large bedroom on the second floor. She and Kim had shown me this room when we'd been given the obligatory tour of their B&B not long after we'd moved in. It was good for Torringham B&Bers to see each other's properties as, when we were full, we could offer recommendations to people we couldn't accommodate. It also proved a useful way to snaffle ideas from each other. Jetsam Cottage now featured minifridges in its guest rooms after we'd put them in ours, while we had a bowl of sweets for guests in the reception area. Saying that, I liked to have a few differences, no matter how small, so we didn't tell anyone that we'd also put fresh milk in the fridges and jars of sweets on the trays, alongside the usual biscuits.

Shona had moved everything but the bulky furniture out of the room. Four imprints on the carpet near the door – and a strip of dust between the carpet and the skirting board – showed she'd already shifted the chest of drawers to the other side. I had a feeling that Kim wouldn't be happy.

"Where are you putting the wardrobe?"

"Over there." She pointed to the other corner.

"Won't it make it a bit tight to get around the bed?"

"Not if we turn it so it's against the end wall."

Taking it in turns to tug at the corners, we manoeuvred the wardrobe away from the wall. With each judder the coat hangers clattered inside and the wardrobe began to wobble as if the MDF backing would come away. Worried it might concertina back to its original flatpack form, we took more care. Puce with effort, Shona grimaced as she heaved her corner an inch or so, pausing while I shoved my end to bring it in line with hers. My neck ached and we'd moved it all of three feet.

Shona thumped the wardrobe panel. "Flipping Nora!"

"What?"

"Can't you see it?"

My heart sank. Was that really a line of yellow daisies beside the sleek silver paper that lined the rest of the feature wall? Whoever had wallpapered had gone to the effort of putting a strip of silver above the wardrobe, so the flowers were well hidden.

"Who put flowery wallpaper there?"

"An absolute idiot, that's who." Shona threw herself on the bed, chin in her palms, elbows digging into her jeans. "I told her not to let him do it, but would she listen? Oh no!" She put on a squeaky chipmunk voice. "Jeremy would be good at it. He did Aunty Martha's and Betty's too."

Whoever she mimicked, it didn't sound like Kim, thank goodness. I didn't want to be there when Shona confronted whoever had recommended Jeremy.

She fell into a morose silence, her fingers pressed into her cheeks so they bulged beneath her eyes.

"Shall we put it back?"

Shona sighed and stood up. "We've not got much choice, have we?"

Once we'd returned the room to how it had been that morning, we headed downstairs. A door on the first floor stood wedged open, the room made up for guests by the look of the pristine bedding, hoover lines on the floor and the tea tray with its cups, biscuits and jar of sweets. Set out exactly as we did next door. Shona had been spying on our website. I chuckled. No flies on her.

As I followed her through to her kitchen to get the promised milk, I asked, "So will you tell Kim about the wallpaper?"

"What would I say? 'Kim, you know your delightful brother swore he'd only need two rolls to do that wall, even when matching the pattern, and then he crowed about how he'd managed it? Well, he did that all right. Just with an old remnant he must have found in our junk cupboard.'" She handed me the milk then slammed the fridge door, making the bottles chink inside. "Worse, we'd stripped it off our room cos Kim couldn't stand the yellow wallpaper anymore. Talk about adding insult to injury that he picked that one. Bet he thought we'd never move the wardrobe." Her eyes lit up and a devious grin spread across her face. "He's coming to stay soon. It'll be payback time."

Even though I'd wasted the best part of an hour, leaving the room as we'd found it was a bonus, especially if Kim hadn't approved the changes. It was safer not to ask about Shona's plans for Jeremy too.

"I'd better go. Jason should be back with the washing machine part and he might need my help."

Shona sighed. "Kim'll be back soon. She'll wonder what I've

been doing all day."

We wandered through to the hallway, where I paused by the Buddha statue draped in trails of fake ivy from the pot above. "Tell her I popped round for a drink. It's not far from the truth."

Giving me a tight-lipped smile, she opened the door, squinting as the sun escaped from behind a grey cloud. The sound of car tyres on wet tarmac scoured the air and droplets from the earlier shower sparkled on the bonnet of Shona's car.

Her expression hardened. "You are kidding me!"

I followed her gaze, expecting to see Kim heading across the drive. Instead, a familiar blue car sat across the road by the cottage. Beside it, the lettings agent I'd helped a few days before stood chatting to an older woman, while a younger couple leaned against the wall puffing on cigarettes. Her children? The girl tossed her cigarette onto the pavement and ground it beneath her boot.

As the lettings agent dropped a bunch of keys into the older woman's outstretched palm, I turned to Shona.

"Who are they?"

Shona's eyes narrowed. "Trouble."

# Chapter 2

SHONA'S WARNING RANG IN MY HEAD each time I thought about our new neighbours. I hadn't spotted them since they'd arrived a week ago. Not that I'd become a curtain twitcher, but I would have expected to see them coming or going, or to bump into them in the town. But the cottage seemed as empty now as when it had been unoccupied. The grime-covered nets hung forlornly in the windows, hiding whatever lay behind.

As I tossed a bag of rubbish into the bin, the phone shrilled from the guesthouse. I hurried inside, stepping over a pyramid of paint pots and a heap of dust sheets, pausing when I spotted the 'Withheld number' on the screen. Recently, we'd been plagued by scam calls from the electricity board or Microsoft technical support calling to save me from a virus. Thanks to Jason changing our phone set-up we were slowly blocking them but, like spores, new ones filled the space. I couldn't risk not answering though. The last time I'd ignored a withheld number it turned out to be the doctor returning Jason's call.

Sighing, I picked up the phone. "Flotsam Guesthouse, good afternoon."

When no one spoke, I added silent callers to the list of things that annoyed me. I went to hang up, but stopped when a feeble voice said, "Hello, hello? Is that the guesthouse? It's me. I need to book a room for next week. I'll be there at noon on Wednesday as I'm coming on the train."

From upstairs came the sound of hammering. Jason must be

putting the floorboards back, which meant the plumber had completed the pipework.

"Sorry but we're closed for renovations." I picked a speck of white paint from my fingernail.

"It's just the one night."

"I'm afraid it's not possible." I had to raise my voice above the sound of Jason thumping and banging upstairs. Surely, she must be able to hear the din.

"It's for my friend's funeral. But… but…"

Silence rang down the line and it took all my willpower not to fill it. What would I say? When the woman found her voice, it quivered as if she was about to burst into tears.

"I always stay with you when I'm down there. At a time like this it would be nice to be somewhere I know, and the wake is at the church hall across...." Trailing off, she blew her nose. "I won't be any bother."

My mouth curled into a 'no' but the word wouldn't come. The poor woman was going to her friend's funeral and wanted to be in familiar surroundings. Our redecoration work in the hall, stairs and landing would be finished by the time she arrived next week. While it would be inconvenient, and Jason would moan – who could blame him? – my wall of objection crumbled. There was no chance of me becoming a doctor's receptionist.

"It'll be noisy because we're working on the place. But if it's just the one night."

She brightened. "Yes, dearie."

"It'll be forty-eight pounds at low-season rates. I don't think you stayed with us last year, so you might not know that we've taken over the guesthouse from Maureen and Jim."

"Jim and Maureen, you say?" She hesitated. "No, I don't know them. The last time I came Brenda and Keith were in charge."

"But you said…" My mouth clamped tight while I replayed our telephone conversation. She hadn't said she was a regular, just that she stayed here whenever she was in Torringham. I scratched my head. One of the other guesthouse owners knew the people who had sold to Maureen and Jim and they hadn't been called Brenda and Keith.

"When did you say you stayed here last?" I asked her.

"Now dear, that's a question and a half. Well, Brenda and Keith were retiring and… I remember now! It was the year Margaret Thatcher got forced out. My friend and I admired her so. That's it. Now what year was that? Nineteen eighty-, no, nineteen ninety one or two. Or was it earlier?"

There was no need to lead me through that period. I'd been alive then too.

I gritted my teeth and swore under my breath. Why hadn't I asked more questions before agreeing to let her stay? Now I'd need to open a room, with all the work and cost of bed linen, towels and breakfast for a single occupancy, one-night stay – all because I felt sorry for someone who'd last stayed here a quarter of a century ago.

The location would be the only thing she'd find familiar. I'd seen the old fire plans for the house, which every guesthouse once needed. Back then she would have had to queue with the other guests for one of the public bathrooms, while each room now had its own ensuite. Not only that, but we'd also painted every surface and replaced all the carpets, the beds, furnishings and furniture.

And what about her friend? How come they hadn't seen each other in all that time? Something warned me not to ask. It might involve a very long conversation.

"I'll need your card details to hold the room."

"I don't hold with all that new-fangled malarkey, dear. I'm popping a cheque in the post as we speak."

The Torringham branch of our bank had closed the previous year, meaning we now faced a ten-mile trek to the nearest branch. I took a deep breath.

"I'm sorry, but we need your card details to hold the room."

It would be either that or no stay.

♦

Wiping my paint-smeared thumb on a cloth, I stepped back to survey my work. Jason had worried it would look too dark or out-of-keeping for an Edwardian building, but the mushroom-coloured walls complemented the stark white skirting boards and architraves. Ready with a 'told you so' I headed off in search of Jason, until the ring of the doorbell stopped me in my tracks.

The outline through the opaque glass was short like Shona, but this person wore her hair in curls rather than spikes. Tentatively, I opened the door. A lady stood on the doorstep, hunched over, clutching a floral holdall in one hand, her other hand planted against the wall. She wheezed and patted her chest.

"I'm getting a bit old for this malarkey."

The voice was familiar, but not her face. "How can I help you?"

"Mabel Richardson." She held out a trembling hand.

"Oh! But you're coming tomorrow."

She frowned. "It's Tuesday. I said I'd be here today."

Although I was certain she'd said Wednesday, I had no proof. She wasn't on email and didn't have a mobile phone, so I couldn't send a confirmation email or text. I could have written but it seemed pointless, especially since her cheque had arrived the next morning, as she'd promised.

In the hallway a ladder blocked the stairs and tins of paint littered a dust sheet. Thank goodness I'd just finished, but the place stank of paint and the walls weren't dry.

"Come in." I took her bag and ushered her into the day room. "There's been some confusion, but we'll get you sorted."

After fetching a registration form, I jotted down her name and asked her to fill in the rest. She took the pen from me and started to write with looped, jagged letters.

"Give me a minute, please."

While the bed had been made and the ensuite cleaned, I hadn't finished the room. Once I'd replenished the tea tray, I smeared the polish cloth along the sides and headboard. There wasn't time for much else. On the way back downstairs, I shifted the step ladder to one side and dumped the dust sheet and painting materials in our lounge.

Back in the day room, Mabel greeted me with a smile and waved the registration form at me. "I've filled it in."

"Your room is ready if you need to get changed for the funeral."

Her forehead creased but then she waved me away with gnarled fingers. "That's tomorrow, dear. It's Wednesday 22nd February. You're getting your days muddled. It comes with age, you know."

I smiled politely at her little joke – at least, I assumed that's what it was – but my focus remained on the funeral. "That means you're going home tomorrow after the wake?"

She unzipped her holdall and drew out a train ticket. "The train is..." She squinted at the ticket and rummaged in her bag, pulling out a pair of glasses which she popped on. "That's better. Six o'clock tomorrow. Do you think that's all right?"

"What time is the funeral?"

Frowning, she delved back into her bag, dragging out a faded nightdress, a crumpled black skirt and a pair of tights, which she piled on the chair next to her. When she drew out a hairbrush tangled with a pair of nylon knickers, she threw me an embarrassed glance and shoved them back. This time she brought out a purse, which she unclipped before rifling through the bits of paper and cards inside, before finally unzipping the central compartment.

Minutes later, she scratched her head, her fingernails rasping on her skin as she stuttered, "I don't know. I must have left the details at home." Her voice quivered and her eyes glistened. "What will I do? Can you find out for me?"

I patted her hand. Her skin was paper thin. "I'm sure I can find out. What was your friend's name?"

She gazed heavenward. "Oh dear. I'm sure it'll come to me."

# Chapter 3

JASON SLUMPED ON THE SOFA, head back, his arm hanging over the side. The remote control lay where he'd dropped it on the carpet. He let out a gentle snore. I envied him his ability to nod off in seconds. Unlike him, I always thought of another job I had to do within moments of sitting down. At least since he was asleep, he couldn't moan about the hours I'd spent this afternoon calling round Torringham trying to track down Mabel's deceased friend. Finally, I'd found her. Planting the telephone between my shoulder and ear, to allow myself to talk and write at the same time, I slid Mabel's cheque to one side of the coffee table and picked up a pen.

"Are you sure it's the same woman?" I asked the reverend. "I mean she might have got her friend's name wrong. It took a while for us to work it out."

"I knew Grace Trewinnard for many years. Mabel used to join her at church occasionally. Grace was in a car accident... let me think, in the 1990s... and moved away to be looked after by her family but she wanted to be buried here." She sighed. "Like I said, Grace died in 2006. She was buried on Wednesday 20th February, so it looks like that date has stuck in Mabel's mind."

I jotted down the details about where Grace was buried. Perhaps I should take Mabel to the cemetery to visit her friend's grave the next day. But what if it upset her? She'd come all this way to attend her funeral, somehow forgetting that her friend had been dead for over a decade.

The reverend must have sensed my concern. "Look, why don't

I come down there and talk to Mabel?"

"That would be lovely, but she's gone out. I don't know where."

"Do you think... No, scratch that. She made it down to Torringham in one piece, so she'll be fine."

Her words sent shivers down my spine. Last year, we'd had a guest go missing when he got lost driving to the car park across the road and somehow ended up taking a ten-mile detour. The following morning he'd disappeared again, only to be located in another guest's bedroom. I'd suspected dementia then too. But, unlike him, Mabel had made it here without a hitch. Except she wasn't meant to arrive until tomorrow – and a couple of hours ago she'd come to ask me about the guesthouse keys, as she couldn't work out which was which.

"Could you come tomorrow morning?" I asked the reverend. "Or I could bring her to you. I think that it's best someone speaks to her before she gets ready for the funeral."

The sound of pages being flipped filtered down the line. "Let me see. I can make it by eleven. Is that okay?"

"Perfect." As I spoke, the doorbell rang. "I've got to go. See you tomorrow."

Mabel stood on the doorstep, twisting her gloved hands. "Sorry to bother you, dear, but I left my keys in my room."

"Are you sure you didn't take them with you? Remember, you asked me to show you how to open the front door again."

"Then I went back to my room. You watched me go." She chuckled and patted my arm. "It's your age. You'll be like me soon."

She grasped the newel post and, wheezing, she lifted her foot

18

onto the first step. By the time I returned with the keys, she'd reached the third step. Thankfully, we'd hung paintings in the stairwell, which gave me something to look at other than the back of her coat. I resisted the urge to pick what seemed to be pet hairs from the fabric. When she reached the landing, she set off as if someone had wound a key in her back, coming to a halt at the bottom of the next set of stairs, where she resumed her painful ascent. She'd scaled three stairs before I realised we'd gone past her room.

"Sorry Mabel." I tapped her back to get her attention and pointed behind us. "Your room's there."

She glanced in confusion at the door below and shook her head. "No, you've put me in the eaves." Gasping with effort, she made it to the fourth step.

I shot into her room to grab her holdall from the suitcase stand. She hadn't progressed any further but stood bent over, her breath whistling as she muttered to herself. I held out her holdall to show her.

"Your things are here. See, that's your room."

"But..."

Taking her arm, I bore her weight while she shuffled around on the stairs. She followed me down, grumbling. When we stepped inside the room, she glanced around bewildered.

"Are you sure?"

I replaced the bag and pointed to her hairbrush on the windowsill and the keys she'd left on the dressing table.

"How about I put the kettle on and you have a sit down. Did you get something to eat when you were out?"

19

She didn't seem to hear me. Her brow furrowed like a ploughed field while she took in the room and her belongings. Then her gaze tracked to the door and the stairs beyond.

I picked up the kettle. "Tea?"

"Yes, dear. And then I'd like to go to my room for a rest."

After convincing her to settle in one of the chairs – although I couldn't sway her conviction that I'd switched her room – I gave her a cup of tea and went downstairs to make her a sandwich. She probably needed a hot meal but I had a feeling she'd be asleep when I returned and a cheese sandwich could be popped into the minifridge. As I'd suspected, she lay with her head resting on the back of the tub chair, her mouth open. Her expression reminded me of Jason downstairs, except his legs spread-eagled onto the lounge floor, while she huddled almost foetus-like into the chair. Her face bore a grey tinge. Poor thing. She must be exhausted – not just after today's long journey but dealing with the vagaries of her mind. What must it be like with the years and memories scrambling into incoherence one minute, while unravelling into lucidness the next?

Later that evening, I padded upstairs to check on her. I hesitated by the door. If I knocked too hard I could wake her but, if I didn't, I might frighten her by entering the room unannounced. I gave the door a light tap and pushed it open. It brushed against the carpet and I peered inside, relieved to find she'd made it into bed.

♦

Mabel hesitated by the breakfast room door. I'd hoped she'd forgotten what she'd travelled here to do, but she wore her funeral attire: the crumpled skirt she'd pulled from her holdall and a black cotton jumper which had somehow evaded yesterday's bag evacuation. She no longer appeared so pallid, thanks in part to the lipstick she'd pasted on. I guessed she'd used it as rouge too because it hadn't blended into her cheeks, lending her the impression of Aunt Sally.

"Sit anywhere you like," I said.

She wavered in the middle of the room, turning while she assessed the possible options. Grooves deepened between her eyebrows and cut along her forehead.

"How about here? You can..." I'd been about to say 'see the sun' but the sky had darkened as if rain was imminent. "People-watch."

She smiled gratefully and slid into the proffered chair.

When I returned with her pot of tea, I found her examining the menu. "Have you decided on anything?"

"Well..." Her finger ran down the menu items and then back up again. When it made its second descent, I added, "What do you like? A full English or an omelette. How about scrambled eggs?" Her blank gaze told me I shouldn't offer too many options.

I took the menu from her. "Are you hungry?"

"Ravenous, dear." She smiled, showing a smear of lipstick on her front teeth.

"How about we make you a full English, and you eat what you can?"

In the kitchen, Jason leaned cross-legged against the worktop, sipping his coffee. He checked his watch and gave me a kiss on the cheek. "Is there anything I can help you with before I get started?"

I grinned. "I can just about manage one breakfast."

"Without burning the toast?" He chuckled. "That'll be a first."

Usually, he cooked the breakfasts but he needed to get on with the renovations, so Mabel would get my – second-rate – version. No way could I do the sixteen breakfasts Jason often had to cook within an hour each morning.

Humming to myself, I made a start. Soon the smell of fried food wafted in the air, accompanied by the sound of bacon sizzling. I'd left Mabel sitting alone in the breakfast room but there was no other option. I turned the sausage on the griddle and popped out to see if she needed more tea.

But she wasn't there. All eight tables were empty and the chair where she had been sitting had been pushed back into place. Puzzled, I headed out to the hallway, where I was buffeted by a gust of wind. Someone – it could only be Mabel – had left the front door open. I sprinted outside and looked up and down the road, but she wasn't among the people clustered by the bus stop. A man from the local garage sauntered by in overalls, nodding hello as he passed, while a pair of joggers headed into town, ponytails flapping in the breeze. Recalling Mabel's tortoise pace the previous day, I couldn't believe she'd somehow become a hare.

Before looking further for her, I needed to turn off the stove and griddle. I headed back through the breakfast room, when the doorbell rang. I heaved a sigh of relief. She'd come back! But Jason stood at the door holding an electric drill.

"I forgot I lent this to Kim." He wiped his feet on the coir mat and shivered. "What were you doing outside? It's freezing out there."

"I've lost Mabel."

"How could you have lost her? She was in the breakfast room a moment ago."

From behind us came a cheery, "Hello dearie" and Mabel appeared at the top of the stairs, clutching the banister as if her life depended on it. Which no doubt it did.

As Jason shook his head and headed off towards our lounge, Mabel huffed her way down the stairs.

At the bottom, she patted her chest. "You need to install a lift. Us oldies can't cope with those stairs."

At least she'd uncoupled me from her age group. We'd had many a request for a lift, especially from guests who lived in bungalows. Some said it in all seriousness, like we could fit a lift into our guesthouse, whereas Mabel had a twinkle in her eye.

Smiling, I said, "Those blooming Edwardian builders were behind the times."

Then the smell of burning reached me. I shot into the kitchen to find the blackened remnants of an egg in the smoking frying pan. Eyes watering, I thrust the pan outside the back door, where the dregs of oil splattered in the chilly air. When the metal bottom popped, I dumped the pan on the ledge to cool before binning it later. The saucepan hadn't fared much better. As I scraped it with the wooden spoon, I cursed the layer of beans stuck to the bottom. Mabel's forty-odd pound payment was turning into a deficit for us.

Finally, I delivered an edible breakfast to Mabel, leaving her to eat it while I scrubbed the saucepan, muttering under my breath. The chink of knife and fork against ceramic and scrape of the chair on laminate told me she'd finished.

"I'm just off out, dearie." My face must have given away my thoughts as she rubbed her stomach and added, "Don't worry. It's just a trot down to the harbour to walk this off."

I handed her an umbrella – in case it rained – and didn't mention I wasn't worried about her getting there, just making it back.

"Don't forget to be back by ten thirty. I need to sort your room."

A lie, but I needed her to return in time for the reverend's arrival at eleven. I hadn't had the courage to tell her about the reverend, especially as it might lead us into a conversation about her long-dead friend. Theoretically, Mabel should have checked out at ten o'clock after her one-night stay but, since we were closed, we didn't have other guests coming in. Also, I wanted to give her enough time to use the loo and freshen up after her walk, but not so much that she disappeared off to the funeral.

Mabel was nowhere in sight when the reverend arrived on the dot of eleven. A short woman with a halo of frizzy grey hair in which she'd buried a pair of glasses, she shrugged when I announced that Mabel hadn't returned yet, told me to call her Catherine and accepted a cup of tea. She exuded calm – an antidote to my jitters – until she went to retrieve her glasses and they snagged on a tangle. At this point she became more Vicar of Dibley than reverential as she told me, in breathless spurts while wrestling her glasses from her hair, how she'd first met Mabel on a church excursion they'd undertaken to Weston-super-Mare. Mabel had been visiting Grace and had led everyone astray by hollering sea shanties from the back seat of the coach, until Catherine had joined in with more suitable songs.

"Weren't you the vicar then?"

As the last strand of hair snapped, she wrenched the glasses clear, only to push them back into her hair like an Alice band.

"No. I've only been a reverend for five years." She corrected me subtly. "Grace and I went to church together years ago, when I was one of the congregation. Back then, the reverend was an old chap. It's lovely seeing it from both sides."

Voices filtered in from the hallway and I went to investigate, finding Mabel clutching a bemused Jason's arm. "This nice man just let me in."

"Haven't you got your keys?"

"I left them in my room. Can you open it for me?"

The reverend stepped to my side. "Mabel, it's lovely to see you again."

Frowning, Mabel scanned Catherine's face without a flicker of recognition until her gaze settled on her dog collar. "You're doing the funeral, dear. How nice of you to pop by."

Catherine smiled. "I've come to talk to you about Grace. How about we get your bag and then we'll go for a spot of lunch?"

After unlocking the door to Mabel's room, I hovered outside wondering if they still needed me, until a red-faced Jason thumped down the stairs.

Breathless, he panted, "I need a hand!" He signalled for me to follow him. "We'll have a flood if I don't get the pipe capped off."

When I turned to go back into Mabel's room, he huffed, "We don't have time for that!"

I couldn't leave without saying goodbye, so I gave Mabel a quick hug and told the reverend I'd be in touch. It felt like I'd passed the parcel to the reverend, except this one held no prizes.

When she realised her friend lay six feet under and had done so for a long time, how would Mabel react?

But I didn't have time to dwell on it. Jason called from upstairs, "For goodness' sake, I need you!"

"Leave the keys in the room," I told Mabel.

♦

After a nightmare day, where we'd ended up taking up the shower tray and the floorboards to track the leak, Jason had gone to bed early. We'd mended the leak, but the ceiling below would need to be sealed and repainted when it dried. It could have been worse. At least we still had a ceiling.

For the past hour, I'd been resting my aching feet on the coffee table while I scrolled through Facebook posts showing delicious dinners, nights out with friends and the occasional moan. I'd regret my late night tomorrow. What was the expression? An hour before midnight is worth two after. My gaze flicked to the time: almost one o'clock. I snapped the laptop lid shut and heard the breakfast room door creak open. Had Jason woken up needing a glass of water or something? Puzzled, I got up. My fingers hovered over the hallway light switch but the glow of a nearby streetlamp through the opaque front door pane gave the hallway a murky half-light, allowing me to see.

As I opened the breakfast room door, Jason pulled it open from the other side, making me jump.

Clutching my chest, I gasped. "Talk about…"

But it wasn't Jason. The person facing me was the same height but had a different build. Jason was muscular, this man skinny. He wore a hooded top, its colour obscured by the darkness. The fetid stench of tobacco and sweat wafted from him. The whites of his eyes widened in the gloom and his arm shot out.

I screamed, "*Jas–*" but he shoved me hard, cutting off my cry. My shoulder smashed into the door frame and I clenched my teeth against the wave of pain. He yanked open the front door and disappeared. I thought to run after him, until sense got the better of me and I paused beneath the canopy, rubbing my sore shoulder. The chill from the concrete slabs seeped through the soles of my slippers and my breath fogged the air. My heart thumping, I tracked his path beneath the streetlamp, where he transformed from monochrome to colour – the hem of his jeans blue against his white trainers – then back to grey as darkness again became his friend and he vanished.

From upstairs came the slam of a bedroom door and Jason appeared at the top of the landing.

Pointing a trembling finger towards the street, I gasped. "A man was in the house."

Barefoot and only wearing a pair of boxer shorts and a T-shirt, Jason took the stairs two at a time and dived outside, coming to an abrupt halt by the edge of the drive. He scanned the road in both directions. I walked over to him, shivering as the breeze cut through my top.

"He went that way." I pointed up the road where too many hiding places lay between the glowing cones of the streetlights.

"We'll call the police," Jason said. "But I'd like to know, how on earth he got in?"

Mabel! She hadn't been able to get into the guesthouse because she'd left her keys in her room. Or so she'd said. After all the palaver with the leak, I hadn't checked her room for them. No doubt she'd dropped them outside and, with the room number on the fob, it would be easy for an opportunist thief to realise they must be B&B keys and to try a few doors. Great! Now we'd have the expense of changing the lock and cutting a new front door key for each room.

"Are you okay?" Jason gave me a cuddle. "Don't look so worried. He's gone now."

Frowning, he picked up the phone to call the police. I sighed. We wouldn't be going to bed anytime soon. Even if we did, I couldn't see myself sleeping. I'd be too worried about the thief coming back again before we got the new lock installed. Mabel's payment had fast become minus forty-eight pounds and rising. I just hoped it didn't rise too much.

# Chapter 4

EVEN IF THE SOUND WAS ON MUTE – which I wished it was – I didn't need to be watching the TV to know the score. Jason's grey eyes reflected the flickering images on the TV screen, his face mirroring each crease of anxiety on the team manager's face. Anxiously, he perched on the edge of the settee, a crisp packet crushed between his thighs. While his hand searched for the open packet, his gaze tracked the ball. He opened his mouth and shovelled a few crisps in.

"Come on, ref," he muttered as he crunched. A sliver of crisp spilled out and sat glistening on his lip.

All being well, in less than five minutes I would have a happy husband. After the day he'd had – I'd heard the swear words above the sound of banging and sawing – he'd earned ninety minutes of happiness.

"What? A penalty? Seriously, ref?"

The sinews on his neck sprang taut and he clenched both fists, his knuckles turning to bone.

I couldn't for the life of me understand why anyone would choose to watch something that ratcheted up their blood pressure to boiling point. Give me a good book any day. Except I couldn't read my book with all the whistling and hollering on screen.

"No!" Jason leapt to his feet, the crisp packet tumbling to the carpet, scattering crisp confetti. As cheers turned to boos, he scrubbed his hands down his face and slumped back onto the sofa. "Thank goodness."

Catching me watching him, he smiled. "That was close."

Then the doorbell sounded twice. Jason frowned and glanced at the clock. From the look on his face, his thoughts echoed mine. Who'd be calling at ten o'clock? Although disconcerted by the thought of a late-night caller, I signalled him to stay seated. He smiled gratefully as I left him to his final minutes of pain.

Even though the *No Vacancies* sign hung in the day room window, we had the occasional evening caller hoping we'd relent and let them stay. I didn't like answering the door at this time of night. I'd always felt that way, even before last week's intruder. With most of our rooms out of action while we carried out the final renovations, my answer would be a definite no. While I didn't like turning down people pleading for a place to stay – especially with many B&Bs closed at this time of year – look where my compassion had got me with Mabel. We'd never found the keys she'd supposedly left in her room. Instinctively, I rubbed my shoulder, remembering the painful bruise.

Then it hit me. What if it wasn't someone needing a room? What if something had happened to Lucy or Emily and I found the police at the door? The night when Emily had been in a car accident the previous year was always at the back of my mind. We'd been stuck hundreds of miles away, helpless and praying she'd be okay, wondering how we could abandon our guests in the middle of the night if we needed to race to her. Thank goodness Lucy had been there.

I opened the door, expecting to see anyone but the person who stood there. It took a moment to register her features, to confirm it was really her. But as those beautiful dark eyes met mine, my hands shot to my face and my heart leapt.

"Emily! What are you doing here?"

"Great welcome, Mum. Nice to see you too."

She sauntered into the guesthouse, drawing with her the chill night air and a wizened leaf which floated onto the coir mat. I glanced outside to see if she'd brought a guest but there was no one in sight.

"How did you get here?"

"Lucy drove me. And before Dad moans, she's coming back on Monday to pick me up. She'll pop by then."

"What's Lucy doing down here?"

"Her boyfriend's just moved to Plymouth, so she dropped me off here."

"Boyfriend? She kept that quiet."

"They've only been dating about three months or so. You should see him." Grinning, she raised her hand to the ceiling. "He's about seven foot and skinny. Walks like Jar Jar Binks. I told Lucy he was gorgeous cos he is. Deep inside."

Her hair glinted auburn beneath the hallway light. She dyed it since I'd last seen her at Christmas. Two whole months ago! I wished she lived closer so we could see each other more. She unwound her scarf and, handing it to me, set about unbuttoning her coat.

The lounge door clicked open and Jason ducked out into the hallway. "Emily? What are you doing here?"

Emily rolled her eyes. "A hello would be nice."

◆

As I emptied the vacuum cylinder into the dustbin, Shona limped across her drive, shoe in hand, muttering to herself. Then she spotted me and hobbled over, grimacing.

"I reckon it's him across the road," she said. When I looked puzzled, she held up the shoe to show me what she'd stepped in. "He doesn't clean up after his dog. Lazy git."

"Are you sure?" The new people across the road had moved in four weeks ago and hadn't caused any bother but, for some reason, Shona couldn't find a kind word to say about them. Not only that, but I hadn't seen them with a dog.

She jabbed her finger towards their house. "Have the police found your intruder? And what about your old lady? Did you ask her about the keys?"

"The reverend phoned me to say Mabel had got back safely but I didn't mention the break in. No point when Mabel couldn't remember the year, let alone what happened to our keys. But someone definitely found them. It's the only way they could have got in."

She looked across the road. "I told you it'll be to do with *them*."

Shona was adamant that the intruder was connected to our new neighbours, but we had no evidence.

From the guesthouse Emily called, "Mum!" and I was grateful to be saved from yet another discussion about our new neighbours.

Emily stepped outside, smiling when she spotted us. She'd pulled her hair into a ponytail and had borrowed one of my old jumpers to help clean the two rooms I'd finished decorating. Upstairs Jason was laying the vinyl flooring in room four's ensuite. He'd be finished with time to spare before the guesthouse reopened the following week. It looked like March would be busier than the previous year had been under the old owners.

"I didn't know you were down. Where's your sister?" Shona stretched to look behind Emily.

"Lucy's gone to see her boyfriend for a long weekend. Work let me have the days off, so I wangled a lift with her. You should have seen Mum's face when she opened the door."

"Hugged to within inches of your life?"

"You're joking. More like..." She pulled an angry face and snarled, "What are you doing here?"

I shrugged. "The welcoming committee were taken off guard."

Emily had no idea how much her visit meant. Being awarded unexpected time with my lovely daughter was amazing, even if it had been spent scrubbing carpets, picture rails and skirting boards. I regretted not taking her out for the day as I'd considered doing, but she'd insisted on helping with the cleaning. After working with us the previous year, she knew what preparing a guesthouse for the season involved.

Wrinkling her nose, Emily gazed at Shona's trainer. "What's that stuff on your... Yuk!"

"I'm gonna find whoever's doing it."

"How?" As the word tumbled from my mouth, I regretted it. "I mean, I'm sure there's more than one. They leave the mess on our drive too."

Shona tapped her nose. "Let's just say, I have a plan. They're gonna get caught in the act."

Grinning, Emily rubbed her hands together. "That sounds fun. I'm here until Monday morning so I'll help if you need it."

33

"Not a chance!" I hissed. I meant it too. No way would Emily get embroiled in this, especially when experience had taught me to take care when Shona had a plan.

♦

At six o'clock the next morning, the three of us sat in Shona's car. When Emily had insisted on joining Shona for her early-morning stake-out, I'd put my foot down. But there was little I could do to stop a determined twenty-one-year old. At least if I signed up too, I could protect her from the worst of Shona's ideas.

Emily perched in the back, her arms slung over the front seats where Shona and I huddled into our coats. Outside it was pitch dark but for the funnel of light provided by a nearby streetlamp. We'd been here an hour already and monitored two people hurrying past, neither accompanied by a dog. My fingers stung with cold and my breath fogged the air, but Emily didn't seem to notice the temperature. Her head bobbed from side to side, craning to gaze through both passenger windows.

If Shona and Kim had invested in security cameras there'd be no need to do this, but when I'd mentioned them to Kim the previous day she'd frowned and glared at Shona.

"Did Shona tell you to ask me? Because if she did…".

Shona had rolled her eyes and dug her finger into my leg. A signal to shut up – which I did. But now I wished I'd pressed the point. In a nearby room, Kim would be nestled beneath a cosy duvet, just as Jason had been when I'd rolled out of bed at four thirty.

"Tell me again why Kim won't let you have cameras," I said.

"She doesn't believe in them. Thinks they're all 1984 and it's the start of a dangerous precedent."

"Bit ironic that she thinks a KGB-style stake-out is okay though," Emily piped up. "With video evidence on a mobile rather than a camera." Sighing, she settled back into the seat. "That's if this person *ever* comes."

Shona's gaze fell on the row of cottages opposite – sitting in darkness – but for a solitary window at the end of the terrace where the imprint of a naked bulb blazed through the thin crimson curtain. Earlier, I'd spotted a shadow flit across the window but had seen nothing since.

I shivered and pulled my coat tighter. My toes had passed the throbbing stage and felt heavy and numb, but we couldn't start the engine to warm up the car in case it gave us away.

"Ooh look," Emily said.

Shona and I spun around but I couldn't see anything.

"What?" Shona said.

"That cat. You won't be able to see it, but Mum will." Sniggering, Emily covered her mouth with her hand. "Get the camera out!"

As Shona leaned over to peer through the window, she smothered me with her coat, burying my nose and mouth in itchy fibres. I twisted around so I could see, although she hogged most of the view. The streetlight didn't reach to the wall, but I could make out a grey shape crouching. It stretched, moving away from the shadows, and with two kicks of its back legs, flicked gravel behind it.

"I don't believe it!" Shona said. "A blooming cat. All this for a cat!" She flung her car door open and jumped out, sprinting after what looked like a huge tomcat. The wind shuddered through the open car door, and we heard her shouting, "Go on, get out of here!" Coming to a halt beneath the streetlight, she threw her hands in the air.

Emily grinned at me. "Mystery solved then."

I clambered from the car, grimacing as I stretched my legs. "I wouldn't bank on it."

Shoulders slumped, Shona headed back. When she reached us, she yawned and patted Emily's shoulder. "Thanks for your help. Looks like chilli powder will be on the shopping list tomorrow. But now I need my bed."

Giving us a wry smile, she turned to go. Emily and I headed across the drive and into the guesthouse. The warmth enticed us inside. Just a few steps and we'd be in bed.

"Well that was pointless. How's she going to stop a cat?" Emily stood on the coir entrance mat while she shrugged off her coat, leaving me stranded behind her with cold wafting across my back. She yawned. "See you in the morning."

"It *is* the morning."

As I turned to shut the door, I spotted an unfamiliar elderly lady shambling along the path. Her terrier strained on its lead to sniff at our wall, but she glanced in my direction and gave the lead a sharp tug before shuffling off into the gloom. Something about the way she'd looked at me before pulling the dog away didn't feel right. But, too tired to think about it, I closed the door and thanked my lucky stars. While tonight had been a waste of time, at least no harm had been done. I couldn't always say that when Shona was involved.

# Chapter 5

THAT NIGHT I HEADED TO BED EARLY, refusing to set my alarm clock, so I slept through until ten o'clock. A luxury we wouldn't have for much longer, as we were set to open in a few days after six weeks of renovations and maintenance. The rest of March looked set to be fruitful and we had a healthy number of bookings for the following months too.

Thanks to the empty milk container in the fridge – the joys of a daughter back at home for a few days – my 'pyjama morning' wasn't to be. I left Jason in the shower and Emily fast asleep in bed and headed out to the shop. An empty crisp packet skittered along the driveway. The icy breeze whipped my hair into my face and I drew my coat tight around me, praying the sun would win the battle as it fought to pierce through the gunmetal cloud.

Gunmetal – my new favourite word – and the colour I'd planned for the guesthouse frontage. Jason had preferred sage. Assuming that Lucy and Emily would plump for my fashionable grey, I'd invited them all to make the final decision. I'd lost 3-1. Not that I minded. Anything was better than the Norwich City green and yellow the previous owners had chosen. At least, sage paint with white lintels gave the building a dignified air.

Thankfully, my attention was diverted from the frontage in time to spot a brown pile on the edge of the driveway. Not from a cat – unless they bred tiger-sized moggies around here. After using a carrier bag as a glove to scoop it up, I found Shona grinning beside me.

"The cat's moved to your drive?"

"This wasn't a cat." Grimacing, I tossed the bag into the wheelie bin. "Your gravel may be the perfect litter tray, but our drive isn't."

For a moment, I thought she'd argue with me but, instead, she nodded towards the cottage across the road. "I reckon it's been them all along. They were watching us in the car. That's why they didn't come out."

"They were asleep, like we should have been."

"When I catch them, I'll show you. What're you doing today?"

"Lucy's coming to collect Emily. We're going for lunch before they leave."

"Shame they're not staying another night. If we were in separate cars on each drive, we'd have more chance of catching whoever it is."

I decided not to question her logic. With the guesthouse opening in a few days, I didn't want to waste any more precious lie-ins.

"I think I'll just have a chat with Jason about getting a camera. Or a fake one. At least it'll be a deterrent."

♦

We'd paired off, Emily in front with Jason, Lucy and I ambling behind. This wouldn't have happened a year ago when Lucy would have attached herself to Jason, possibly with Emily on the other side, while I took up the rear. Now my lovely stepdaughter didn't mind being stuck with me. In fact, she seemed to relish the chance to tell me about her new boyfriend, Lester.

"He's moved from Normansby to become the general manager

at a restaurant in Plymouth, but he wants his own place. He reckons it's do-able within a year."

"In Plymouth?"

She shrugged. "He's not tied to anywhere. He likes the coast, though."

As we rounded the corner, the harbour came into view. Set within a natural bowl, the colourful buildings crammed the hillside: a thuggish fuchsia, lime green or navy frontage interspersing the riot of pastel shades. The cottages led in disorderly tiers down to where the restaurants, shops and pubs ringed the harbour wall. The tide had gone out, leaving the small rowing boats slumped to one side, while the larger boats and yachts perched on twin keels or were held upright by poles. From where we stood it appeared as if you could sink into the muddy harbour bed but, when we got closer, we could see a layer of pebbles. A man in yellow wellies and blue overalls crouched below the rudder of his boat. Behind him the approaching tide glimmered as it crept beneath the afternoon sun.

The fish quay sat just outside the entrance to the inner harbour. From where we stood, I could see the tips of the upright derricks, which would be lowered when the boats went out to trawl for fish. Opposite, yachts and sailing boats of all sizes lined up beside the pontoons in the marina. Their masts swayed in the breeze. Beyond them lay the shingle beach where we would skim pebbles with Emily, too far away to be seen.

"Look!" Three swans gliding across the water by the inner harbour entrance caught my attention and I tugged at Lucy's sleeve. "They've been here all winter. Odd isn't it."

Squinting against the low winter sun, her steel grey eyes – the same colour as Jason's – tracked my finger. "Swans?" She sounded deflated, as if swans were an everyday sight at the seaside. Then she added, "Oh, I see what you mean! You know, my Lester would love it here. He likes fishing, he likes the sea."

We followed Jason and Lucy into 'TorViva', which had opened the previous week, to be greeted by the aroma of food and the faint smell of fresh paint. Around us copper tabletops glinted and glasses chinked. The buzz of chatter suggested a summer's evening packed with tourists, rather than a late February afternoon. Most of the customers must be Torringham folk keen to see what the owners had done to the place, while Jason and I would also be assessing whether we could recommend it to future guests. Not that one visit would prove anything as the restaurant could be having a good day or teething troubles, which is why we tried to ask guests about their evenings out and how their meals had gone.

"He'd love this," Lucy gasped. "This is sooo his dream."

Looking at the harassed faces of the waiting staff, I couldn't imagine why anyone would want to work in a busy restaurant. I found it stressful enough serving sixteen people for breakfast each morning, especially when they all came down in the space of ten minutes, which had happened half a dozen times in the past year. It didn't sound a lot, but those mornings had been branded in my mind like a weal. Thank goodness we'd agreed to recruit someone to help this year, even if it was just part-time. Along with some of the breakfast services, they'd also be doing the rooms with me, which meant that Jason could get on with other jobs. We didn't have enough spare cash for much more, not after spending all our money on renovations.

Lucy slid along the polished bench and picked up her menu. I sat opposite and took the wine menu from the waiter, my gaze stealing to the right of the page.

"Have you brought your credit card?" I grinned at Jason. "People keep saying Torringham is on the up. I think we now have proof of it."

"People pay these prices?" Lucy gasped. "I am definitely telling Lester to open a restaurant here. He'd make a bomb."

Emily focused on her menu which she held in front of her face, but I could make out pinpoint blotches on her cheeks. What had upset her? We'd said this would be our treat, so she couldn't be worried about the prices. Her eyes glistened – with tears? – and she muttered to herself. Just as I leaned across to check she was okay, Jason butted in.

"What are you having, Katie? The lamb sounds nice. Or the vegetable lasagne."

How could he not notice the vibes rolling from Emily? Wave after burgeoning wave, until her menu crashed onto the copper table and she folded her arms.

"So, you're thinking of moving here with Lester? What about your job?"

The waiter put a pitcher of water on the table and scooted away. Without meeting Emily's gaze, Lucy pursed her lips and picked up the jug of water. A waterfall of ice and a solitary lime plopped into her glass. She took a sip and placed her glass on the paper coaster. Then she settled back into her seat mirroring Emily's folded arms.

"Who knows what the future will bring? It's early days yet. The lamb does look lovely, but I think I'll have the turbot."

Emily scrutinised her older sister. "I thought you didn't like roll-neck tops." Her hand shot to her mouth. "Oops, did I spill the beans?"

We all looked at Lucy, who flushed and tugged at the collar of her top, covering the purple bruise on her neck.

"What's eating you?" Lucy hissed. "Are you jealous of me and Lester?"

"Hardly. I'm glad he's eating you and not me."

I sighed and Jason shook his head. So much for our cosy family get-together. We fell into an uneasy silence, with the girls examining their nails or the view outside the window, while Jason hummed to himself while he reread the menu.

Unable to bear the strained atmosphere any longer, I said, "We had more mess on the driveway. Shona wants to do another stake-out."

"Gross," Lucy said.

"Mum! Times and places." Emily shook her head and turned to Lucy. "Mum and Shona are fixated with dog mess."

I opened my mouth to respond – after all, Emily had been the one wanting to do the stake-out with Shona – then clamped it shut. At least they had spoken to each other. Whatever had upset Emily seemed to be forgotten for now.

♦

In the end, we had a lovely meal. Lucy had stuck to water due to facing a long drive back, while Emily and I shared a bottle of Prosecco. With each sip, Emily had become more animated and fizzed with excitement as she recounted recent exploits with friends. And she allowed Lucy to mention Lester without being snarky.

When we stood outside the guesthouse to wave them off, Shona rushed over from Jetsam Cottage, followed by Kim, to berate the girls for trying to leave without saying goodbye. While Shona tiptoed to kiss Emily's cheek, Kim's cerise fingernails rested on Lucy's shoulders as she bent to embrace her. Kim had wrapped her braided hair in a gorgeous orange and pink scarf, which coordinated with her pink ballet pumps. Goosebumps prickled her arms below her short-sleeved white shirt but, unlike Shona, who jumped up and down rubbing her arms as her Metallica T-shirt flapped in the wind, Kim remained her usual serene self. I edged away. If I was comparing her and Shona, would someone be so judgemental about me? After a winter of eating too much food, the waistband of my trousers cut into my flesh and, if I prodded my stomach, my finger disappeared into a mound of fat.

But it kept me warm while the girls did goodness knows what. Lucy still hadn't made it into the car but bent over the driver's seat, bum in the air, rummaging around in the footwell, while Emily sat in the passenger seat checking her face in the mirror.

"Unless you want to wait half an hour while Lucy faffs around, I suggest we go in." Jason turned to Kim. "Coffee?"

As she followed Jason indoors, Shona pulled me aside. "Don't tell Kim but I've set up a secret camera." She pointed to a first-floor window. "I borrowed it from a mate."

She pulled out her mobile phone. It flickered into life to show an impressive picture of the driveway and footpath outside Jetsam

Cottage, with the tip of Lucy's car bonnet on display, while Shona and I were out of shot. A bus trundled past on the screen – wafting us with fumes – followed by several cars and a van.

"I can sit in bed and watch this instead of TV."

A tickertape of questions scrolled through my mind. Wouldn't it still be dark at six o'clock in the morning? Did the camera have night vision? Wouldn't Kim notice? But I let them roll away unvoiced. At least Shona wasn't involving me in her scheme.

"That sounds a brilliant idea."

# Chapter 6

A FORTNIGHT AGO WE'D PUT AN ADVERT in the local newsagent's window asking for a part-time cleaner. We'd had five responses. After a brief chat with each person, the numbers had fallen to one. Understandable, noting we couldn't offer definite hours. If we didn't have guests in, we couldn't afford to pay someone for doing nothing and, come the low season, the work would be sporadic. However, Sarah already had a job cleaning holiday lets and simply needed a few extra hours each week.

She arrived for her trial session fifteen minutes ahead of the agreed ten o'clock, catching me in my pyjamas. In my defence, I was making the most of the final morning before we opened for the season. Unlike last year, when we'd taken on the guesthouse, I had some idea of what lay in store for us. When I apologised for not being ready, Sarah breezed into the hallway, waving me away with, "You should've seen what I've seen in some of the places I've worked at." And left it at that.

While I closed the front door and popped the mail onto the sideboard, she stood in silence clutching her handbag. I gazed at her doubtfully. Even though we'd be sharing the work, would this tiny woman be up to the grind of cleaning eight bedrooms and showers, including lifting heavy mattresses?

Jason came into the hallway. A tall but not a thick-set man, he dwarfed Sarah in height and build. When he welcomed her to Flotsam Guesthouse, she held out dainty fingers tipped by manicured nails so perfect that Kim would drool with envy. Her blonde hair had been pulled into a ponytail and she wore minimal make-up: a touch of mascara and a dab of lipstick. Two stud earrings pierced her lobes, while a third perched at the top of each ear, in line with her perfectly arched eyebrows. I wished I'd bothered to brush my hair.

Thanks to Emily's help earlier in the week, we had just four rooms to service. A perfect number to see if this job would suit Sarah. I showed her the first bedroom, told her where to find the linen and left her to get started on the bed, while I dashed to my room to throw on a pair of jeans and an old top. On my return, I found a ghostly spectre waving its arms at me: Sarah inside the duvet cover. With a grunt, she flung the white cover over the duvet. Clutching the corners of the duvet, she swiped an arm across her face to brush away strands of hair that had escaped from her ponytail. Then with a grimace, she flapped the cover hard until it wafted onto the bed. My mouth fell open. I could never get a duvet to do that. I might have twenty years on her, but she could show me a few tricks.

She dabbed her forehead with a tissue, which she tucked back into the pocket of her jeans. "I find it easier to turn duvets inside out and work from inside. The superkings get me, though. How many of those have you got?"

"Two. We do those in pairs."

"That's good. I can never find my way out." She grinned. "Right, tea tray or polishing next? Or the ensuite?"

♦

The next hour flew by in a blur of beds, loos and showers, while Jason went out to buy provisions for the weekend. After agreeing pay and hours – just one day a week to start with, going up to three or four days a week during the high season – I waved goodbye to Sarah at eleven forty. Had the clock stopped? Nope. Somehow, we'd finished four rooms and had a chat over coffee in under two hours. If Jason could be freed to get on with shopping and ironing, while Sarah and I did the work upstairs, the coming season wouldn't seem quite so challenging.

As Sarah headed over to the bus stop, Shona scurried past. She'd dyed the blonde tips of her hair puce, which seemed to leach all the colour from her skin. Unless she was unwell.

"Shona!" I hurried out.

She turned, giving me a wan smile. "I didn't see you there. I'm just off to the chemist. The doctor reckons I've got a chest infection."

"You poor thing. By the way, did you catch anyone?" When she gave me a puzzled look, I added, "With the camera."

"Oh that." She squirmed as if she didn't want to tell me, but her downfall was an inability to lie to me. "Sort of. I've got to go."

Thanks to Sarah I had an unexpected hour free. "I'll walk with you. I could do with a bit of fresh air."

Frowning, Shona waited while I shut the front door. When I joined her, she set off at speed, making it impossible to talk. How she walked so fast with a chest infection, I didn't know. She left me panting for breath and all but running to keep up with her. When the chill cut through my top, I wished I'd brought a coat, but at least her speed meant we got there quickly. Shona pulled open the chemist door and ushered me in first. I let her go ahead, while I savoured the blast of warm air from the overhead heaters. Just like getting out of a bath into a cold room, the moment I stepped away the first icy shivers crawled down my spine. I found Shona handing her prescription to the shop assistant.

"So? What did you see on the camera?" If she thought I'd forgotten, she didn't know me well.

Shona pursed her lips. "You've come all this way just for that? You must be desperate." Sighing, she said, "Okay, but don't tell Kim."

She retrieved her mobile from her back pocket to show me a grainy picture of a shadowy, stooped figure half-lit by the nearby streetlight. Unmistakeable nonetheless.

"I've seen her before. The morning we did the stake-out, when we saw that cat," I said. "What happened?"

She flushed. "It turns out I can't solve either the cat or dog issue. At least the cat buries it, whereas she can't bend over to pick up the mess. She's old and lonely and the dog's her life, so I couldn't be mean. I've agreed that she'll put a note through our door each time it happens, so I'll know to clean it up."

I chuckled. "That's very sweet of you."

Shona growled. "That's what she said. Mug, more like."

I decided not to point out that from the size of the deposits, the cat and the old lady's terrier weren't the only ones involved in foul play. I made a mental note to buy a bulk load of doggy bags from the pet shop the next time I went shopping.

Shona grabbed my arm. "Watch out!"

Instinctively, I whirled around.

49

"Don't let him see you looking," she hissed.

"What's the matter?"

"It's him. From across the road."

A lanky man lumbered towards us, his greasy blond hair snaking along the collar of his khaki bomber jacket. Shona turned to inspect the baby medicine section, nudging me to point out I should do the same. While I'd seen the woman and her teenage children several times, I'd not met the man before. I positioned myself so I could surreptitiously watch him, but when the smell of stale cigarettes and grime wafted over to me, I edged away.

He handed a crumpled prescription to the pharmacist. "How long will it take, mate?"

Like Shona, he had an Essex accent. But that's where the similarity ended. The frayed hems of his dirt-engrained jeans draped over his ancient workman's boots and he scratched his chin with fingertips yellowed by nicotine.

When the pharmacist called Shona's name, she pushed me towards the counter. "You get it."

With that, she left. A few minutes later I joined her outside where – not bothering to take the bag from me or ask what she owed – she hauled me away by the arm.

"What's going on?" I hissed.

She jabbed her head towards the chemist. "He's back out."

He wasn't following us, but Shona rushed off as if we were about to be ripped apart by a pack of wolves. If she'd had a whip, I was sure she'd use it but instead she tightened her grip, her fingers digging into my skin. The pace of my enforced trot increased until we all but galloped along the street. Thankfully, she pulled up by the pedestrian crossing, where she gasped for breath.

"You know, the new family that moved in. He's one of them. I'd heard he got out of prison a few weeks ago, but this is the first I've seen of him since." She clutched her chest and inhaled deeply. "I'll fight my corner with anyone but not him. He used to do drugs. Then he got put away for burglary and GBH."

"He beat someone up?"

"A householder stumbled upon him in the middle of the night." Furtively, she checked behind us. "I just *knew* that family would have something to do with your burglary. And him being back proves it. Count yourself lucky he just ran away."

"How do you know it was him."

She rolled her eyes. "Who else would it be? He probably needs money. Look, take my advice and keep well clear."

# Chapter 7

WE WERE BUSIER THAN EXPECTED for our first weekend of the season. By the eight o'clock deadline for checking-in, five of our six couples had arrived. Earlier, I'd tried calling the final couple – followed by a text – to see what time they were arriving, but they hadn't responded. Frustrating, to say the least. We valued the few hours we had to ourselves each evening after all the guests had arrived. It wouldn't be long until we headed upstairs, knowing the night would fly by and the next morning we'd stagger from our warm beds to start preparing and cooking breakfasts, before moving onto the other jobs that stretched throughout the day.

Jason's stomach rumbled and he threw me an exasperated look. "It's a minute past eight. Can we eat now?"

"Give them half an hour more."

"They've ignored our calls, text and email. Do you really think they're coming?"

Our first guests had turned up on the dot of four o'clock, with all the other couples arriving within half an hour of their agreed arrival time. Not bad for a Friday, especially with the usual heavy traffic. After the penultimate guests had arrived at seven, I'd suggested to Jason that we wait before eating. I didn't want to be mid-mouthful when the doorbell rang only to return to a cold dinner, especially when I'd picked fresh Dover sole from the fishmonger. After we'd been closed for weeks, I'd forgotten what a busy check-in day could be like. Now I remembered why we ate so much pizza last year. It's quick to cook and can be eaten hot or cold. In fact, there was probably one in the outside freezer.

"Fancy pizza instead and the fish tomorrow?"

"I'd eat a paper bag if it filled me up."

The late arrivals didn't disturb our pizza dinner. When they hadn't turned up by nine thirty and a further call went straight to answerphone, I retrieved my bottle of pinot grigio from the chiller while Jason spoke to the booking company about our missing guests.

Half an hour later, with the guests clearly a 'no show', I settled down to watch a recorded episode of *Death in Paradise,* my current favourite programme, although not Jason's, by the sound of his snoring. The suspects were all waiting to hear the whodunnit verdict, when our doorbell rang. I glanced at the time. Five to eleven! If this was the missing guests, they'd arrived three hours after our deadline. I considered ignoring them but, if they kept ringing the doorbell, they'd annoy any guests who'd settled down for an early night.

Sighing, I pressed pause on the remote control and, leaving Jason asleep on the sofa, I headed out. At the front door, I forced a smile. It's no good welcoming guests with a frown or a tart 'Do you know what time it is?' even if that's what you're thinking. People wouldn't dream of turning up for a flight several hours after it left or a meal two hours after they had reserved a table. But some guests – thankfully very few – assumed a guesthouse was the same as a 24-hour hotel. Both offered a bed for the night and breakfast in the morning, but there was the small matter of staffing. The people who bid you goodnight at a guesthouse are the same ones who say good morning and good afternoon. Every single day.

"Hello." My lips stuck to my teeth, probably making my smile more like a grimace.

A young couple stood on the porch. The man towered over his girlfriend, like Jason did with me – but that was the only likeness between us and these guests. The woman's hair had been pulled back into a ponytail so tight, her eyebrows arched in surprise. Mascara clumped her eyelashes and speckled her skin. When her startling blue eyes met mine, she held her gaze without smiling. Unnerved, I turned to the man. A dark fringe flopped over his eyes which he flicked away with long fingers.

"Sarah-Louise and Vincent Hamilton."

He carried a small case, but I couldn't see his car outside.

"Have you come by car or pup…" My tongue tripped over the words. "Public transport?"

He pointed to the car park over the road. "We've parked over there, like your email said."

So, they'd seen my email. Strange that they'd spotted the offer of free parking but missed the paragraph above stating check-in times.

"Come in. I'll give you a passing…" I swallowed. "Sorry, *parking* pass to put on your dashboard." For some reason, I felt the need to explain my mistake. "Three Ps are too much for me after a glass of wine."

I held out my hand but Sarah-Louise stiffened and, sticking her arms behind her back, she stepped behind Vincent. Was it because I'd mention alcohol? Then I realised there were only two Ps in parking pass, not the three I'd said. She must have thought I was actually drunk!

Vincent gave me a tight-lipped smile – with the same insincerity I'd greeted them – and held out his hand. A lettuce leaf a month past its sell-by date would have had more life than his handshake.

"Nice that you get to drink when you're working," he said.

"I'd be teetotal if I didn't." I didn't temper my comment with a smile.

This time I took care to enunciate my words, which probably made me sound more inebriated. "I'll check you in and take you up to your room. Hold on while I get the card machine."

Vincent glared through the curtain of his fringe. "What? We pay now?"

He reminded me of two lads who'd stayed the previous year. They'd turned up late, quibbled about paying, and had been no end of trouble. I'd had a bad feeling then, just like I did now.

"That was also in the email I sent." My cheeks burned – heat, alcohol or annoyance – I couldn't tell. "Look, it's eleven o'clock. We don't usually accept people at this time but it's your call. It's payment on arrival or there are hotels nearby."

He drew a card from his wallet and tossed it onto the table. In return, I handed him his registration form. "Fill this in. I'll get the machine."

When I came back, I took his payment and form, gave them the room keys and a quick rundown about the guesthouse including breakfast times.

"I only drink soya milk," Sarah-Louise said. She folded her arms like a barricade.

"I'm sorry but we don't have that. We ask about dietary needs in advance so we can buy things in. I'll have it in for breakfast on

Sunday though."

"But you said breakfast was from eight. Don't the shops open around seven?"

"You're right, they do. I'll be setting up for breakfast then, but you're welcome to pop out and get some."

I took them upstairs where they surveyed the room with blank expressions. Glad to leave them, I headed back downstairs, muttering to myself. Why on earth had I answered the door? I should have done what we'd agreed to do when people arrived far too late without good reason: let them find somewhere else to stay.

◆

Our first breakfast service of the season started in the manner it would no doubt continue. While I raced about, Jason counted out twenty-four pieces of bacon and twelve sausages and slotted the trays into the oven. Three times I opened the fridge door to stare at the laden shelves, unable to recall what I needed. Only after I shut the door each time did I remember.

Cursing that I hadn't got up half an hour earlier, I chopped the melon and slid the pieces from the chopping board into a bowl. Two cubes splatted onto the floor, but I left them. If I picked them up, I'd have to wash my hands again and I didn't have time. As I hacked into the pineapple, I checked the clock. Somehow the minute hand had leapt ten minutes in the space of two. Guests would be arriving soon to find a half-filled buffet table.

Jason scooped the pieces of melon from the floor, tossed them in the bin and gave his hands a quick wash before heading over.

"Slow down. You'll hack your fingers off at this rate."

Knife in hand, I swung around, forcing him to leap back. "Instead of telling me what to do, why don't you help? We start service in five minutes."

"I was just about to offer as a safety measure." Grinning, he held his palms inches from my cheeks. "If you were a nuclear power station, I'd give you a minute until meltdown."

"Milk and orange juice need to go into the jugs." I shot another look at the clock. Two minutes wasted. "And the yoghurts into the chiller. Then the butter in the dishes."

Thirty-five minutes later, we leaned against the kitchen worktops staring at the walls. We'd set everything out with seconds to spare, but our rush had been for nothing. Half an hour into the breakfast service, we didn't have a single guest. The second hand on the clock bounced sixty times, counting out one boring minute, before moving onto the next. Beside me, Jason gazed at his mobile chuckling to himself. I'd already run through my Facebook timeline. Not much had happened since I'd gone to bed the previous evening.

A herd of footsteps clattered across the laminate floor. I stuffed my mobile phone into the drawer, grabbed my pen and notepad and headed out. Four guests milled by the buffet table while another two strolled into the room. The bang of a door upstairs told me more would be arriving soon. It would be one of those mornings.

I'd served half a dozen breakfasts and had put a round of toast on Vincent's table – he'd told me Sarah-Louise wanted to shower in peace so he was eating alone – when I turned to find another guest, Eddie, hovering by the door, wringing his hands. When I pointed towards a vacant table, he shook his head and signalled for me to come over.

"We've got a bit of a problem," he hissed.

These were the last words I needed to hear when Jason had several orders lined up and wouldn't be able to help. I led Eddie out to the hallway, away from prying ears.

"I'm sorry about that. What is the matter?"

"There's no hot water. Rita was in the shower and it suddenly went cold. It's too chilly for her to rinse the suds out."

"Do you mind waiting, just for a moment?" I hurried into the kitchen, where a red-faced Jason was tackling four full English breakfasts. Frowning, he flipped the sizzling bacon while I relayed the issue.

"There's only two rooms on the tank, so how the water's run out, I don't know."

"But what are we going to do about it?"

He gave me one of his looks. "I can't leave these breakfasts. The water will be hot again in fifteen minutes."

With four pans on the hob and the griddle crammed with sausages and bacon, he had a point. But that meant I had the unenviable task of telling Eddie that Rita would have to wait until the water heated up.

After my hurried explanation with 'sorry' interspersed between every other word, Eddie's eyebrows shot up.

"Fifteen minutes!" When I apologised again, he sighed. "There's not much you can do about it. But will you hold on for us?" He jerked his head towards the breakfast room.

"It's the least we can do."

Summoned by Jason's bell, I headed back into the kitchen and took Vincent's breakfast out to him. He folded the scrambled egg on toast like a wrap and crammed it into his mouth. When I next swung by carrying two plates to another table, his cheeks bulged like a ravenous chipmunk. Slapping his hands together, he slid from the chair. I gave him a cheery goodbye but, when I came back into the breakfast room a moment later, I found him hovering by the door. Did he have a problem too?

"There's no need to clean our room," he said.

"You don't need anything?"

"No," he said. "There's no need to go in there."

We always poked our heads into a room once a day to check for taps left running or extractor fans left on, but just as I was about to tell him that, Eddie appeared with Rita clad in a turban towel.

"We decided to have breakfast and then shower. At least by then the water will be—"

Vincent pushed his way between them, forcing them aside. Puzzled, Rita, Eddie and I watched him dash up the stairs. He hadn't removed the labels from the soles of his boots.

"I would ask if it was something we said," Eddie said. His gaze alighted on Rita's towel. "But I have a feeling it may be the way we look."

◆

I'd finished cleaning the first floor ensuites and was about to head upstairs when I spotted Jason had wedged room three's door open. Polish cloth in hand, he stood by a bedside table.

"I forgot to tell you, they didn't want this room cleaned."

"Too late." He gave the side a quick wipe. "It's all done bar the hoovering and the ensuite. Not that I needed to do much. They haven't touched the cups or glasses, so I just did the bed and the bin." He frowned. "Odd. They'd filled it to the brim with wipes."

I gazed round at the spartan room. Apart from a slightly crumpled look to the remade bed and the suitcase zipped shut on the stand, the room looked just the way it had on their arrival the previous night. When Vincent had said it didn't need to be cleaned, they'd been right. I had no reason to check the ensuite.

"I'll leave a note to apologise."

When Jason gave me a puzzled look, I added, "Just to explain that I didn't pass the message on in time."

The telephone shrilled downstairs. I dumped the cleaning tub on the floor and sprinted off in search of the handset, which I found on the coffee table in the lounge, next to Jason's half-finished mug of tea. As I picked it up, the answerphone clicked in and I had to listen to the message before I could speak.

"You sound like a right old woman on that," Shona said. "You need to change your message."

"Thanks. Haven't you got any work to do?"

"We're dead here."

"We're not," I said, hoping she'd get the hint that I didn't have time to talk. "What do you need?"

"Nothing," she said.

I rolled my eyes, safe in the knowledge she couldn't see me. I had two ensuites left to clean, a breakfast room to set up while Jason vacuumed, a dishwasher to empty and refill, and a breakfast room to set up. Only then could we sit down.

"If it's not urgent, I'll call you after lunch."

"Who said it wasn't urgent?"

"Is it?"

"Well it depends on your point of view."

I sighed. "I'll call you later." And cut the call.

♦

The next morning the weak March sun pierced through the clouds.
I prayed it would win because I fancied an afternoon walk around
the harbour. We didn't have any check-ins, so the ironing pile could
wait. Maybe Jason could be persuaded to have a meal out
somewhere too. Plans in place – subject to the weather and Jason –
I cheerily handed two guests their breakfasts and turned to check
on another couple. My heart lurched. Eddie stood at the breakfast
room door. Rita hovered beside him in her familiar turban towel.

"I put my hand under the shower before I got in and it was hot,"
Rita said. "I kid you not, I'd just put my conditioner on and it went
from warm to freezing." She patted her turban. "It's meant to be
left on for two minutes but it won't harm having twenty while we
eat."

"I'm really sorry. I'll get Jason to speak to you. We can't be
having this happen for the rest of your stay."

Behind us Vincent scoured the ceramic from his plate. He'd
come to breakfast alone again as Sarah-Louise hadn't slept well and
needed a lie-in. After ordering a full English he'd fallen into a
contemplative silence, watching passers-by meandering along the

street, while he sipped his coffee. But now he shifted up a gear. The clang of metal on plate made us turn to watch him scrape the last of the bean juice onto his knife and wipe it along his tongue. In one fluid move, he threw the last dregs of coffee into his mouth and shoved his chair back.

We parted like waves as he dashed past without an 'excuse me'. Odd how each time Rita and Eddie appeared, he shot off.

Eddie watched Vincent take the stairs two at a time. "It *is* us!"

Rita patted the towel wrapped around her head. "I'll have a shower after breakfast tomorrow. Maybe's he thinks it's inappropriate to wear this to breakfast."

"I doubt it," I said. "Anyhow, they're leaving this morning."

After taking their order, I headed into the kitchen to tell Jason about the water issues. His gaze didn't stray from the pan of scrambled eggs he stirred, but he frowned.

"Again? But we haven't run out of water in a whole year with five showers on the tank and now we've only got two, this is happening."

I dropped the bread into the toaster. "Poor Rita's down with half-washed hair again. We need to sort it out."

After serving all the breakfasts, I took a tray and headed out to start clearing the empty tables. From the corner of my eye, I spotted Sarah-Louise and Vincent rushing out of the front door with their suitcase. This wasn't unusual; guests often packed their bags into their cars before coming back to say goodbye. But something made me follow them. If they were leaving, I needed our guesthouse keys. By the time I reached the front door, they'd made it to the car park across the road. Vincent pointed his keys towards the car and its lights flashed. He tossed his case inside the boot as if it contained nothing but air. When the boot closed with a thump, he raced round to the driver's side door, to find me standing there.

I couldn't help but smile at his surprised expression. "Are you off?"

"The keys are in the room door." Giving me a strangled smile, he arched past into his seat and closed the door.

I tapped the window and he muttered something to himself – or to Sarah-Louise, who'd already made herself comfortable in the passenger seat – and wound the window down, giving me a 'what now?' look.

"I need the car park pass."

He snatched it from the dashboard and handed it to me. I tucked it in my pocket and held out my hand, which he shook without comment, while Sarah-Louise stared out through the windscreen.

Irked by her rudeness, I raised my voice, "Have you had a nice stay, Sarah-Louise?"

Startled, she turned around, to find my hand held out towards her. She looked from my face to my hand and, biting her lip, shook my hand with the tips of her fingers. They felt like sandpaper rasping against my skin. When she pulled away, holding her arm out as if it was contaminated, I noticed her chapped fingers, the tips raw and ragged with dry skin.

"Hope you both have a safe journey back."

The moment the window clamped shut, Sarah-Louise spat something at Vincent and held her palm inches from his face. He shrugged and jabbed his thumb in my direction. The car accelerated away, leaving me with the image of her mouth, a dark pit of anger as she bellowed at him.

Dumbfounded, I stood for a moment, until I collected myself and headed back.

"Are you ignoring me?" Shona called from the front door of Jetsam Cottage.

"Sorry, I forgot to call!" Completely true, but it sounded false. "We haven't finished breakfast service, but I'll speak to you at lunch time. Honest."

I didn't wait for her to respond. I'd left the guests unattended in the breakfast room for long enough. Shona had waited a day, so what were a few more hours?

♦

After breakfast, a red-faced Jason flagged me down on the landing. In silence, he led me into room three where, like Vincent had told me, the key hung from the door. The duvet cover lay in a tangle on the bed – nothing out of the norm – while the bin resembled a volcano: a mountainous heap of facial wipes overflowed from it onto the carpet. But otherwise the room appeared to be in good order.

Jason stomped through to the ensuite where, hands on hips, he glowered by the doorway. In the gloom of the windowless space, I could make out a large mound in the shower cubicle. I snapped on the light and my mouth dropped open. The heap wasn't the usual towels but a twisted mass of, what appeared to be, clothing too. I hauled a pair of jeans from the pile, along with a cream jacket, and held them up to Jason. He looked as confused as I felt.

64

He scratched his head. "Why would anyone leave their clothes behind?"

"They're in good condition too."

Among the tangle of towels were T-shirts, underwear and a solitary trainer: its companion lurked somewhere, no doubt. When I dragged the pile onto the ensuite floor, the other trainer thudded down. Four empty containers littered the shower tray. One of them was familiar.

"She's emptied our shower gel and three of her own too."

Jason pointed to the pedal bin where two empty plastic bottles poked from beneath the half-open lid.

"There's more in there. At least we know who ran the tank dry both days. She must have been showering for ages to use this much gel."

He disappeared, returning with a bin bag, which he held out to me. When I gave him a look, he sheepishly picked up the trainers and dropped them into the bag.

"I doubt she'll say yes, but we'll write to see if she wants this lot back. I'm at a loss why she'd leave them," I said.

If she'd didn't want to pay for anything to be returned, I'd wash the jeans and jacket and take them to the charity shop. They were too good to bin.

Two small bottles lay in the sink. I examined them. Hand sanitisers. Empty, of course.

Jason tossed them in the bin. "She must have OCD. There's no other explanation. Maybe she thought these clothes were contaminated somehow."

I clamped my hand to my mouth. "Poor woman! No wonder she

didn't look happy when I shook her hand to say goodbye. And you cleaned this room yesterday when Vincent asked us not to. Now I feel terrible."

Jason shook his head. "We're not psychic. At least there's one positive. Rita can have a shower with hot water tomorrow morning."

# Chapter 8

As I WANDERED THROUGH THE HALLWAY with my sandwich in one hand and cup of coffee in the other, the phone rang. A familiar number showed on the screen. I considered ignoring it, but it was pointless. She'd simply knock on the door instead. Either way, my lunch would be disturbed. It was my own fault. I should have called when I'd promised yesterday. I laid the plate down and picked up the phone.

"Flotsam Guesthouse, how can I help?" Pretending not to know the caller would give me a few seconds more to formulate an apology.

"Okay, what have I done?"

I took the defensive. "Nothing as far as I know. We've just been busy."

"A call only takes five minutes."

Shona might be known for being blunt but she wasn't usually this prickly. Something must be up. "I'm sorry. I should have phoned. Is it urgent?"

"It's starting to get that way."

I took a sip of coffee and winced when it scalded my mouth. "How about I come round to talk when I've finished my lunch? Give me ten minutes."

"No more than ten though, or else Kim'll be back."

My guilt transformed into unease. If Shona didn't want Kim to be involved, then I shouldn't be either.

After a hasty lunch, we squared up to each other on her doorstep.

I'd been practising my use of the word 'no', but the minute I saw her face, I realised my hunch had been right. There was more to this than a simple favour. Beneath Shona's palpable anger, grey bruised the skin below her eyes and her usual pasty complexion was ashen. When her gaze fell upon the cottages across the road, she narrowed her eyes and her lips thinned to a blanched line.

"Are you okay?" I asked.

"Yeah." She swept her hand around as if she didn't have a care in the world, but her pinched expression told me otherwise.

She ushered me in. On the sideboard, the Buddha statue laughed beneath the trails of fake ivy from the pot above. Beside him sat a guestbook which hadn't had a new entry for weeks. From the look of it, if I smeared my finger along the sideboard I'd find a ribbon of dust. Unheard of when there were guests about.

"Are you closed?"

"You'd think so. We've got our first busy weekend coming up. But before then I get the honour of Kim's idiot brother coming to stay."

Shona led me through to the lounge. They'd replaced their old sofas with a corner unit. Their old one had a broken strut beneath the cushions, which plunged the unsuspecting visitor into the depths of the frame. This one looked like it could take the weight of a rhino. It was a similar colour too: slate grey.

I'd been invited in to see it on delivery day a week ago, but I hadn't been around since. The smell of new leather hung in the air, no longer overpowering but still noticeable. From the dips in the cushions at either end, I could tell Kim and Shona liked to lie against each armrest, which meant one of them would have to crane their neck to see the TV. Most likely Shona. For all her belligerence, she had a core of kindness.

She led me through to their kitchen. It smelled of detergent and the soles of my trainers stuck to the floor – a tell-tale sign that Shona hadn't diluted the floor cleaner enough.

"Used too much again?"

She rolled her eyes. "I keep forgetting its concentrate. I swear it works out cheaper to buy the usual stuff." She held up a mug. When I nodded, she popped a tea bag in each.

"So," she continued as she poured the water from the kettle. "Are you free tomorrow afternoon?"

It seemed like a throw-away remark, but I took care with my response. "I'm not sure. Jason mentioned we were running low on a few items."

"Jeremy's coming tomorrow. Kim's brother."

"Wallpaper brother or another one?"

Arching her eyebrows, she said, "Only little bro Jeremy would decorate three-quarters of a wall and hide the fact he'd run out of paper."

She went through to the lounge. Shona took the end I thought she would, then burrowed into the cushions and stretched her legs along the sofa, giving me a view of the dirt-stained soles of her socks.

After taking a sip of her tea, she said, "She paid him to do that job, you know. I asked Kim how much and it was over seventy for materials with labour on top. But he only bought two rolls and they're twenty quid each. I'm spitting." Oddly, she'd calmed down from earlier and looked quite serene. "Apparently she's offered him

69

more work when he comes down tomorrow. I've got a job for him too, to help him pay back what he owes. I've managed to get a ladder that'll reach to the roof."

"Where did you get it?"

"Well I hoped from you," she said. "But when you didn't return my call, Maggie and Jeff up the road agreed to loan me theirs."

"Ours wouldn't have been long enough."

"You can still help me, though. Jeff's done his back in and Kim'll be out picking up Jeremy, so can you give me a hand getting their ladder down the road tomorrow?"

"What will he be doing on your roof? Jason can help if there's something that needs fixing urgently."

Shona smiled. "That's lovely of you but, honestly, this job will be easy enough for Jeremy."

♦

Jason had insisted on going with Shona to collect the ladder rather than letting me do it. When they returned with the ladder hoisted between them, I followed them up the lane that ran beside our guesthouse to their back gate, where Shona led the way into her lovely courtyard garden. The sun warmed the tall stone walls. In the raised beds below, trumpet daffodils bullied clumps of Tête-à-tête and grape hyacinths. Beside Shona's circular patio table stood two glazed pots filled with clumps of leaves which promised an abundance of flowers over the next few weeks. Already a few red and yellow tulip cups swayed in the breeze. Shona and Kim must have bought the pots from the garden centre during a recent trip, along with the hanging baskets filled with winter-flowering pansies which hung on either side of the solar lights on the wall.

Many a time I'd gazed from one of our guest bedroom windows at the rear of the house and compared our desolate patch with their little Eden, although I wouldn't trade if their ground floor yard was part of the deal. Due to the hill behind our properties, our courtyards lay level with the first-floor rooms, accessed from steps that led from the ground floor. Luckily, the garden was inaccessible to guests as – unlike our guesthouse – if you tripped over the low wall by their steps there was a deathly plunge into the concrete abyss.

"Mind out!" Shona angled the ladder down. A small flat-roofed extension had been added to the second floor and it was this that Jeremy would be working on. I didn't envy his ascent above the mammoth drop.

Once the ladder had been placed against the roof, Jason turned to Shona. "What do you need doing? I've got a bit of time."

I grimaced at the drop below, but Shona patted his arm. "No need. Jeremy will be only too happy to help."

She took us down the steps into the high-walled dungeon just outside their back door, where the limewash was no longer visible through the green algae staining the walls and ground. Jason wrinkled his nose as the fusty smell hit us. Each day Shona and Kim passed through this hellhole to reach the gorgeous courtyard above, yet they seemed not to notice their dank surroundings.

We stepped into the utility room where paint tins littered the worktop, some with rusty lids. Maybe they were having a much-needed cupboard clear-out. I remembered Shona telling me that she didn't have to worry about guests marking the walls as they had leftover paint from when Maggie and Jeff owned Jetsam Cottage years before.

After flicking on the kettle, she took us through to the lounge. While Jason admired their new settee, I went to use their loo. On my return, I found they had been joined by Jeremy and Kim. She slipped off her coat to reveal a gorgeous short-sleeved yellow top that reminded me of the daffodils in her garden. Her brown arms shimmered. She'd showed me her new powder the other day, telling me she needed to liven up her dull skin after spending the winter shrouded in jumpers. The sparkle dimmed as she moved away from the window into the centre of the room, where she bent to give me a welcoming kiss.

"Nice to see you," she said. "Have you met Jeremy?"

I shook his hand. Black grime embedded his fingernails and his palm felt clammy, yet rough. He must have come straight from work; the tang of oil wafted from his grease-stained jeans and a tatty brown leather jacket. When his wide smile lit up his dark eyes, I could see the likeness between him and Kim.

"Looks like Shona will be keeping you busy," Jason told him.

Shona hurried in from the kitchen, wiping her hands on a tea-towel. "Not really. Kim's got plans for a walk to Shadwell Point, a trip on the steam railway and a couple of small jobs. So, he won't have time for much else."

Jason frowned. When he went to speak, Shona butted in. "Except when Kim's out tomorrow. I'll be looking after him then." She swivelled around to Jeremy. "We'll have a fab time, won't we Jezza?"

She received the flickers of his uncertain smile with gratitude. "It's always fun when Jezza's here."

After we finished our coffee, Jason and I headed out the front door. After Kim said goodbye and her attention turned back to Jeremy, Shona came over.

"I don't suppose I could grab you just to give me a hand for ten minutes tomorrow. Just while Jeremy goes up the ladder."

Jason scratched his jaw. "I've got to get the shopping in once the rooms are done, so it depends what time."

"I was thinking Katie could help. It's easy now the ladder's in place."

Something *was* up. She'd been too keen to turn down Jason's help.

"Okay," I said, but when Jason sauntered on to the guesthouse, I turned back, grabbing her by the front door.

"I'll help but just tell me this won't lead to trouble."

"What do you think I'm gonna do?" She shook her head and chuckled. "I'm only asking him to give me a hand. Kim'll thank us too."

♦

The next morning the phone rang on the dot of ten o'clock. We'd only just finished cleaning the kitchen. Glancing at the number – Shona's – I thought twice about answering, but it was pointless. She knew we'd be in at this time.

"Can you pop round now?" she said, without so much as a 'hello' or 'are you busy?'.

"I'm just about to start on the guest rooms."

"It'll only take a minute. Honest. Come round the back"

When I slipped through the back gate into her courtyard, I found Jeremy shielding his eyes from the glare of the early morning sun and surveying the roof.

"Moss, you say?" He brushed his hand over his cropped afro hair.

"Kim's been worrying about it. She forgot to ask but it has to be done this morning. The ladder needs to go back."

A dubious look clouded his face and a V cut between his eyebrows. For a moment, I thought he'd refuse, until he turned to me and flashed a smile.

"If you're here to hold the ladder, I've nothing to worry about."

I felt like a fraud. A liar too. Especially as the least trustworthy person stood beside me beaming an angelic smile. She gave him a gentle prod.

"Thought I'd try to kill you, did you? You should know me by now. Come along. Once you're up there, I'll throw you the broom."

Shona and I planted our feet at the foot of the ladder and gripped the rails. The ladder bowed beneath Jeremy's weight. With one tentative foot following another, he edged his way up.

Grinning, Shona said, "He doesn't like heights."

I gazed down. "I don't blame him."

The ladder rattled as Jeremy clambered onto the roof. He brushed his palms together and looked around. "I can't see much moss."

"It'll be on the pitched section," Shona called. "Stand back while I throw you the broom."

She turned to me. "We'll let you get back to work. I'll give you a ring when he's finished."

"Okay." I gave Jeremy a quick wave and headed towards the gate, pleased to escape without incident or injury.

Even so, something didn't feel right.

♦

With no arrivals due and just four occupied rooms, Jason and I undertook the servicing in just over an hour. While he headed off to the shops, I found an old episode of *Call the Midwife* on catchup and got on with the ironing. When he arrived back a few hours later, he carried a tray. Wincing, he stared pointedly at the TV.

"It needs to be that high or I can't hear them speak." The iron hissed as I lifted it.

He slid two plates from the tray and placed them on the coffee table. Perfect timing. With one last swipe, I finished the duvet and switched off the iron, only to be hit by the blast of the TV. I jabbed the volume button on the remote control and settled down beside him. He'd crammed my tuna mayonnaise sandwich with fresh lettuce, so it crunched when I stuffed it into my mouth. I added 'nom nom' noises for effect, to let him know how lovely it tasted.

Moments later, someone hollered, "Oh shut up!"

"What's that about?"

Jason shrugged. "I think Shona's having a barney with someone. Maybe you should close the window."

Shutting the window wasn't an option – the air hung thick with condensation from the steam iron – so I turned the volume back up on the TV. The afternoon news masked the noise, but it wasn't long before Shona's dulcet tones rose above the sound of Middle Eastern bombs. What on earth was she doing? I shoved the last of the sandwich in my mouth, took a glug of coffee to wash it down, and headed upstairs to one of the unoccupied guestrooms at the rear of the house.

Through the gauze-like voile, I spied the ladder leaning against the tall stone wall. Shona couldn't have needed my help to get Jeremy off the roof. She stomped up the steps into the courtyard, carrying a magazine which she tossed on the patio table. Muttering, she plonked herself down onto a chair, wrenched open the pages and pretended to read. I say 'pretended' because her body stiffened as if she was listening to someone or something.

Her mouth opened like she spoke to somebody, but she didn't move her gaze from the pages on her lap. Carefully, I eased the latch open on the window, holding my breath when she jumped up and slammed the magazine down on the patio table.

She cupped her hands around her mouth and bellowed, "How many times do I need to say it? Tell Kim what you did and how you'll be rectifying it at your own cost this week. Then I'll let you down."

Jeremy must be stuck on the roof! And I'd helped get him there. Why hadn't she just spoken to Kim? No doubt Shona's logic would lead her to think that Jeremy would wangle himself off the hook. But this wasn't the way.

I dashed down the stairs, passing a bewildered Jason, and ran up the lane to Shona's back garden. I expected the gate to be unlocked – after all it had been when I'd left – and almost broke my shoulder as it met the unyielding wood. I stepped back, grimacing and rubbing my bruised arm. This time I knocked. No answer. Then I hammered the gate with my fist, rewarded by a tiny splinter embedding itself in my skin.

"Come on, Shona. Open up."

"I'm stuck up here!" Jeremy shouted.

Shona remained mulishly silent. I leaned against the gate, nibbling at the splinter in my hand while I considered my next step. Inspiration hit me.

"Shona! Kim's on the other end of the line. She couldn't get hold of you for some reason, so she called me."

A scraping sound told me Shona was easing the bolt across. A clank told me she'd succeeded. The gate juddered open and she stood there, frowning.

'Kim?' she mouthed.

I put my finger to my lips and stepped into the courtyard. Jeremy sat on the small area of flat roof, cross-legged like a child, his chin in his hands. He perked up when I appeared.

"Why's he still on the roof?"

"Shush." She pointed at the phone. Her expression darkened as she spotted the screen. "You lied to me."

"And you co-opted me into helping you take him hostage."

"I can assure you no Jeremys will be harmed in the teaching of this lesson."

"You'll have to let him down," I hissed.

She sank back into her patio chair. "If he's done that to Kim, who knows what rubbish work he's done for his poor aunties? They all tell me how wonderful Jeremy is. Then they're calling Kim

77

because their new fridge has blown up or the belt's gone on the brand-new washing machine Jeremy bought just two months ago. Except Jeremy can't find the warranty, so he gets his mate over to fix it at a knock-down price. They don't realise he buys second-hand stuff that looks new and then he pockets the difference. Kim falls for it too. It does my head in."

"They probably do know. But he deals with all their issues, so they accept it." I sat down in the chair opposite.

A red bloom stained her cheeks, the only colour in her face. "I don't agree. He's taking advantage of his family. They might think he's the golden balls but I don't."

*Golden boy*, I almost corrected her, but stopped myself.

She clenched her fists and turned to him, raising her voice. "Well, he's sorting this out or he's not coming down."

"You don't need to shout," Jeremy said. "I heard every word. And, okay, I'll do the work. I'll phone Kim and tell her, like you asked. Just let me down."

"What's the passcode on your phone?" Shona said. "And I'll text her for you. Then there's no getting out of it."

"1-2-3-4." Jeremy sighed.

Shona shook her head at me. "I should have guessed. He's the Brain of bloody Britain. Bet that's his PIN number too."

# Chapter 9

THE FOLLOWING DAY I POPPED AROUND to Jetsam Cottage, worried that Kim would be annoyed about the unintentional part I'd played in yesterday's hostage situation. Heading across the driveway, I spotted the new neighbour leaning against the wall of his house, puffing on a roll-up. His knee poked through a tear in his jeans. He flicked his cigarette into the road and crossed his legs, so one leg of his jeans lifted to reveal a white trainer. Something about it seemed odd, but I couldn't say what. Not taking his eyes from me, he crossed his arms. When I rang the doorbell, I turned around, unnerved to see him still staring in my direction. Kim answered the door, but she didn't glance out and I decided not to mention the strange neighbour. Maybe he'd watched because I'd been looking at him?

From upstairs came the sound of someone whistling. When I was a child, older men used to whistle as they sauntered past, winking innocently and giving me a cheery hello, but it was odd hearing it now. Most people would have the radio on instead. At least that would conceal the bang of cupboard doors and the clatter of cutlery coming from the kitchen. Something would get broken soon.

Kim raised her eyebrows. "She's been like this for a few days now." She kept her voice low. "I think the man across the road is getting to her."

And Jeremy. But I let that thought remain unvoiced.

"He seems to appear each time Shona is outside," she continued,

"Apparently, this morning he stood there smoking and watching her as she cleaned the front windows."

"I saw him just now. Maybe he's got nothing else to look at?" As I spoke, it occurred to me that the man might have watched me because of where I headed: Jetsam Cottage. He hadn't been bothered with Jason or I before.

She shook her head. "That makes three of us. He's making a point and it's winding her up."

Something metal crashed to the floor, followed by an expletive. Kim ignored it. "I think that's why she behaved so oddly with Jeremy yesterday. I can't believe she did that. But he's upstairs sorting out the problem, so that's something."

Kim knew! But would Shona have told her everything or just the sanitised version?

The devil herself stomped into the lounge. "Coffee?" she barked.

Kim patted the cushion. "Here, I'll do it. You sit down."

"I don't need to sit down." Shona flexed her fists with agitation, then took a deep breath and turned to me with a smile, her tone almost saccharine. "I'll make tea instead. I know you prefer that, Katie."

She disappeared into the kitchen to treat us to the sound of water pelting the metal sink and the chink of mugs on the countertop, but the furious smashing had died along with her anger. The cupboards would live to see another day.

Kim exhaled and leaned back into the seat. "I could do with getting her away from this place for a few hours, but I don't think a day out with Jeremy would help."

Shona bustled around the kitchen. Even though her mood had lightened, her complexion seemed paler than usual and her jawline tensed as if she was clenching her teeth. Perhaps I could offer a solution.

"Emily phoned last night. She's popping down tomorrow while Lucy's seeing her boyfriend for a few days. Perhaps we could take Shona out for a walk? We've been promising ourselves a trip to Dartmoor."

♦

Ten minutes earlier, an optimistic Emily had ignored my warnings about Shona's timekeeping and had thrown her coat into the car boot, along with the walking boots and woolly hat I'd texted her to bring. Now she hopped from one foot to the other, rubbing her arms to keep warm, while I leaned against the car searching Jetsam Cottage for signs of life.

"Get in the car if you're cold," I said. "Or put your coat on."

"There's no point unless you put the engine on to warm it up." She kept up her Tigger impression until the front door of Jetsam Cottage creaked open, whereupon she dived into the car to secure the front seat.

I'd not seen Shona wearing a hat before, especially not one in fetching pink. She stomped over swaddled in a matching scarf and gloves and a thick navy duffel coat.

I hid a chuckle. "Pink suits you."

She grunted and pulled open the rear door.

"Ooh," Emily said. "Pink. I've not seen you in that before."

"Blame Kim," she muttered.

As I eased the car into the busy road, Shona's gaze didn't leave the cottage opposite, although nothing twitched behind the grubby net curtains. Her jaw clenched tight until we headed past the Toll House and out of Torringham, when she perked up.

"Do you mind if we take a diversion to a walk I used to do? There's a lovely stream and a little waterfall and hardly anyone goes there."

Emily threw me a pleading glance. I'd promised her a trip to Haytor and a cream tea at Widecombe-in-the-Moor. With the cleaning finished, thanks to Emily's extra pair of hands, and Jason dealing with the one check-in later in the afternoon, we could squeeze in Shona's walk – if it wasn't too far from civilisation. I had a feeling Shona's request had more to do with the need to be away from people, whereas Emily's choices would take us to Dartmoor's busier areas.

"Is it on the way to Haytor?" I said.

"Sort of." Shona settled back into the seat, then added, "I couldn't give you a place name, but I know how to get to it from here."

I didn't want to let Emily down. "Okay, we'll go to your choice first and then Haytor."

Over an hour later – much of it on winding roads – Emily and I clambered out of the car, thankful to stretch our limbs and turn our faces into the fresh breeze. Lush hills rolled before us, interwoven by hedges and dotted with copses and the occasional farmhouse. A car engine scarred the air as it rumbled along a winding lane, until it disappeared into woodland. Our world fell silent until a bird chirped nearby, its call returned by another.

"Beautiful," Emily whispered. "Look at those tors over there."

I turned from the greenery to where Emily pointed. Dartmoor's dark hills stretched along the horizon, some like mounds, others craggy. Later, when we drove into Dartmoor, we'd see the granite formations. I couldn't wait to see them up close, along with the free-roaming horses and sheep.

"Do you think that's Haytor?" Emily pointed to a rocky outcrop.

I shrugged. We'd find out later.

Behind us, Shona slammed her car door. She'd taken off her coat, scarf and hat in the car after complaining about the heat, but when we'd pulled into the car park she'd insisted on putting everything back on again before she got out.

"Bleeding cow pat." She gripped her calf while examining the sole of her boot. "Did you park next to it on purpose?"

"You chose to come here." From where we stood, concealed by the open boot as we put on our coats, I shared a secretive grin with Emily.

Huffing, Shona wiped her boot on the grassy verge. Once clean, she led us through a wooden kissing gate and onto a narrow track that wound around a field, from where we strolled through another gate and down a slope. While Emily chatted to Shona, I gazed around, enjoying the transformation from a landscape of enclosed fields into peaty-smelling woodland, in which bracken and twigs crunched beneath our feet and we had to keep a watchful lookout for trip-hazard tree roots. When we clambered over a broken-down stone wall, the landscape changed again and the air became damp. The gurgle of water echoed from the valley while ferns uncurled on the ridge nearby, soon to swathe the valley sides. Through a patchwork of branches a stream appeared, churning against the granite boulders strewn along its path. As I got closer, I realised it was wider than I'd first realised, and faster-flowing.

On our side the footpath headed upwards, away from the river, but Shona edged crablike down the bank and onto a flat rock that leaned towards the churning water. Did she expect us to cross by leaping from rock to rock? I didn't fancy our chances.

"Take care," she called "It's a bit slippery here."

She hadn't even reached the water's edge when her feet shot out from under her and she crashed down. Shocked, Emily and I raced over to her. As I neared her, my feet slithered on the slimy rock. No amount of arm circling could save me from landing with a sickening thump. Pain fired up my spine and down my legs and I gasped in shock.

Behind, Emily squealed with laughter, while Shona scowled. "I told you to watch out."

Shona planted her knees on the rock and got up, one foot at a time. Turning to me, she held out a hand covered with algae and slime. Mine matched hers. As I clutched her squelching palm, her feet slid from beneath her again and, eyes wide, she toppled onto me, crushing my legs.

When Emily's laughter became witch-like cackles, Shona's stony gaze met mine. She kept her tone menacingly low.

"I'm going to keep calm. Even though right now my feet are in the water and it's fricking freezing."

Using my shoulder as a crutch, Shona pushed herself free and stumbled to her feet. Emily's manic hooting had faded to snorts.

"Give your old mum a hand." Panting, Shona waved Emily over.

Rather than argue that Shona and I were the same age, I let them tuck their hands beneath my armpits and heave me to my feet. Pain and cold had numbed my bones and I felt ancient.

While Shona stood in drenched socks banging her boots against the rock in a futile attempt to dry them off – not caring that she showered us with droplets – I brushed myself down, before inspecting my throbbing elbows and rubbing my frozen backside. Satisfied I'd survive to see another day, I hobbled onto the bank.

"Do you want to go back?" I gazed at Shona's water-stained boots.

"I'm not gonna let a bit of water stop me." She peeled off her sodden socks and stuffed them in her jacket pocket without wringing them first. A bloom of moisture appeared through the material.

Shona looked at the rocks and the gurgling water and sighed. "How about we keep to this side of the bank and see where it leads?"

My backside still ached. I rolled my hips from side to side to ease the stiffness, wondering whether to mention going back. But we'd come all this way for a walk. If Shona could manage it in wet boots, I could deal with a few grumbling bones.

To the sound of Emily's chuckles, I followed Shona as the path angled away from the stream. When the path split in two, she didn't hesitate to take the left branch. When the track dipped around a corner, we could hear the familiar burbling of the river again. It grew louder until a waterfall appeared through the trees, cascading down a rocky incline. A wooden fence bordered the drop. I checked it stood firm before leaning over to gaze into the gorge. While not on the scale of the waterfalls I'd seen on holiday, it was stunning, especially since Shona hadn't breathed a word about what we would find.

The water dropped no more than twenty feet to splash onto the rocks below, churning and roiling as it rushed over stones and bubbled around boulders until it reached the calm beneath a canopy of trees. There it curved around a bend which led to where we'd tried, and failed, to cross the stream.

We stood for ages entranced by the water tumbling down and the birds that flitted among the trees. On the other side, a dog poked its head through the fence. Its owner waved and called out to us, but his words were swallowed by the waterfall. Woken from our reverie, we turned to move onwards, up a steep hill and into woodland. From there the path led us into a grassy field. Muttering something about not being caught out twice, Shona side-stepped a cow pat and stomped on ahead.

Emily slowed to link her arms through mine. "How's your bum?"

I grinned. "Sore."

She nodded towards Shona. "She's funny. One minute she's in a right grump and the next she's soaked and freezing but, for some reason, it makes her happy."

"I think it's given her something else to think about, other than whatever has been getting her down lately."

Emily shook her head. "I can't believe that man is so nasty to her."

There was little point mentioning how unsettled I'd felt when he'd watched me go to Jetsam Cottage. "It's odd. I've only seen him a couple of times, but Shona bumps into him all the time."

Ahead of us Shona shouted, "What is it with these cows and their sodding shit!" She lifted a brown-stained boot.

"Just like she does with cow pats," Emily chuckled.

While Shona wiped her shoe on the grass, Emily pointed to half a dozen cows grazing on the slope below us. "I haven't seen ones like that before."

They looked like every other brown cow until the sun's rays touched their silken coats. Then they glistened auburn, but the tips of their tails were frayed and blond.

Emily headed down for a closer look, but I hesitated.

"Take care," I called. "Don't go too close."

"Okay, Gran." Shona nudged Emily. "Your mum is becoming a right old woman."

But they came to a stop about ten feet away from the herd. The cows paused to assess them with curious gazes, but soon the sound of grass being torn from its roots once again mingled with the birdsong. Feeling more confident, I edged forward to stand by Emily. Flies buzzed around the cows, flicked away by an ear or a swish of a tail. Up close they smelled of manure – or was that Shona? I was about to make a joke when I spotted a dog haring down the hill. His flapping ears and lolling tongue reminded me of the cartoon dog, Roobarb, and he wore the biggest grin I'd seen on a dog. *Let me at those cows!* Behind him, his owner sprinted, arms flapping, screeching, "Fenton, Fenton!"

Fenton. Where had I heard that name before? Before I could

dwell on it, I realised we stood yards from huge beasts with hooves that could pound us into the earth.

"Run!" I hissed and grabbed Emily's arm. She'd spotted the dog and didn't need much convincing. We sprinted to the left. The beat of hooves told me the cows were on the run. Towards us or away? My heart thudded. *Please let us be okay.*

"Stop, stop!" Emily shouted. "Shona!" Instinct told me to keep going, but Emily pulled me to a halt.

Shona raced in the other direction, arms pumping, her face taut with fear. Behind her the cows picked up speed. Around their pounding hooves, divots flew into the air as if sliced by a knife, rather than torn by a huge beast. How would she survive being trampled by them?

"Go left," I shouted. One of the cows veered off towards Shona, but the silly woman (I nearly called her cow!) swung right.

"Left!" we screamed.

One cow overtook Shona, then another. Four others were on Shona's tail as she skirted a thistle. If she swung away, she'd be out of their path, but she followed the route of the two front-runners.

"Left" we bellowed again, using our cupped hands as microphones.

But still she ploughed on. The thud of hooves drove her forward.

When Shona became enclosed in a V formation by the cows, Emily covered her eyes. "Why won't she move?"

"She can't. She's trapped."

Unable to see anything other than the spikes of her hair and her boots behind the gleaming muscular frames that thundered beside her, I bit my knuckle and watched as our friend ran with the cows.

The cow surged forward, followed by another. Finally, they overtook Shona. Still she ran.

"She's chasing them!" Emily laughed. "I've got to get a picture of this."

As Emily whipped out her phone, I grinned with relief. "How long before she notices she's been beaten into last place?"

Moments later Shona jerked her head backwards, then to the other side, and her pace slowed. She pulled up and bent over, wheezing heavily. In the distance, a figure strolled up the hill and away from us, his dog now on a lead. If the man had been closer I would have wrung his neck, but instead I headed over to Shona and patted her back.

Her chest heaving, her eyes bloodshot from bending over, she straightened up. Her puce cheeks glistened and she swiped her forehead with the back of her hand, flicking away beads of sweat.

"Who'd have thunk it!" She gasped for breath. "Bloomin' Fenton's at it again. Isn't that the dog who chased the deer?"

Nonplussed, Emily and I shrugged at each other. Shona grinned. Her eyes sparkling with excitement, she slapped my shoulder. "That was flipping amazing. What are we doing next?"

# Chapter 10

KIM HEADED TOWARDS US, pushing a trolley laden with multipacks of cereal and loo rolls. Smiling, she drew alongside Emily who was endeavouring to persuade me to change our napkins from two-ply to three-ply to make the guesthouse 'posher'. Emily wouldn't win, and nor would we be getting the flowery loo roll she'd suggested.

"Look, Kim goes for the normal stuff." I pointed to the loo rolls stacked on her trolley.

Kim chuckled. "Don't talk to me about these. Shona's always moaning about the amount of toilet roll we go through."

Even when shopping, Kim was dressed beautifully, with her braids tucked inside a vibrant azure and lime headscarf which complemented her emerald blouse. I felt like a peahen in comparison.

She clutched Emily's arm. "Talking about Shona, you need to come back more often. I don't know what you did yesterday, but it's worked wonders."

Emily laughed. "Believe me, she did it all herself. I've never seen anyone run with the cows before."

"She gave me a garbled account. What really happened?"

While Emily told her about the day's adventures – we'd never reached Haytor as Shona was worn out – I sneaked the two-ply napkins into my trolley, re-joining the conversation at the part where Shona had kept running because she hadn't realised that all the cows had overtaken her. Kim's throaty chuckle had become a raucous laugh when Mike and Josie, friends who owned another guesthouse, turned the corner. Josie came over to give us all a kiss, smothering us in a waft of perfume, while Mike followed with a tall lad I hadn't seen before.

"What are you all laughing about?" Josie said, not waiting for an answer. "You must meet my Tom." Grabbing the lad's arm, she dragged him forward. His eye roll told us he wasn't impressed with the forced parade.

"Our son," she continued. "He's back from a year in Australia."

When we welcomed Tom, Emily hung back, clutching her hands. After a swift poke from me, she stepped forward with flushed cheeks to mutter, "Hello."

When our conversation moved on to chat about how our B&Bs were doing, Kim flashed a grin at me. Tom had wandered over to Emily.

"So, what do you make of this B&Bing lark?" he said.

She shrugged. "I'm not involved much now I live with my sister. I don't know how long for though, as she's talking about moving in with her boyfriend in Plymouth."

Startled, I tried to eavesdrop on their conversation, but Josie thwarted me by asking after Jason. As I stuttered my response, my mind reeled. Did that mean Emily would come back home? That would be a dream come true – if she could be happy in Torringham – but she'd given no indication that she wanted to do so. It also seemed a bit soon for Lucy to be considering a move to Plymouth.

Our conversation ended with the usual vying about which B&Ber had the most work to get back to. When Emily pushed the trolley away, her eyes sparkled and a pink stain tinged her cheeks. We moved on to the next aisle where I picked up a box of coffee sachets.

"And?" I asked.

She gazed down the list. "Tea bags?"

"I mean, how did your chat go?"

"You're so old-fashioned," Emily said. "Put a boy and girl together and they can't just have a platonic chat."

Her glow didn't suggest she'd just had a conversation about the price of eggs but I let it slide, until she elbowed me.

"You may as well know that we're going out for a drink later. And don't worry, I told him I couldn't go out until I'd seen Uncle Bert."

♦

True to her word, Emily stayed in until Uncle Bert appeared with Doreen. As he stepped into the hallway, he slipped his flat cap from his head and folded it in two, tucking it in his jacket pocket. He was my final link to my mother – his sister – who'd died years before. We'd bumped into each other by chance the previous year, after losing contact for decades, only for me to face losing him within months. He'd gone through so much since his operation to remove a kidney late last year, followed by the subsequent cancer treatment. Thankfully he'd started to look like his old self again. Eyes gleaming, he leaned forward to plant a kiss on my cheek. Now in retirement, he no longer carried a scent of grime from the building site. Instead he smelled of Old Spice, but his roughened palms remained a testament to his years of manual labour.

While he moved on to hug Emily, Doreen stepped forward,

drawing with her the faint scent of rosehip. A petite woman with a ready smile and grey hair set in curls, she seemed like my childhood idea of a grandmother, even though her son was a year or so younger than Emily.

She grasped my hand and gave it a squeeze. "Isn't he doing well?" Smiling, she watched Bert shake hands with Jason. "I never thought he'd get to see spring and his favourite tulips but..." She swallowed and her eyes brimmed with tears. "Look at me getting all maudlin when we have so much to celebrate."

She paused for a moment to compose herself and smiled. "It's lovely to see you and your gorgeous Emily. I wish I'd convinced our Callum to come now but he couldn't give up his evening at football."

"Emily can only stay for an hour – she has a date."

"Mum!" Emily said. "It's not a date. It's a chat."

As Jason ushered us into the lounge, Emily took up the rear with Doreen, explaining the reason for her visit – Lucy's boyfriend, Lester – and talking about her job. Although Doreen listened, she didn't take her eyes off Bert as he hitched up his trousers and eased himself onto the sofa with a sigh.

"Beer, wine, tea, coffee?" Jason said.

When he reappeared with the drinks, Bert sipped his cup of tea and gasped in appreciation.

"Nice brew that."

The sofa creaked as, mug in hand, he settled back into the cushions. Not a man of many words, he sat in silence giving the occasional chuckle or nod of his head while Emily relayed the story of Shona and the cows – this story was in for the long run – and

Doreen told us about Callum's recent driving test.

When the doorbell rang, Emily bounced to her feet. "That'll be for me!"

She planted a breathless kiss on Bert's and Doreen's cheeks, pausing by the lounge door to give us all a little wave before she left.

Bert tapped Doreen's arm. "That'll be our Callum next. Have you noticed he's been mentioning that lass, Chelsey, quite a bit?"

"Talking about Callum." Doreen cleared her throat. "Now Bert's well enough, we'd like to take a trip to Scotland. Bert's dream has been to visit the lochs. We've a favour to ask you though. Don't feel obliged to agree."

Her gaze moved from me to Jason, who gave a gentle nod for her to continue. She twisted her wedding ring and I felt a jolt of apprehension. What sort of favour would make her so nervous?

"Callum." Her hand moved to smooth the hem of her skirt and she cleared her throat. "He's old enough to look after himself but with him failing his driving test, he won't be able to get to work easily. He's started a job on a site in Berrinton. Could he stay with you both for the week? It's not until next month."

Relief flooded me. Was that all? Jason must have felt the same way, because he laughed. Our eyes met and we both knew the answer.

"Of course, we'll have him," Jason said. "We're pleased you thought of us."

"We trust you." Without a hint of humour, Doreen added, "I'm sure he'll behave."

Later when Jason and I lay in bed, he twisted round to face the window. Moonlight cut through a crack in the curtains and was mirrored in his eyes. His hand reached out for mine and he gave it a little squeeze, then he gently kissed my shoulder. Too tired to talk, I let my eyes flutter shut and I felt myself sink into the warmth of the bed.

"Did you think it was a bit odd the way Doreen said about Callum behaving?"

At first, I didn't hear Jason. Then his words seeped deeper into my subconscious and I woke to find he'd shuffled to the other side of the bed, drawing the duvet with him. Moments later his breathing eased and soon a faint snore told me he'd fallen asleep. While I – eyes wide as I gazed into the darkness – replayed Doreen's words and wondered what she'd meant by 'I'm sure he'll behave.'

# Chapter 11

A PETITE WOMAN WITH A PERFECT BLONDE BOB stood at the front door, leaving her husband sitting in their crimson Audi. If they'd read my booking email, they'd wouldn't have arrived two hours before our earliest check-in time but maybe she couldn't read as she'd also ignored the sign on the door which showed our check-in times in large red letters, which I'd printed after the episode with Vincent. Even more frustratingly, they'd arrived slap-bang in the middle of my lunch break. If I hadn't been expecting a parcel, I would have ignored the doorbell.

"We're a bit early." Wafting expensive perfume, she held out a manicured hand. "Patricia and Dan Davies."

As I smiled, I hoped the remnants of my hurriedly swallowed sandwich weren't jammed between my teeth.

"No problem at all. Let's get your bags."

I took the pass out to give to her husband, who'd apparently grown roots in the driver's seat and couldn't get out of the car. Helpfully, he pulled a lever to pop the boot open to allow me to unload the suitcases. When I saw their size, I regretted nominating Jason to attend the meeting about the new tourism strategy for Torringham and Berrinton. The tourist board had promised it would be short but, even if the presentation was brief, the question and answer session was a shirker's dream. They should ask 'who doesn't want to get back to work?' That would elicit the same number of hands as 'any questions?'.

The luggage must be my pay back for laughing at Jason's

misfortune when I'd waved him off an hour earlier.

"I'd take mine but I've hurt my shoulder." Patricia rubbed her shoulder and upper arm and mouthed 'ouch' to make sure I understood her predicament. Her breath warmed my ear as she hissed, "He's a lazy bugger at the best of times but, apparently, he's on holiday now, so he's doing sod all."

"Not to worry." I hefted both cases from the boot. They weren't heavy, just bulky.

We stepped aside, making room for Mrs Hollacombe who trundled past in her mobility scooter, with the usual adverts pinned to the sides of her vehicle. Today's offer wasn't the typical discounts at Gary's café or cheap fishing trips, but a never-to-be-repeated 50% off at Doggy Dogs' grooming parlour. To complement it, she'd tied numerous cuddly toy puppies to the rail on the back of her seat with green twine, but one dangled upside-down and bashed against the number plate. Open-mouthed, Patricia gazed after her. I chuckled at her expression. It was typical of the reaction when people met Mrs Hollacombe for the first time. Her eccentricity showed in her determination to support her family's various businesses.

While Dan drove across the road to park the car, I abandoned one of the cases in the hallway and took Patricia up to the second floor, giving her a brief rundown about the room before leaving her with a promise that the other case would be arriving soon.

By the time I made it downstairs, Dan stood in the hallway gazing at a black and white print of Torringham harbour in the 1920s. When he'd sat in the car, I hadn't noticed anything odd about his height, but he towered above the door frames on either side of him. In any other room this wouldn't be unusual – anyone over six foot had to duck to get through some of our squat doorways – but our hallway ceiling was at least eight-feet high and his head skimmed the lampshade. Why on earth had he booked the smallest room in the guesthouse? Not only would his feet be hanging off the end of the double bed, but he'd also picked the only room advertised as having a low ceiling due to the eaves. Patricia hadn't mentioned anything when I'd taken her into the room. She hadn't even raised her eyebrows or looked concerned.

"Your wife's upstairs." I hesitated. Should I warn him about the room before he went in? "I should let you know that you've booked a room with a height restriction. We don't recommend that taller people book this room."

One eyebrow lifted. "You'll need to move us then."

I gave him an apologetic look. "We're full or I'd do what I could. The issue is that guests book specific rooms and you've booked our smallest room which has a sloping ceiling by the bed."

"You mean my stupid cow of a wife has."

I had no idea how to respond, so I shrugged. "Shall I take you up to the room?"

"Be my guest."

A thick gold chain dangled from his outstretched arm as he stepped aside to let me pass with the second suitcase. He followed me, grumbling about the stairs not doing his knees any good, but he obeyed instructions to duck at points where the ceiling jutted into the stairwell, which meant he didn't have to worry about banging his head too. While I was used to climbing the stairs, I found myself panting because of the heavy suitcase, so I slowed on the pretext that he couldn't manage my pace.

"Let me guess – my wife booked a second-floor room."

Dousing the fire with a hefty glug of petrol, I said, "It's an Edwardian townhouse over three floors. We advertise that it's not suitable for people who cannot manage stairs."

We turned the final corner to room nine, when he stopped and bent over as if nursing a stitch. From where I stood on the stairs, his bald patch shone like a rosy apple under the landing light.

"Are you okay?"

He straightened up, his eyes watery, his face puce. "Not really."

"If this isn't right for you, you could book elsewhere."

"What's the likelihood of us finding a place in Torringham this weekend?"

He had a point. The Torringham Music Festival meant a bumper weekend for hotels and pubs.

"What about Berrinton?"

"That'd suit Pat but don't tell her that. I'd rather kill myself climbing these." He grimaced. "Although now might be a good time to tell her I cancelled the life insurance, so she needn't bother with this silly game."

We battled the last half-a-dozen steps in an awkward silence. My arms aching, I lugged the suitcase step by step, while he huffed behind me. When we reached the second-floor landing, I signalled for him to go ahead into the room and handed his suitcase over.

"When you're ready, come and check-in. No hurry."

To the sound of raised voices, I slipped downstairs. Hopefully, they'd spend so long unpacking that Jason would be back from his meeting and he could deal with them.

My wish was granted. An hour later my saviour came into the lounge pulling a face. I grinned. If he hadn't believed my story about the strange couple, he did now.

"They're a happy pair." He sank into the sofa. "Can you believe he refused to pay? She all but threw her card at me. I've left them bickering about whose idea it was to come down for their friend's wedding. They probably haven't noticed I've buggered off."

The guesthouse door slammed and Jason and I gazed at each other.

"How many days before they leave?" he said.

Half an hour later the doorbell rang. Two smiling faces greeted me at the door, suitcases at their feet. The woman held a long cerise dress on a hanger, while the man had strung a suit carrier over his shoulder.

"John and Mara Kennedy." He nodded towards a blue Fiesta parked on the side of the road with its hazard lights flashing. "I parked there while we unpacked. I'll move it in a minute."

"You'll need this to park across the road."

Jason handed him the pass and took the cases upstairs, leaving me to usher Mara inside, where we stood in the hallway making small talk about the traffic on the motorway until John returned. He wiped his feet on the mat and handed Mara a pair of sunglasses.

"Thanks, I'll need those."

After checking them in, I led the smiling couple upstairs. Jason came out of our bedroom and pulled a face and hissed, "They're back and still rowing."

"We've come for a wedding. My cousin's." Mara said in a cheery voice.

"I wonder if it's the same one our other guests are attending," Jason said. "Is it at Shadwell House Hotel?"

"That's the one," Mara said. "Ooh, you must introduce us at breakfast. It'll be lovely to know other people at the wedding."

As the strains of an argument filtered down the stairs, I grimaced. They'd get to hear from Dan and Patricia before then. Their rooms neighboured each other.

♦

The next morning, I came down to a breakfast room bathed in brilliant sunlight. Through the window, an azure sky promised a gorgeous wedding day for our guests' friends. Then I remembered Patricia and Dan and it was like a grey cloud passed across my mind. Would they be argumentative at breakfast? I tried to tuck my worries away and concentrate on the job in hand – setting up the buffet table – while reminding myself that we had no check-ins and the ironing could wait. This afternoon I would be walking in the sunshine, clambering over rocks, listening to the waves rushing over pebbles and breathing in the tang of seaweed. Afterwards, we'd head to the music festival and have a few drinks. Stuff our unhappy couple. They'd be gone tomorrow.

I headed into the kitchen. While Jason started preparing the hot food options, I sliced the fruit and decanted the orange juice and milk into jugs, taking them and the yoghurts and jams through to the breakfast room. The dairy products and juices sat on a chilled tray, while all the condiments and fruit were in bowls in front of the cereals. It was more than ample for our sixteen guests, especially with a range of hot options, but I added another jug of orange juice, just in case.

The smell of bacon floated from the kitchen, where I could hear Jason singing along to the radio. At five minutes to eight, I unlocked the door to find Mara and John standing outside.

"We're a bit early," she said. "We don't mind waiting out here until eight."

Often guests would stampede into the breakfast room the moment I opened the door. I'd taken to locking it after I'd come out of the kitchen once to find a couple sitting at a table waiting to be served, twenty minutes before breakfast time. When I'd explained that we weren't ready, they'd volunteered to sit and wait, silently tracking my every step until I offered them coffee while I set up.

Mara and John didn't move, so I ushered them in and invited them to take a seat. After chatting about their evening watching a local band at a pub, I left them tucking into yoghurt and fruit while I went through to make them a pot of tea.

Then a loud squeal from the breakfast room made me jump and boiling water splattered from the tea pot. Nursing my throbbing hand, I raced into the dining room to find Mara with a huge grin on her face.

"I don't believe it! Of all the people to bump into."

She got up and dashed over to Patricia, who stood rooted by the breakfast room door, wearing a look of dismay. Her expression turned to horror when Mara pulled her into a hug. How Mara didn't notice she was cuddling a statue, I don't know.

Trapped by Mara's wave of affection, Patricia couldn't see Dan's impression of a grinning Jack-in-the-box as he bobbed around taking great delight in his wife's discomfort.

"Aren't you going to introduce us, darling?"

Mara draped her arm across Patricia's drooping shoulders. "We work together. Can you believe it? Two hundred miles and we've chosen the same place."

"She's the receptionist," Patricia said. For my benefit, she added, "I'm required to attend high-level meetings, so I'm rarely in the office."

Mara cackled. "Ooh, listen to you. If I go out to pick up supplies, can I be high level too?" Not waiting for an answer, she pointed to her husband. "We're just by the window. Let's see if we can pull the tables together."

"I prefer it over there." Patricia pointed to the other side of the dining room. "Away from the sun."

Dan wheedled his way between the women. "Don't be silly, darling. We came down early to get a window seat. Let's join them." He pointed at me. "Can you move those tables together?"

Mara and I took the table, while John left his half-eaten breakfast to drag the chairs across the floor. A glob of blueberry yoghurt clung to his bottom lip.

"Look at you. What are you like?" Mara wiped his lip with her finger and stuck it in her mouth. "Yum. Which one is that?"

Deflated, Patricia crumpled into her chair. After taking her order for a strong, black coffee and Dan's for an Earl Grey tea, I rushed back to the safety of the kitchen, where Jason wilted beside an oven belching the smell of sausages.

"Sounds like things are getting as heated out there as in here." He stepped into the courtyard to fan himself, rolling his eyes when another squeal came from the breakfast room.

"That's amazing! We're going to the wedding too!" Mara said.

"We're getting a taxi. You should join us," Dan boomed and I could picture Patricia's expression.

"Just pray it doesn't reach boiling point," I said.

♦

After a busy breakfast service, I came out of the dining room to find Dan and Patricia hissing at each other in the hall. Hoping I hadn't been spotted, I stepped back in retreat but Patricia pounced.

"We're leaving."

For a moment I wondered what she meant, then it clicked. "What about the wedding? Where are you going?"

"Anywhere but here."

I gazed from her to Dan who stood with his arms folded, displaying the same stupid grin that he'd worn when he'd seen Mara with Patricia. I wasn't going to be part of their sport. The sooner I dealt with them, the quicker I'd get the rooms serviced and Jason and I could get out for the afternoon. They'd paid and they wouldn't be getting a refund.

"I'm sorry to hear that. Can we help you with your luggage?"

She flung her arms out like an opera diva. "Is that all you can say?"

Did she want me to beg her not to go?

Her expression became a snarl. "Call that customer service. The room is small, it's on the second floor, built for hobbits, and we were forced to breakfast with people I wouldn't choose to talk to, let alone dine with."

I kept my voice calm, although inside I shook with anger. "You booked a small room. You knew it was on the second floor and that it had a low ceiling too. When we spoke about it you thought a low ceiling would be in your words, 'delightfully quaint'." I air-fingered the quotes.

"Then, you agreed to sit with your friends. In fact..." I glanced at Dan – a big mistake as it made me want to scrub the smirk from his face – your husband asked me to put the tables together because you two seem to get some perverse enjoyment from being nasty to each other."

I'd gone too far. Her eyes narrowed and she clenched her jaw. Dan flushed. I may not like them, but this was our business and they were our guests. I searched for a way to lighten my furious words.

"That was a bit harsh, but—"

"Harsh? Bloody rude more like. We demand a refund." Dan stretched to his full height to intimidate me.

No way would he win. Although it cricked my neck to do so, I locked my gaze onto his and kept my voice level, my tone low.

"A: Patricia knew everything about the room and B: you asked to join the other guests this morning. Everything you are unhappy about is what you have chosen. If you leave, it won't be with a refund."

Behind us, the stairs creaked. Mara came into view, dabbing her eyes. How long had she been there? It didn't take long to find out. She pointed a quivering finger at Patricia and said in a trembling voice, "You're no better than me. Don't forget that I know you got your friend to access the boss's computer and give you the interview questions. And you lied about your qualifications."

Beside us, the door creaked open and Jason stepped out. His smile faded when he saw our serious faces. "Is everything all right?"

"Not really," I said. "I think these people need some privacy."

I manoeuvred him back into the breakfast room and leaned against the door, sighing with relief.

"What—"

"Shush!" I put my finger to my mouth and began to whisper an explanation. But there was no need. Mara's recriminations filtered through the door, becoming louder and louder as her list of complaints about Patricia grew. Even Patricia's occasional muttered, "Sorry, sorry" couldn't calm her. Not a peep could be heard from Dan, but I bet he'd lost his stupid smile, whereas I'd found mine.

After a few minutes I got bored and headed to the kitchen to join Jason, where he was piling the cups and glasses onto trays to take to the rooms. Snatched words echoed from the hallway.

"We're trapped in here. Unless we can somehow get through them."

"I think the whole guesthouse is in hiding. That Mara has a good pair of lungs on her." Grinning, he pointed through the back door. "Follow me. We'll go around them."

Jason took a tray and headed out. I grabbed a set of keys from the side and followed him with the other tray. We climbed the steps to our tatty little courtyard on the first floor, where he placed his tray on the top step. Between the tall stone external wall and the guesthouse, ran a thick concrete ledge, the width of a path, that led to what must once have been a doorway to the first floor. Now half-bricked up, it had become one of the windows in our bedroom. Thankfully we'd left it ajar to air the room. Shielding my eyes from the sun, I watched him clamber inside then passed him both trays.

"Teamwork." I followed him into the dark room, feeling the sun's warmth fade. Our lucky guests had a lazy day ahead beneath the incredible sapphire sky. I couldn't wait to join them.

I'd worry about Dan and Patricia later. If they stayed, fine. If they left, great. But regardless of what they did, I would have my afternoon in the sun.

"Let's get this done. I need to get out."

The cleaning took an hour longer than usual, not helped by many of the guests barricading themselves in their rooms until the rumpus died down. Even after it had, it seemed that no one wanted to risk bumping into the unhappy group, so they hung on until they were certain of a safe exit. Jason and I started on Mara and John's room then moved across to Patricia and Dan's. Strangely, they had not packed a single item.

We didn't see either of the warring couples before we left for our walk, even though they would need to get dressed for the wedding. I didn't give them a second thought as we headed out into the glorious sunshine, sunglasses on, book in bag, and Jason's hand holding mine.

♦

A set of room keys sat on the reception desk. After checking the room number, I did a little happy dance. Bouncing the keys in my palm, I waltzed into the kitchen where I hung them on the rack with a "Ta-da!". Not only did it mean two fewer people for breakfast but, even better, the keys were Patricia and Dan's. I turned the radio on to find Madonna's *Holiday* playing. Humming along, I opened the fridge and started breakfast preparations.

Mara and John were the last through the door, a few minutes before service ended. When I took their drinks order, she gazed around the dining room.

"Are Dan and Patricia not coming down?" Oddly, she sounded disappointed.

"They've checked out."

Her shoulders drooped. "After Dan left the wedding early, we had a good old chat."

She saw my puzzled look. "Of course, you wouldn't know! Patricia came over to me at the wedding and apologised. We had a right good time and she told me something too." She winked at John and laughed. "Don't worry darling, she hasn't given me ideas."

She dropped her voice to a whisper, but it still rang through the room, turning a few heads. "Patricia's going for a divorce. Dan doesn't know yet, but…" She tapped her nose. "He will by the end of today. Apparently, he doesn't treat her well. He's got a serious heart condition. He might kick it any day, but he cancelled his life insurance, just to be spiteful. Can you believe that?"

So, not only had Patricia booked a second-floor room when Dan had dodgy knees, but he also had a heart problem. He was probably safer without life insurance.

Mara gazed at me. She'd just told me juicy gossip and obviously expected a response. My mouth opened and closed while I thought of standard phrases – 'that's interesting' or 'how shocking' – but I couldn't lie. She'd fallen for Patricia's 'love-in' at the wedding, not realising it was to elicit sympathy and to stop Mara from telling her colleagues about Patricia's interview lies. 'Can't you see she's playing you like a puppet?' I longed to say, but it wasn't my place to do so. Like a hairdresser, a B&B owner should listen but not offer unasked-for advice.

Instead, I simply said, "I'll get you a pot of tea." and hotfooted it into the sanctuary of the kitchen, where Jason sweltered by the stove.

"From now on I'm changing the expression to 'If you can't stand the heat, get into the kitchen,'" I told him. "I don't think I can bear to hear any more about poor little Patricia. How about I cook and you serve?"

"You've heard the one about too many cooks?" He turned the sausages on the griddle. "Well in your case, you can't even manage toast."

As he spoke, a burning smell filled my nostrils and I shot over to the toaster, groaning at the blackened slices.

To my horror, I heard another squeal from the breakfast room. Mara! Maybe Dan had gone home alone, leaving the keys, and Patricia had just appeared in the breakfast room. I wouldn't put anything past that couple. I hurried out to find all eyes on Mara who clutched her mobile phone. She held it out to me.

"Look, look!"

I took the phone from her. A smiling Mara and John gazed from the screen. His cheeks were flushed and his forehead glowed under the camera flash.

"Lovely pic," I said.

"Noooo!" She snatched the phone from my hand and jabbed the screen. "Here!"

I squinted at where she pointed. If my eyes didn't mistake me, it looked like Patricia in an embrace with a man two foot shorter than Dan.

"Oh!" I said.

"Oh indeed." She grinned. "The girls in the office will *love* this."

# Chapter 12

A STAIN BLOOMED ACROSS ROOM THREE'S CEILING. Shaking my head, I headed off in search of Jason, who shot me a look of despair when I told him the bad news. I'd painted the ceiling less than two months ago and now it would need repainting. But while I felt hard done by, Jason faced a day of pulling up floorboards in the room above to track the leak we thought we'd solved.

An hour later, he ducked through the lounge door and slumped onto the sofa. I waited in expectant silence while he rubbed his eyes.

In the end I had to ask, "Is it sorted?"

He shook his head. "We'll need to get the plumber back again. The pipe needs welding."

Sarah appeared at the doorway. "Have you got the…" Her gaze rested on the duvet cover.

"Just this last bit to do." Steam hissed as I gave the duvet a final swipe. "I'll just do the pillowcases and then I'll move onto the room trays."

After I'd finished the pillowcases, I left Jason talking on the phone to the plumber and went upstairs to find Sarah holding a towel ring. Two screws sat in the cupped palm of her other hand.

"Sorry." She grimaced. "I bumped into it and it fell off."

I shrugged and placed the towel ring and screws on the side. "Don't worry. If it was that loose, anyone could have done it."

As the doorbell rang, I left Sarah and hurried downstairs, surprised to find Kris the plumber standing on the step. His

111

muscular build filled the door frame. He'd tucked his tight black T-shirt into his jogging pants. Perhaps he'd stopped off on his way to the gym? Wherever he was heading, he must be in a rush, because he'd abandoned his van across two spaces on our drive. I was just about to remark about coincidences when the lounge door creaked open and Jason appeared.

"When you said one minute, I didn't believe it," Jason said.

"You struck lucky I was passing. An hour more and I'd be stuck at the job in Berrinton."

While Kris hoisted his toolbox into the guesthouse and followed Jason up the stairs, the scent of aftershave trailing in his wake, I headed off to the kitchen to collect the cups and glasses for the rooms. The dishwasher had finished its first run, so I put everything away and reloaded it. Then, to the sound of cups and glasses chinking on my overloaded tray, I made my way back upstairs where I found Sarah in room five.

"You never said you were arranging eye candy," she said.

"Eh?" I settled the tray on top of the chest of drawers.

"That man. He's gorgeous. He caught me borrowing this from his toolbox." She held up the screwdriver. "I thought it was Jason's, so I took it to mend the towel ring."

I could have sworn she'd had her hair in a ponytail a moment ago. Now her blonde tresses settled over her shoulders and her lips glistened. Since when did she wear thick lip gloss to clean the rooms? She flushed under my scrutiny.

"Sadly, I think he's accounted for."

"All the best ones are. But a girl's gotta hope. He said I can borrow his tools anytime."

"If that's the case, we could do with his blow-torch. Just in case he leaves us with another leak."

"Blow-torch!" she chuckled. "Strange how tools are all named after sex. No wonder men don't stop thinking about it. Tool, screw, blow, nuts." She counted them out on her fingers, hesitating when she reached the fourth digit.

"You're stretching the point there. Hammer, saw, plane."

"Well, you hammer away at it. And..." She hesitated. "If you saw a guy and fancied him, it would be *plane* what the next step would be."

I chuckled. "I can see you've thought about this a lot."

"Probably too much." Her expression became wistful. "I'm being silly, I know. But it would be nice to meet a guy who isn't taken. I miss being in a relationship."

◆

At lunchtime, Jason and I decamped to the lounge with our sandwiches to watch TV. Jason had replaced the floorboards and the carpet but needed to go to the hardware store in town to buy stain sealant for the ceiling in room three, while I made a dent in the ironing pile. Later we had two couples checking in, but Jason would be back in time to help.

"Did you hear Kris talking to Sarah?" Jason said.

"What about?"

"Apparently, he needs a cleaner on a Friday afternoon. Sarah asked if I minded and I said no."

That didn't make sense. Why would he need Sarah to clean for him and why ask all of a sudden? "Hasn't he got a wife and children?"

"What's that got to do with it? He needs a cleaner to help now his wife's just had child number three."

While there might be a good reason for Kris's need for a cleaner, I felt uncomfortable that he'd asked Sarah. She'd glowed with excitement after he'd chatted to her and seemed so vulnerable when she'd said how she missed being in a relationship.

Kris bothered me. But I couldn't explain why.

Jason got to his feet and brushed the crumbs from his trousers, ignoring my frown when they spilled onto the carpet. "Right, I'm off."

My plans for an afternoon spent ironing were put on hold after I took a call from Kim. Their car had broken down and she needed to get a set of jump leads to Shona. I'd volunteered – Jason had enough on his hands with mending the ceiling. But our guests arrived early, so Jason ended up dealing with them and the ceiling, while I had a pleasant drive out to Kentingbridge followed by the obligatory ironing.

That evening, Jason and I ate our lasagne dinner on our laps while watching a film. I'd chosen a romcom, but neither of us were enjoying it. When my mobile beeped and a message from Sarah appeared on the screen, I frowned, hoping she wasn't texting to cancel her next shift. It sounded again. A second message? How odd.

I placed my knife and fork on the plate and picked up the phone, swiping the screen so the full message appeared.

*I heard back from that plumber. He doesn't need a cleaner. Not*

114

*sure if it's a compliment or I should be annoyed. Either way, it's a no. Thought it might make you laugh. X*

She'd copied a message from Kris and sent it to me too. I read it twice before tossing the phone to Jason. Laugh? It made me furious.

*Hi Sarah. It's Kris (we met today). Well... I told the Mrs about you... I might have said you were fit! Now she won't go for it. She doesn't trust me with a hot cleaner. Sorry about that. Take care though. X*

"Why on earth is he telling his wife that the new cleaner's fit and then going back to Sarah like that? His wife's only just had a baby for goodness' sake."

Jason's forehead creased as he read the texts. "Maybe it's his way of encouraging his wife to lose weight." Spotting my darkening expression, he quickly added, "I'm not saying I think it's right. Just that might have been his plan. It's a bit off to send that to Sarah, though."

"Maybe we need a new plumber."

His eyebrows shot up. "You try finding one who turns up when called. Like I said, it's a strange thing for him to say but..." He shrugged. "It's not like he's actually done anything terrible."

I took the phone from him. "Even though she's laughing about it, she'll be gutted. It's odd. She's young, but she doesn't seem to go out. She'll never find a relationship if she's stuck in watching TV every night."

"Who knows what people get up to in their private life."

Jason stuffed a forkful of lasagne into his mouth, following it with a slab of garlic bread. The conversation had ended. Hopefully, the leak had stopped too. That would solve a lot of potential problems.

♦

The next morning, an elderly couple hovered by the breakfast room door in thick coats, a newspaper tucked beneath the man's arm. This was not unusual, as many of our guests took an early morning walk to buy a paper or get some fresh air. The couple gazed into the room, looking confused. They must be the ones who'd checked in yesterday while I'd been helping Shona and Kim with their car. Everyone else had come in within minutes of the breakfast service starting, so the breakfast room buzzed with chatter, which could be discomforting for some new guests. I headed over and gave them a welcoming smile.

"There's a few seats to choose from." When they didn't move, I pointed to a nearby table. "Why don't you sit there?"

The woman followed me. Grunting, she stooped to place her handbag on the floor and with gnarled fingers began to unbutton her coat. The man shrugged off his coat and strung it across the back of the chair, refusing my offer to take it. He sat down, folded his arms, and gazed around.

Frowning, he hollered to his wife, "Where's Bert and Edith?"

"Maybe they got caught up?" The woman made a show of looking up and down the breakfast room, although they'd both scanned it earlier. Then she craned her neck to look out of the window. "But I would have thought they'd be here by now."

Edith and Bert must be arriving soon to take this couple out. We often had people staying at the guesthouse when visiting family and friends living nearby. Once we'd come back to find a bunch of strangers sitting in our day room – friends of our guests who'd gone upstairs to change before going out. Another time we'd accommodated a family who asked if a relative who lived nearby could join them at breakfast. But Jason hadn't mentioned anything this morning.

"If you need to get away, I can take your order now." I whipped the pad and pen from the pocket of my trousers.

The woman cast a final gaze to the window and turned back to the man. "Maybe they've come and gone." She pursed her lips. "I didn't think we'd been that long."

The man eyed my pen hovering above the pad and sighed. "The same as yesterday, please."

"Yesterday?"

He gave me a hard stare and pointed to the kitchen. "Ask your friend."

Maybe they'd been at a different guesthouse the day before. Many guests spent a week travelling around the south-west, stopping for a few days here and there. I decided not to point out they'd arrived the previous day and they must be confusing us with another B&B.

"I'm really sorry. Can you just remind me?"

In the kitchen, I slapped the sheet on the counter next to where Jason cracked eggs into a frying pan. "When you've done that, here's your final order. Unless you've agreed to let anyone else come to breakfast."

His "Eh?" told me all I needed to know.

When I headed back into the breakfast room, a couple I'd never seen before sat at a table at the back of the room. Confused, I counted the guests. Two had already left – they'd gone moments before the elderly couple had arrived – but eight people sat in the guestroom. We had five rooms in. Ten guests. But we had twelve guests for breakfast.

I did a swift about-turn back into the kitchen, where I grabbed Jason by the arm and signalled for him to follow me. He jabbed his finger towards the frying pan to show me he was busy, but I hissed, "I need you for one second. That's all."

He threw his hands in the air but obeyed. We stood at the entrance to the breakfast room, where he gave me a blank look.

"Do you know them?" I whispered and pointed to the couple who'd just arrived."

Puzzled, he said, "What? The Petersons? What about them?"

"We've got too many guests."

"How can we have too many guests? Look, I really have to get on."

"What about those two?" This time I surreptitiously pointed towards the elderly couple.

"No idea. I've never seen them before." He swung back into the kitchen, muttering about eggs.

I hovered in the doorway. The couple who'd just arrived in the breakfast room caught my eye and threw me uncertain smiles – most likely wondering why I didn't come over to take their order – while the other couple sat in silence, tapping their fingers on the table. No doubt missing Bert and Edith, whoever they might be. I swung by the Petersons' table, promising to be back in a moment

118

to take their order.

My nerves churning, I cleared my throat and crept over to the other table. What was I supposed to say? "Excuse me." I kept my voice low. "It appears that you don't seem to be staying at this guesthouse."

Startled, they looked at me.

"What on…" The man clenched his fist as if to bang the table but stopped mid-air. Slowly, his mouth formed an 'o' and his eyes met his wife's.

"Oh gawd," she said. "I thought it was all a bit odd."

"I'm so sorry," he stuttered. "The door was open. The couple said to go through."

He scrambled to his feet, tugging his coat from the back of the chair. "This isn't Jetsam Cottage."

"That's next door." I handed the woman her coat and ushered the couple out. In the kitchen, Jason sounded his bell but I ignored it. "An easy mistake to make."

As I went to close the front door on them, I caught the woman's shrill cry, "Bert! Edith! There you are! You won't believe—" The door clicked shut, cutting off whatever 'unbelievable' tale was being told.

Jason had given up waiting for me and had taken the two breakfasts out. I bustled past him, ignoring him shaking his head at me.

"Sorry about the wait," I told the Petersons. "What can I get you?"

The man grinned. "Not what they ordered."

An hour later my mobile phone dinged. I picked it up to find a message from Kim containing half a dozen 'crying with laughter' emojis. She didn't need to say any more. We'd be the butt of all the B&Bers' jokes for weeks to come.

# Chapter 13

THE TEASING LASTED FOR JUST A DAY, until Jason turned the tables by telling Kim and Shona that their guests had no doubt heard about our fantastic breakfasts and hoped to sneak in unnoticed. Usually, Shona would burst out laughing, offer a witty retort or even punch him on the arm, but she seemed to take umbrage and Kim had to point out that he'd been joking. Shona's sense of humour failure seemed part of a wider pattern of ups and downs.

Later, Kim caught up with me outside the guesthouse. "I think something else has happened with that nasty man across the road. Can you speak to her? She won't talk to me."

Jason and I rarely saw him. Apart from the one episode when he'd stared at me when I'd visited Jetsam Cottage, he no longer even glanced in my direction but shuffled off down the road, the mandatory roll-up hanging from his mouth. Occasionally a strong aroma hung around him, which smelled suspiciously like weed.

Kim twisted a braid of hair around her fingers. She'd had her hair restyled, her braids entwined with lighter strands. Her dark eyes held mine. She didn't need words to show how much Shona troubled her. But what could I do? Shona wasn't the touchy-feely type. If I asked about their neighbour, she'd probably become defensive or just tell me he was horrible, without any explanation of what he'd done to be awarded that label.

Behind us came the sound of gravel crunching and Shona stomped towards us, kicking stones across the drive. A corner of her shirt hung from the waistband of her ill-fitting jeans, which sagged at the knees.

She gave me a fleeting smile. "You okay?"

Not waiting for an answer, she turned to Kim. "I could do with a hand."

"With what?" Kim said.

Shona's gaze flickered over to the cottage opposite. "I can't find the corkscrew."

"It's in the drawer."

"It's not."

Kim sighed. "Come on then. Is it really that urgent at three in the afternoon?" She paused as she turned to go, resting her hand on my arm. Her pleading eyes met mine. *Do something, please.*

"I'll call you tomorrow."

I gave her a hopeful smile. "We've got Callum arriving then. I'll bring him round to say hello and we can have more of a chat."

♦

Even though we'd met Callum half a dozen times, he lagged behind Doreen and Uncle Bert at the door and had to be coaxed into the lounge, where he perched on the edge of the sofa in between his parents. He'd got this from Bert, who usually sat on the edge of a seat, as if ready to spring to freedom at any time, but today Bert settled back into the cushions, his flat cap folded on the armrest. Callum ran his fingers along his fringe, curling it away from his eyes and gazed around the room. He had Bert's eyes: deep blue, the same as my late mum's too. It unnerved me to think I'd spend the next week gazing into her eyes.

Doreen tugged the hem of her dress from where it had been pinned beneath Bert's thigh and smoothed it. For some reason, she always looked as if she'd dressed for church. On the occasions I'd visited her at home she wore a flowery dress and, if she popped to the shops, she'd tuck her curls into a hat and fasten her belt around her coat. She reminded me of my childhood in the seventies, when sixty-year-olds wore the uniform of their age. From what I gathered, she'd met Bert in her early forties, when he'd just turned fifty and they'd married soon after. Neither had children from previous relationships and Callum was their only child. Sometimes, like now, he seemed younger than his twenty years.

"I feel like a child being babysat," he said, echoing my thoughts. "I could have taken time off work and not bothered you."

Bert sighed. "I told you, lad. You can't let Len down when he's at this point in the build. How would you get to work each morning?"

Callum shrugged and turned to me. "I don't mean to be rude, mind. It's just that it feels like a lot of bother."

I smiled at him. "It'll be nice for your parents to get away. And for us to get to know you too."

Bert poked his arm. "And that lass you liked at college. Weren't she from Torringham?"

Callum rolled his eyes. "Da-a-d! That was years ago!"

Doreen smiled. "Perhaps that's part of his reluctance to stay in Torringham."

As poor Callum's blush deepened, Bert grinned. "My parents used to have a field day embarrassing me. I swore I'd not do it to my own, but it's too much fun." His chuckle became the familiar *he-he-he* that he and Mum shared. Bert turned to me. "I remember when they caught your mum creeping into the house in the early hours after a wild night out with Tom Jones."

My mum? Wild? Those words were like a square peg in a star-shaped hole.

Since Bert was my only living connection to Mum, I leaned forward, desperate to hear more. "What happened?"

"Well, not much. This were your mum after all. She and her mates had missed the last train back after the concert." He rewarded me with another bout of laughter until, catching my expression, he slapped his leg. "Bet you thought I meant she'd been after Tom Jones. What are you like?"

I had. But not *that* Tom Jones. I'd assumed he'd been talking about a local lad, rather than her going to see a concert.

Callum grinned, pleased not to be the centre of attention for a change.

"Our parents used to tease her rotten about fancying Tom," Bert said. "Not realising how close they was to the truth, being that's where she met your dad, Tom."

He added the last part, as if I didn't know my dad's name. I shifted forward. While not prone to long chats, Bert seemed to know how much I loved hearing about my mum. He hadn't told me this story before and he wouldn't be going anywhere until he'd spilled the whole tale.

"Tell me about it."

"I'll put the kettle on," Jason said.

♦

124

Life didn't alter at the guesthouse: Callum set off to work early in the morning and didn't get back until late afternoon, when he'd disappear up to his room to get washed and changed before going out to do goodness' knows what. Apart from making an extra dinner each night – which Callum gulped down after reheating it in the microwave – Jason and I continued our routine of breakfasts, cleaning rooms, washing and ironing, and checking-in guests, before watching TV or reading a book. I had my book club once a month, the occasional night out with friends or I popped to someone's house for a coffee. Jason went out with Mike and a few others, or occasionally got co-opted into maintenance issues at Mike and Josie's Seaview B&B. During free afternoons or evenings, we made it out for a walk or a meal, but that wouldn't last for much longer.

May loomed like a thunder cloud – except this cloud would pour a torrent of work and guests. Or so we hoped. Soon, the washing pile would take over the utility room each morning and we'd struggle to make time for activities on top of our everyday workload. While we valued our time to relax, we needed the money from the high season to carry us through the quiet winter months. But, after our first tough year, we'd promised to try harder to achieve a better work-life balance.

With the Easter break well behind us, and a quiet week until the May Day bank holiday, I felt we should make more of an effort with Callum. When he got home later that afternoon, I rushed out from the lounge.

"Callum!"

Startled he paused at the foot of the stairs, his dust-stained fingers clutching the newel post. A thick strip of cement smeared his cheek and speckled the rest of his face in an ashen mask that made his eyes unusually bright.

"Do you fancy going for a drink later with Jason and me?"

Chewing his bottom lip, he checked his watch. "What time?"

"We've got a check-in at six, so how about seven thirty? We could grab some food while we're out."

"Umm." He swept his fringe out of his eyes. "Okay, I'll be back here for then."

On the dot of seven thirty, Callum stepped into the lounge. He'd changed into a checked shirt and black jeans, which passed for trousers. Jason gave him a wave from the sofa, where he was on the phone. He ended the call and stood up.

"Good day at work?"

Callum shrugged. "It's work."

"I won't be joining you two yet. Our six o'clock arrivals have decided they were hungry and, rather than come here, have gone straight into Torringham and are currently eating. I've given them until eight fifteen to check in. You go on ahead. I'll join you later."

After grabbing our coats, Callum and I headed outside. A gust whipped through the front door and I tugged the collar of my coat up and clipped it into place. Heads down, we battled down the street, our hair lashing our faces. A crumpled can of Stella clattered across the road and smashed into the kerb, while an empty crisp packet danced in the air, dipping and swirling.

I raised my voice. "You didn't say it was this windy."

"It wasn't earlier!" Callum shouted.

We turned the corner into Lower Walk, surprised to find

ourselves out of the wind tunnel now sheltered by surrounding buildings. Above us, a sign creaked.

We swung in the direction of the harbour where, once again, I battened my coat tight, bracing myself against the squall. My hairstyling had been in vain. Move over Aunt Sally: Worzel Gummidge would be featuring tonight.

When we stepped into the calm of the pub, Callum laughed and pointed at my hair. Checking myself in the mirror behind the optics, I ran my fingers through my battered strands, wincing each time I hit a tangle.

"Yours isn't much better." I laughed. "Your fringe is like Tin-tin's."

"We've got a table booked, but we're having a drink first," I told the young woman at the bar.

She glanced across at Callum – who also used the mirror to restyle his fringe – and her face lit up. "Oh, hello! I'd heard you were around."

After being served, I paid and went over to a table by the window, leaving them to talk. Mesmerised by the colourful harbour lights shimmering on the scudding water, I'd all but forgotten about Callum so the screech of chair legs on the tiled floor startled me. He smiled and sat down.

"Tara's an old mate," he said. "I'll probably hang on later and have a drink when she's finished. I've told her that we'll wait for Jason before ordering."

Callum happily chatted about college, his work and friends for a while before juddering into silence, his gaze tracking a lanky man who shuffled along outside, his tatty jeans scuffing the path, his jacket collar pulled over his face like mine had been earlier.

It was the man from across the road. He headed towards us.

"He's not coming in here, is he?" Callum said.

"Do you know him?"

Callum's mouth had settled into a grim line. His voice was flat. "Not really."

By now the man had reached our window, where he paused and pulled a tobacco tin from his jacket. Sheltered beneath the outside balcony, he rolled a cigarette and popped it between his thin lips. The wind shuddered and the masts of the boats in the inner harbour swayed from side to side. The man flicked his lighter several times and swore – we didn't need lip-reading skills to register the F-word. Then he unzipped his jacket and ducked within. After a flash, an orange glow and a puff of smoke, he reappeared. Pinching the cigarette between nicotine-stained fingers, he zipped his jacket back up and ambled away.

"He's gone." Callum let out a long breath.

Splats of rain hit the windowpane. Poor Jason would get soaked. The man hitched his jacket over his head and crossed the road. From where I sat, I could track his route down the brightly lit street, until he flicked his cigarette away and ducked through a pub doorway.

This time it wasn't a question. "You know him."

Callum slurped the froth from his beer. "Not really."

It was the second time he'd uttered these words, but this 'not really' told me more.

"How do you know him?"

Callum's gaze slid to the window. "I don't. Well, not to talk to.

But your neighbour does. You know, the spiky woman next door."

# Chapter 14

SHONA CAST FURTIVE GLANCES in the direction of the cottage opposite and shot down the road, her arms in step with her legs like a soldier. Except a soldier would run towards conflict. Her speed picked up until she was all but running down the street. After hearing what Callum had told me, I could understand her caution. But this fleeing figure wasn't the Shona I knew. I'd seen her, chin jutting, fists clenched, bouncing on her drive like a boxer when she'd confronted people who'd left their car on her drive. And she'd been banned from the book club (although no one had the courage to tell her) for arguing about books she hadn't read.

Kim opened the door and frowned. She'd tied her hair back in a lime green headscarf and still wore her 'work' crocs.

"Finished already?"

"Not quite, but we wanted to catch you."

Her frown deepened. "Mysterious. A Sunday morning visit too."

We stepped into the hallway, moving to one side as two of her guests appeared on the stairs. The man ducked beneath the low ceiling of the hallway, which cut into the stairwell, smiling when he spotted Kim. A woman followed behind him. She turned to the wall as she climbed down, so she could grasp the handrail with both hands.

While Kim asked them about their plans for the day, Callum picked up the smiling Buddha statue and upturned it, no doubt to investigate its provenance. Bored, he moved on to twiddle the trailing ivy and read the guestbook. A moment later, he elbowed me. Grinning, he pointed to the pages. I scanned a few lines but couldn't see what he thought so funny.

He chuckled and whispered loudly in my ear. "What a name! Who'd call themselves Herbert?"

The man frowned at us. I glared at Callum.

"I don't think they would've had much choice in the matter," I hissed and put my finger to my lips to silence him.

When Kim opened the door to let the couple out, the man glanced back at Callum and shook his head.

"That's Herbert and Ellen," she told us. "They come all the time. She's getting a bit frail now but she insists on staying here."

My hand shot to my mouth. While I wilted inside, Callum looked confused.

"Don't people fill in the guestbook after they've left?"

"By and large," Kim said. "Why?"

When Callum pointed to Herbert's name in the book and the comment – *Had a wonderful stay yet again. Thank you.* – Kim's finger slid across the page to the date.

"They came last month. She's got an elderly auntie here, so they're down quite often."

I glared at Callum, willing him to shut his mouth. I could predict his thoughts. How could people that old have an elderly relative? Young people thought forty-year-olds decrepit. At that age I hadn't questioned the brutal social engineering in *Logan's Run*. I would have been surprised if Callum – at the grand age of twenty – hadn't marked Jason and me down as geriatrics, while Bert must be an antiquity at seventy.

131

Kim led the way into the lounge, where she flicked on the light switch. She picked up two piles of towels from the sofa and placed them on the ironing board.

"I haven't finished the rooms. Do you want a cup of tea or anything?"

"We won't keep you long. It's just that we know you've been worried about Shona and that man across the road. I was going to speak to Shona but then I thought it might be best to talk to you first. Callum's overheard something."

"Okay." Kim sank onto the sofa and steepled her fingers in her lap. "What did you hear?"

Callum's eyes widened. He shrugged, not knowing where to begin, so I helped him. "Callum was sitting in the doorway of the church hall." I didn't add that he had been smoking. He was twenty, so it was no one's business but his own. "That's why they didn't see him."

Callum sat, finger in mouth, tugging at a hangnail. I'd never noticed his jagged fingernails before. His hands were already hardened from working at the building site. As a crimson bead bubbled, he sucked it away. I pulled a tissue from the box on the coffee table and handed it to him.

Kim leaned forward, her elbows on her knees, palms outstretched. She lowered her voice, speaking gently, so her voice became husky. "What did you hear, Callum?"

He didn't respond until he had finished bandaging his finger with the tissue.

"Well..." His gaze alighted on my face, then Kim's, before settling on his injury, where a red bloom seeped through the tissue.

132

"That man, I don't know his name, passed her in the street. He shouted…" Callum blushed. "Look, I'm sorry but this is what *he* said, not me, okay?"

Kim nodded. Her fingers nipped the edge of her sleeve.

"He said, 'Still not said anything, you stuck-up cow. You think you're so much better than me, but we both know who you are. But does your … umm … lover know?'" Callum flushed scarlet. "By the way, the 'umm' was me, not him."

"Know what?" Kim asked.

Callum shrugged. "He said twenty quid would keep him quiet till he got back the next week. But she told him to shove it."

"Good on her." Kim shot him a watery smile.

"That's when he shouted. 'If your guests find out, what will they think?'"

"What did she say?"

"Nothing. She just stuck her finger up at him and carried on walking."

"Oh, that's bad," Kim said. "Shona's never been one to walk away from a row. I wonder what he knows about her."

# Chapter 15

WE AGREED THAT KIM WOULD SPEAK TO SHONA. Whatever the reason for the man attempting to blackmail her, it was nobody's business other than hers and Kim's. When Callum and I left, Kim clutched his arm and thanked him, tears welling in her eyes.

Our gazes fell on the cottages opposite. If it wasn't for the solitary hanging basket outside one cottage, anyone would think the terraced row was unoccupied. Usually, there would be life: the young couple at the end edging their pram out through the narrow door, the woman with the yapping dog, the stooped man who shuffled down to the betting shop each day.

Except for the cottage in the middle. The one with the flaking door, dirty nets and grubby render. Rarely did the door yawn open to reveal the occupants inside. I'd spotted the woman and her children twice since she'd moved in and the man a handful of times, which was odd as there was no way they could go in and out unseen; even the rear alleyway access led to the road. But Shona seemed to bump into him every day.

"He shouldn't get away with treating her so badly. She's nice."

I smiled at him. "She is. But don't let her hear you say that. It'll ruin her street cred. Anyhow, I'd better get back to work. We've got guests arriving in an hour."

♦

Jason walked across the road clutching a bundle of carrier bags. If he'd waited until the first guests had arrived, we could have gone to Sainsburys via M&S. I needed a few summer tops and there were five hours between our day's two arrivals. In vain I tapped the glass, but he couldn't hear me from my position on the second floor. Instead, I tried to pull the handle of the window, but the voile thwarted me. By the time I'd made it through the mass of material, he'd reached the car park. I weighed up my options – shout for him to come back, race downstairs to call him from my mobile, or finish the cleaning and moan at him when he returned – and settled for the latter.

Two hours later, he arrived home laden with provisions. I didn't say a word to him. If he'd waited for the guests to arrive, we'd still be sitting here twiddling our thumbs.

I pushed the last of the tins into the crowded cupboard, praying the contents wouldn't topple out the next time we opened the door, while Jason popped the kettle on.

"Fancy a walk soon?"

"The guests haven't arrived yet."

"I'll give them a ring."

He left, then came back a few moments later to tell me they hadn't answered. "I've sent them a text saying we're going out until our check-in starts, unless we hear from them in the next few minutes." He glanced at his watch. "Not that it gives us much time for a walk."

Most days we had a few hours between servicing the rooms and three o'clock, the start of our check-in time. In the summer season this time would be taken up by shopping or ironing, but in the shoulder season we had time to go out for a walk or to spend a few

135

hours reading or watching TV. If we accommodated an earlier arrival, we expected guests to turn up at the time they'd requested. With a flash of annoyance, I recalled that we'd already agreed to a late change of date for these guests.

"How about we forget the coffee and go now?"

"If you want." But then a sly smile crept over his face and he drew me into his arms, enveloping me in the waft of his aftershave. "Or we could go upstairs for a lie-down."

I laughed. "Let me think. A walk or a lie-down? Definitely a walk." But I hugged him closer, enjoying the warmth of his body next to mine.

Then the phone shrilled. Sighing, he extricated himself from my arms.

He answered the phone. "Mike! Great to hear from you. … Yes, yes, not a problem. We were just popping out anyhow. … Okay, see you in five."

He ended the call. "They're having a bad day. Josie's put her back out, their freezer has broken down, and Mike needs a hand to pick up a new one from Berrinton. He has to get it urgently, so he can't wait for Tom to get back."

Now it was my turn to sigh. While sympathetic to their plight, I fancied a walk to the harbour, rather than an hour in Josie's lounge while Jason drove to Berrinton. What were the chances of persuading her to get out for a stroll if she was laid up with a bad back? His departure also meant I'd be left to deal with the guests myself – not a huge deal, unless they'd bought a mountain of cases and needed me to carry them upstairs.

The phone rang again and Jason grabbed the handset from

136

where he'd left it on the worktop.

"You're in Torringham? Lost. Where?"

I chuckled. If they knew where they were, they wouldn't be lost, would they? At least if they arrived now, we could check them in and then go out.

"I mean, can you see anything around you?" Jason said. "Like a pub or a signpost. Hold on, I'll hand you to Katie and she can tell you how to get here."

He held out the phone to me, but I shook my head. He'd answered it, he could deal with it. But he pushed the phone into my hands.

"I've got to go now," he hissed. "The freezer is urgent."

Giving him a menacing look, I took the phone. "Mr Simpkin," I said with forced jollity. "I'm sorry to hear you're lost. Did you manage to find a road sign or anything?"

Jason popped his head through the door to wave goodbye. I stuck my tongue out at him.

Mr Simpkin must have got out of his car to look for a road sign or other identifying feature. Panting, he told me. "Number 23. Now it's 21. I'm going the right way at least." A passing car drowned out his monotone recital.

"Number 9, 7, 5. Shadwell Drive. That's where I am!"

I sighed with relief. I knew that road and could direct him to the guesthouse without resorting to Google.

"You missed the turning when you entered Torringham. Turn around and head back the way you came. At the roundabout take a right and then an immediate left and then at the junction another right and you'll see our sign along the road. See you soon."

He wouldn't be more than five minutes, so I wandered through to the day room to wait. After a gloomy few days, the sunshine had perked everyone up. Even the terraced row opposite glowed, except for the sullen cottage in the centre.

My mobile beeped and I pulled it from my pocket. It was Josie, telling me she'd put the kettle on. *'Guests arriving in five'* I typed and smiled, anticipating the warm sea breeze wafting away the claustrophobia of a morning tucked in ensuites, scrubbing showers and loos. Once I'd checked in these guests, I'd have more than a few hours spare until the next arrivals at six o'clock.

My attention strayed to a family walking past, the father pushing a buggy, the mother skipping behind with a small child. In the other direction, a couple strolled arm in arm, their eyes masked by sunglasses. When the woman threw back her head and laughed, her teeth glinted in the sunlight. Strains of impatient tooting filtered through the window and I tracked their confused gazes. Mystery solved. The couple stepped into the safety of our driveway to avoid Mrs Hollacombe who trundled past on her mobility scooter. The usual posters decorated the front of her shopping basket and the back of her seat. The rear one advertised an unbeatable offer of a Devon cream tea and a drink for just £4.95 at her son's café.

I rather fancied a salted caramel ice cream from the ice-cream parlour next door. Perhaps I'd make a detour there before going to Josie's.

Fifteen minutes later, I slumped into one of the tub chairs, resting one elbow on the chair arm, my chin in my cupped palm. How could it take them so long? Twenty minutes later, I gazed anxiously through the UPVc bars on the window to my prison, hoping the clouds massing in the distance wouldn't head this way. If only the Simpkins would hurry up. Thirty minutes later, I sighed with such feeling, I surprised myself.

Where on earth were they? This was ridiculous.

I decided to phone the guests. It rang through to answerphone so I left a message asking them to call me. Then I texted Josie '*They're not here yet*' along with a sad-faced emoji.

Had they got lost again? How difficult could it be to follow the signs to central Torringham? At this rate we'd have to rename it the Torringham Triangle. So many guests seemed to disappear when navigating through it.

I tried calling again. This time the phone didn't even ring before the answerphone cut in. Either they'd turned their phone off or they were stuck somewhere without a signal. Neither boded well.

Leaving a message, I kept my voice light. "Hi, this is Katie at Flotsam Guesthouse. I'm a bit worried. It's been over an hour since we spoke and you were coming straight here. Can you give me a call when you get this message?" I sent a text too, just in case, then shoved my mobile into my trouser pocket. As if by magic, a black car outside slowed, its indicator flashing. Instead of pulling to a stop outside, it veered into the lane that ran beside the guesthouse. My desolate gaze swept the street. Where were they? A bus rumbled by, followed by a white van, then Mrs Hollacombe trundled towards home in her mobility scooter, her basket stuffed with groceries.

The clock showed five to three. Almost the start of our standard check-in time. My hopes crushed, I sighed and texted Josie to apologise for being unable to make it. Muttering darkly, I dragged the ironing board from the utility room cupboard, jabbed the remote control at the TV – making sure the volume was low enough for me to hear the doorbell when the guests finally arrived – and made a start on the ironing pile.

An hour, an old episode of *Ramsey's Kitchen Nightmares* and six duvets later (I'm not a speedy ironer), I'd all but forgotten about the guests when my mobile beeped. I picked it up.

*'Found your place and decided to go for a late lunch. Just walking it off.'*

What did they mean by 'found your place'? Had they really driven past when they'd asked for an early check-in and knew I was waiting for them. My hand hovered over the phone. I longed to punch out an angry response or at least demand to know how long they would be. But it would be pointless. Unless they planned to go further than Shadwell Point, they would be here within an hour. And an hour after that, the six o'clock check-in would arrive. I tugged another duvet cover from the ironing pile. At least someone would get a walk in the sunshine. Just not me.

A while later, the lounge door creaked open and Jason ducked beneath the frame. His gaze took in the pressed duvet covers and the steamy atmosphere, thanks to me forgetting to open the door to vent the room. He also noted my expression and grimaced in response.

"How come you didn't go to Josie's?"

I growled, "Don't ask." But then fury got the better of me. "Because our selfish Simpkins decided to get lost and then go for lunch without bothering to tell me. Now they've gone for a walk."

"Really?"

"You can check them in. If I do, I'll… I'll…" I slammed the iron onto the board. "Say something I regret."

"You don't need to say a word. Just give them the look you're giving me. Scary." He grinned. "Why don't you go and see Josie? I'll take over the ironing."

The credits started to roll on the TV. Another episode of *Come Dine With Me* had ended and I couldn't say what the contestants had eaten, drunk or whinged about. After spending the whole afternoon praying I'd get the chance to see the sun, I wasn't about to turn Jason down. I put the iron in the holder. When I tiptoed to give him a kiss on the cheek, he cuddled me tightly, burying me in his chest. The faint tang of beer had replaced the scent of his aftershave.

"I am sorry they messed you about."

"Did you stop off at the pub?" I didn't wait for an answer. "I'll just grab my cardi. It'll get nippy later."

As I shouldered my arm into my sleeve and opened the front door with my free hand – multi-tasking at its finest – I found a woman standing there, finger poised above the doorbell. Looking startled, she stepped back. Behind her a man sat in a blue Fiesta. I tried not to glower at her. This could be the six o'clock arrivals coming early or the noon arrivals finally making an appearance.

"Marion Simpkin." No hello, sorry for being late.

"Hold on." I left her on the doorstep and headed back to the lounge. Finding it empty, I stomped off to the utility room where I found Jason dragging towels from the tumble drier. I kept my voice low, although I longed to shout, "The Simpkins have finally arrived."

I took the pile from him, determined I wouldn't be the one to check in Marion sodding Simpkin, and dumped it on the ironing board in the lounge. I re-joined him at the door, where he held out his hand to the woman.

"Hello, I'm Jason."

She offered him a limp hand. "I thought I was stuck here for the duration."

I hissed under my breath. "No, that was me."

No way could she have heard but her brow furrowed. I sidled between them.

"Nice to meet you." I didn't shake her hand, but I did smile at her. Or, at least, proffer a passable version. "I'll see you at breakfast. I would stop but I'm the opposite of a vampire. I need to get out before sunset."

# Chapter 16

IN THE KITCHEN THE NEXT MORNING, Jason shook his head. "What on earth made you say, 'I'm the opposite of a vampire?' You should have seen the look she gave you."

I couldn't face a rerun of the previous evening. Every ten minutes or so he'd chuckled and asked if I'd gone mad. What he didn't know was that I'd spent the whole walk yesterday cringing and kicking myself for saying such a stupid thing. I had been so annoyed that it just came out. Even after sleeping on it, I still felt ruffled, especially as I had to plaster on a smile and serve the Simpkins breakfast within the next hour.

Hearing chair legs scrape on the laminate floor, I went through to the breakfast room to greet the first guests of the morning. Kevin stood at the buffet table pouring orange juice, while Janet sat at their table. Holding the glasses, he gave me a wave with his pinky.

"The usual for me." This was their fourth visit and Kevin had maintained an unbroken run of full Englishes. For such a lithe person, he could fit in a lot of food and often tucked into Janet's breakfast if she ate too slowly.

Janet grimaced. "Heavy night. I'll stick with toast. And I'll have coffee instead of tea."

I glanced at Kevin, half expecting him to coerce her into having a breakfast for him, but he rubbed his stomach. It must have been some night for him not to want extras. She did look a bit peaky.

I laid a sympathetic hand on her shoulder. "Hope it was a fun night, though."

Voices echoed from the hallway – more guests making their way down to breakfast. I hurried through to the kitchen and handed the order slip to Jason, clicked the kettle on, popped bread in the toaster and took a milk jug and butter dish from the fridge.

As I poured the boiling water into the cafetière and teapot, Kevin's voice filtered into the kitchen. "Janet, Janet! Look at this!"

A disgusted voice filled the air. "It's shocking."

I placed the tea and coffee on the tray and headed into the breakfast room. A small crowd huddled by the window all gazing to where Mr Simpkin – I'd forgotten his first name – pointed.

Kevin turned to me and grinned. "Not quite Banksy."

Puzzled, I followed their gazes to the centre cottage across the road. 'ABUSER' had been sprayed in black across the front of the cottage. Whoever had undertaken the artwork clearly didn't have a ladder – the 'B' was splashed across the door while the 'E' covered the window. They'd finished it off with a squiggly underline. My expression mirrored Janet's: she stood mouth open, eyes wide in disbelief.

"I've always thought Torringham was a sweet little place," she muttered.

Marion Simpkin wrinkled her nose and sneered. "You like it here?"

Her lipstick had bled into the lines around her lips so, when she opened her mouth, she reminded me of a map of the M25 with all the roads feeding off it. For a fleeting moment, I had an intense wish that she'd take one of them and disappear.

Janet flushed. "This is a lovely guesthouse. Why wouldn't we?"

I hadn't considered that Marion didn't like the guesthouse. I'd

144

assumed she referred to the town. While the tiered cottages in the harbour were quaint and there were stunning coastal walks, Torringham also had a sizeable fishing industry and with that came noise and smells. Most people thought that part of its charm, especially as the restaurants served locally caught fish and mussels. I much preferred living in a thriving, honest town than one filled with trinket shops and tat, with not a pub or chip shop in sight come winter. Perhaps Marion didn't agree.

She jabbed a finger towards the offending graffiti. "I had to spend all morning looking at that."

Of all the guests to be in the guestroom facing the cottages, of course it had to be her. If it had been Janet and Kevin or any of our other wonderful guests, we wouldn't have heard a peep. Our selling point was our proximity to the town and harbour, not the view. We'd put the voile in Marion's window to obscure the row of unattractive cottages – in particular, the centre one – but she'd obviously chosen to lift it.

Sighing, I headed back into the kitchen, to be greeted by the waft of burnt toast. I flapped my hands to clear the air. Jason glowered and prodded the bacon with his spatula.

"If you want me to check on the toast, tell me. I'm not psychic."

"Sorry. We've got a bit of an issue out there." I tossed the toast into the bin. "Someone's graffitied the cottage opposite. You won't believe what they've put."

"What's it got to do with us?"

I shrugged. Nothing – if our guests could walk outside blindfolded. Then a positive struck me: at least the cottage would be painted now. Surely, no one would leave it looking like that.

When I took Kevin's breakfast to him and apologised to Janet for her toast taking a bit longer than expected, Marion Simpkin beckoned me over.

"You'll have to move us to another room. We can't be facing that."

♦

After breakfast, Shona came over. Her usual hedgehog spikes had been flattened to one side, so it seemed she had the short back and sides of an old-fashioned schoolboy. She held a letter out to me without ceremony.

"What is it?"

"Read it. Then tell me what you think?"

She cut past me into the hallway, where she waited until I shut the front door before walking through to the lounge. As I followed, I pulled out the crumpled sheet. *Abel & Soames* read the letterhead. *A tradition of excellence* trumpeted the strapline. From its tatty appearance and last week's date on the letter and envelope, she'd had it a few days at least. I scanned the three short paragraphs.

"You have a bequest?"

Shona nodded.

"Is this Ronald Bevans a relative?"

"An old friend, but he moved to be closer to family last year. He used to have a boat in the marina which we used to go out on."

A bang shuddered through the ceiling and both of us gazed upwards to where the lampshade swung.

"Sarah, our cleaner," I said.

"Does she work for the local demolition company?"

"She and Jason are moving a guest room around after they agreed it would look better that way. I think it's fine as it is, so I've left them to it."

"You've got your cleaner in. Are you busy then?"

"Full."

Shona sighed. "We've only got three rooms in."

Why we were full while Shona and Kim struggled for business, I had no idea. We'd managed to move Marion Simpkin to a room at the back of the guesthouse, but that meant today's arrivals would face the graffitied cottage. I'd apologise to them at check-in, but there was little more I could do.

I changed the subject. "When are you meeting the solicitor?"

"I came to see if you'd go with me."

"What about Kim?"

A flush crept up Shona's neck, but her face kept its usual pasty complexion. Her eyes didn't meet mine, until I said, "I don't want to cause a problem with Kim."

"Look." Shona took the letter from me. "You won't. It's just that Ron was a fan of jazz, which Kim detests. He's probably left me his collection or something. If it's worth a few quid, I know she'll want me to sell it. We could do with the money."

Finally, her eyes met mine. "I will tell her. I just want a bit of time to think if it turns out that's what he's left me. But I don't want to go alone. Just in case there's more to it."

"More to what?"

She shrugged. "No idea. I've never had a bequest before."

Then the lounge door opened and Sarah stepped into the lounge.

She gave Shona a warm smile and turned to me. "You should see the room. It looks miles better."

Shona got up. "I'll come round at two thirty, then."

"What today?"

"Of course." She rolled her eyes at Sarah. "What is she like? We've just had a whole conversation about it."

After Shona had left, I realised she hadn't mentioned the graffiti on the cottage opposite. It couldn't have escaped her notice. Had she done it? After all, Callum had told us the neighbour had been hassling her. But surely Shona wouldn't deliberately do something that would harm her business?

I'd have a word with Callum. He'd come in late last night and gone off to work early this morning. Perhaps he'd seen something.

Sarah stood expectantly by the door. "Coming?"

As I got to my feet to follow her upstairs, a mobile phone dinged on the coffee table. Its screen brightened.

"Shona's left her phone behind," I said.

I couldn't help seeing the message on the screen: '*Looking forward to our love-in later. K*' followed by three love hearts.

Sarah flushed and snatched the phone from my hand. "That's mine! That's where I put it. I've been looking for it."

She hurried away, head down, gazing at the phone. Smiling to myself, I followed her upstairs. She had a boyfriend. How lovely.

# Chapter 17

WE SAT IN THE CORNER OF THE WAITING ROOM. Shona tapped the envelope she'd pulled from her jacket pocket against her thigh, while I gazed at the paintings dotted around the room. One depicted Berrinton in Edwardian times, with couples promenading by the sea, women with parasols and children darting ahead. Another showed a sailing boat – not a red-sailed vintage trawler that would have come from Torringham – but a tall ship with a dozen white sails that billowed in the breeze.

The painting above the stone fireplace was different from all the coastal scenes. A portrait of an elderly woman filled the frame. She wore a black bonnet, her hair parted tight to her skull, the black collar of her dress reaching just below her chin. The woman's black beady eyes locked on mine and I glanced away, only to look back to find her scrutinising me. A shiver ran up my spine. I crossed the room to view the tall ship in more detail. When I turned back, the woman's gaze fell upon me and tracked me back to my chair. Stupid, I know, but I couldn't explain my discomfort.

Beside me, Shona's knee bounced up and down as she hummed what sounded like a funeral dirge. Apt really, considering why we were here. But the noise, combined with the menacing portrait, set me on edge.

"I'm going to wait outside," I murmured.

Her brow crinkled in confusion. "Why?" She checked her watch. "He'll be out in a minute."

I slumped back into the chair. Determined not to face the woman in black, I looked at the carpet – a red and yellow swirly affair – and the foot-high mismatched skirting boards. The ones with ornamental details were clearly Victorian originals, while other sections had been replaced by basic planks with a simple curved edge. Oddly, the carpet no longer met the skirting in places.

A door creaked open and a squat, balding man stepped out. His polished black shoes gleamed. He wore a white shirt and grey waistcoat and a pressed crease ran up his grey tweed trousers. His dark, beady eyes met mine. Just like the woman in the portrait. An ancestor? Or, judging by his age, perhaps his mother. I chuckled to myself until, feeling the woman in the painting glare at me in approbation, I whispered an apology.

"Sorry about what?" Shona hissed.

I shrugged and stepped forward to shake the man's outstretched hand.

"Clarence Abel."

Introductions made, he showed us through to an office that smelled of old paper and teak. His desk sat by the window, his chair facing outwards so he had a view of roof tops and the distant sparkling sea. Above the fireplace hung another portrait, this time of a man. He stood, pipe in hand, his waist-coated chest puffed out, his other hand resting on a fireplace mantel. His bushy grey moustache had been twiddled into points at each end. Then it struck me. The fireplace in the picture, was the one in the room we were in.

Mr Abel – he didn't look like a Clarence – pointed to three chairs, set in a semi-circle in front of a large bookcase that ran the length of the wall. A quick glance confirmed it contained dusty legal tomes.

"Please, take a seat."

Shona took the chair in the centre. It looked like a typical office tripod chair but for its high curved back and wide seat. I wouldn't have picked that one; it seemed unstable, especially the way it wobbled when Shona moved. I chose the winged armchair furthest from him – Shona was the important person here. It creaked when I sat down and with every slight twitch. I shuffled forward to perch on the edge of the seat.

"Tea or coffee?" He picked up the phone.

Once he'd given his secretary our orders, he settled back into his chair and clasped his hands.

"It seems we had a mutual friend in Ron. A lovely man indeed." He spoke clearly, enunciating each syllable precisely.

"Yes, he was." Shona tried to mimic his speech, but she couldn't get rid of her Estuary undertone.

"We shared a mutual love of jazz."

"He did love his jazz." Still speaking slowly, Shona leaned forward. Her eyes sparkled with curiosity and her fingers drummed the chair arm. Knowing Shona, her façade wouldn't last. Any moment she'd tell him to get on with it.

"Do you have an affinity for jazz too?"

Shona mirrored him by clasping her hands in her lap. "Not so much as Ron but we can't all be afishionaries like him."

Mr Abel frowned. "Quite."

I chuckled to myself. Did she mean aficionados? While Shona rarely confused her words, if she was going to do so it would be under stress. Like now. Her flushed cheeks and the way she worried her lip revealed her nerves bubbling beneath the surface.

The door opened and a woman stepped into the room carrying a tray which she settled on the low table in front of us, pointing out which cup belonged to each of us. Shona leaned forward to pick up her coffee, grimacing when her chair wobbled. She edged onto her seat, taking care not to spill her drink. I left my tea on the tray.

Mr Abel cleared his throat. "Shall we get on with the business in hand. I'm sure you'll be interested to know what Ron has bequeathed to you."

Shona waved him away as if she didn't care but eyed him greedily above the rim of her cup. Mr Abel lifted some papers off the desk and perched his glasses on the tip of his nose.

"Let me see." His finger tracked the contents of the will. "Ah yes, here we are. If we're all sitting comfortably, I'll begin."

For some reason, Shona chose that moment to plump heavily into the back of her chair. It began to topple and her eyes widened, her mouth forming an O of shock. Her arm shot upwards as if to balance herself, but she still held her cup of coffee. The liquid flew over her head in an inexorable journey towards the bookcase. It splatted across the books – with the lovely faded blue and red spines and the embossed gilt lettering – and splashed to the floor.

We froze in a shocked silence, broken by Shona jumping up in panic and all but throwing her cup onto the table. Blotches stained her neck, rising like a tide to just below her jawline.

"Give me a cloth!"

In contrast, Mr Abel sat ashen faced on the other side of the room, as if spellbound by Narnia's evil White Witch. Except with her flattened schoolboy hair, his adversary, Shona, looked more like Edmund.

Shona called over to him. "I'll sort it. Don't you worry."

He sat motionless, his eyes shimmering with unspilled tears, his mouth an arc of desolation.

I snatched my handbag off the floor and pulled out a packet of tissues. Shona grabbed them from me and set about dabbing the books. Knowing his secretary might be able to find a cloth, I headed towards the door.

"Those books belonged to my great-grandmother," Mr Abel said quietly.

"The woman in the painting outside," I murmured. It wasn't a question. I just knew.

When he nodded, a shiver ran through me. The brass handle warmed beneath my grip, but I couldn't turn it in case I found *her* standing on the other side. She'd been dead for a century but, unnerved by her portrait and her ruined books, my imagination had got the better of me.

"We need more tissue!" Shona pleaded. Sodden clumps sat in her outstretched palms and coffee dripped between her fingers.

Head down so I couldn't meet the accusing gaze of the woman in the portrait, I yanked the door open and flew through the waiting room, along the corridor with the creaking floorboards, down the stairs and into the reception area.

"There's been an accident. We need cloths," I panted.

Without a word, the woman stopped tapping on the keyboard and swivelled her chair around so she could step away from her desk. With precise movements, she headed through to an adjacent kitchenette where she took a kitchen roll from a cupboard. Her crimson fingernails were like blood against the tissue.

"I think we may need more than one," I said. "It was a full cup of coffee over the bookshelves."

She frowned in disbelief. "Over them?"

I nodded. "Yes. Over them."

♦

I'd never heard Shona apologise so many times. We'd emptied the bookcase and the receptionist took the damaged books away to dry them out. It wasn't just the spines that had been pounded by the coffee tsunami; it had sprayed the tops of the books, staining them sepia and rippling the upper sheets.

Once we'd finished cleaning, Mr Abel read out Ron's bequest in a monotone voice. When Shona squealed with excitement and jumped out of her chair – she'd moved onto the spare chair which had four legs – to give him a hug, he drew back from her, his eyes straying to the two rows of the bookcase visible above the chairs. The dark gaps where coffee-stained books had been extracted looked like missing teeth, making the bookcase grimace at us.

Overwhelmed by Ron's gift, Shona muttered, "I can't believe it!"

I felt dreadful about Mr Abel's loss, even though it hadn't been my coffee. But Shona bounced down the stairs giving the woman, who'd helped us clear up, a cheery wave goodbye.

"Sorry about the books," I hissed, spotting the tomes laid out on dishcloths and towels on every available surface, including her desk and the countertops in the kitchenette.

"I can't believe Ron left me his flipping boat. It's amazing." Shona giggled. "And the mooring fees too. He thought of everything."

Then she shuddered. "But I can't believe I did that. I mean…" She clasped her hand over her mouth. "I ruined his grandmother's books. That poor bloke. I feel terrible but I was *so* excited. No one's ever left me anything before."

"Great," I said.

She frowned. "Why is it great?"

"It's his great-grand—"

Cutting me off, she shouted, "Oh no! I've got a parking ticket."

She hurried across the road. I caught up with her as she unpeeled the pouch from her windscreen and waved the ticket in my face. "I blame those books. If we hadn't spent so long cleaning them, we wouldn't have got this."

We? That word made me nervous. I'd come along to support her, but that didn't stretch to paying half the fine.

"What a shame *you* got a ticket." I put the bill firmly back in her court. "But you arrived with nothing and you're leaving as the owner of a boat."

# Chapter 18

WE MUST HAVE SEEMED A MOTLEY CREW standing on the pontoon beside Shona's yacht, posing for a photograph. Ranging from tall to short, it would be Lester, then Jason, followed by Kim, Emily, Callum, me, Shona and Lucy. But Lucy had taken her position between the gangly Lester – who had a lot of Peter Crouch about him, minus the football skills – and Jason, so when the neighbouring yacht owner handed Kim's mobile phone back to her, Shona chuckled at the photograph.

"You look like a little girl, Lucy."

"Thanks!"

"Aww, did she call you a little girl?" Lester bent over to envelop her in a hug.

Her voice muffled by his clothing, she cried, "Leave it out!"

When she broke free, she set about straightening her top and tidying her hair. Gritting her teeth, she said, "Next time I'll stamp on your toes."

A bemused Jason stepped away from them, while Emily stood at a distance, her expression unreadable as Lester gave Lucy a sloppy kiss on the cheek, swiftly wiped dry with the back of her sleeved hand. They'd been like this ever since they'd arrived with Emily last night: either poking fun at each other or mock wrestling. Emily, Jason and I had ended up squeezing onto one sofa leaving them to jostle and cuddle on the other. Callum had snuck out with a friend. With him staying until Sunday, we'd been lucky to find space for the girls. But, thankfully, they'd given us a few days' notice of their intended arrival, so I was able to close off the final two rooms, before they were snapped up by last-minute bookings.

I turned my attention back to the boat. Ron had named it *Jazzed Up* but it no longer lived up to its name: the once-white deck had yellowed with age and the edges of the rolled-up sails were spotted with mildew. The navy paint work on the outside appeared in good condition but Shona informed us that the boat suffered from a bit of osmosis.

"Nothing to worry about though," she said.

"I've got contacts if you need anti-fouling paint or anything," Callum said. "My friend, Ella's cousin's boyfriend, Dave, works at the chandlery in town."

Paint. It struck me that Shona still hadn't raised the subject of the graffiti across the road. I hadn't seen her since we'd gone to the solicitors but, thinking back to our return journey, she hadn't once mentioned the horrible artwork that faced us each time we stepped outside the guesthouse. But neither had I. We'd spent the journey to Berrinton wondering what the bequest would be, while on the return trip she had been full of excitement about the boat and sadness about the parking ticket, which she believed was 'karma' for the damaged books.

Kim sidled over. "What do you make of it?"

"Eh?" I said, distracted.

Emily had moved away from the huddle around the boat and joined us. Her new fragrance wafted in the air. She wore a top I hadn't seen before and she'd styled her hair in wide ringlets.

"Love your new look." Kim fingered a strand of Emily's hair. "Very glam."

As Emily smiled in thanks, Kim continued, "I was just telling your mum that it's odd Ron not only left the boat to Shona, but he paid for the marina fees and other costs for two whole years." She narrowed her eyes. "Somehow he covered every possible argument I could raise about why she shouldn't keep it."

Emily chuckled. "It could sink. Especially if you pull the plug on Shona having it."

Shona stood chatting to Jason by the bow of the yacht. I didn't need her stepping unseen into the middle of this conversation. I knew Kim was worried about their finances. When Shona thought Ron's bequest would be jazz paraphernalia, she'd hinted that Kim might want her to sell items to raise money. But I'd seen Shona's excitement at being given this yacht, so it would be a shame if she couldn't use it for a while.

"Didn't she sail with Ron quite a lot? He would have known what she needed."

Kim shrugged. "A bit. But he sailed with other people too."

"And the yacht could break down, like you and Shona did last year." Emily nudged me. I wouldn't need to keep a diary with her on hand.

"That was a little boat," I said. "Not a thirty-foot yacht. This could sail back if the engine failed."

Emily pointed beyond the wooden wave barrier at the edge of the marina. "Try sailing through that lot to get back."

She had a point. Past the marina lay the outer harbour, which was dotted with yachts and boats of all sizes. Unlike the marina where yachts and speedboats lined the pontoons, these boats were spaced far apart and tied to moorings, so they could swing around with the tide and the wind. Shona wouldn't be expert enough to sail through the channel between the moorings, along which a large red trawler now chugged. A flock of seagulls kept up with the boat, wheeling and swooping in anticipation of swiping a fish or two when the catch was landed. Another trawler left the fish quay, its derricks upright but ready to drop to each side so it could trawl for fish when it reached the open sea. I'd learned a little about fishing after chatting to some fishermen who'd stayed at our guesthouse.

The tang of diesel filtered into the air as the Berrinton ferry revved its engines and moved into a space on the pontoon. The crew jumped out to tie its ropes to the bollards, while passengers waited to disembark. When a nearby brightly coloured boat tooted and began to reverse, they turned to watch. Unlike the ferry which had a constant back and forth journey to Berrinton, this boat was heading out of the bay on a trip to spot seals, sea birds and, hopefully, dolphins. As it passed us, one of the tourists stood up to photograph a cormorant which teased him by diving beneath the water.

The boat joined the traffic in the busy channel. When Shona took her yacht out, she'd need to travel along it too. I didn't envy her.

When Shona came over, I pointed to her yacht. "When are you going out on it then?"

"After I've had a few lessons."

Kim hissed, "She's getting them from Pete."

"Is that bad?"

"Well, he's managed to sink two boats so far."

"Third time lucky with this one then. Or you'll be boat-less

159

again before you know it."

Shona patted Emily on the shoulder. "Next time you come down you can go out on it." She turned to Lucy and Lester. "And you too."

Emily grinned. "Can Tom join us too? He's done sailing before."

Tom? Then I remembered he was Josie's son. I knew he and Emily had gone for a drink after meeting at Booker, but I hadn't realised they'd kept in touch.

"Do you still talk to him?"

"He's coming out with us later." Then she corrected herself and pointed to Lucy and Lester. "I meant us three – Callum's off elsewhere – but you and Dad are welcome to join us if you want."

In other words: please don't.

◆

As it happened, Josie had texted to see if Jason and I wanted to join her and Mike for a drink, so the children went to the cocktail bar while we headed to a pub. I found it disconcerting that Josie seemed to know so much about Tom's 'relationship' with Emily, although he did live with them and Josie was pretty nosey.

Although our Sunday morning guests tended to arrive a little later than normal in the breakfast room, we decided not to stay out too late as, without exception, they also plumped for full Englishes. It proved a wise decision as the morning didn't go well. Half an hour after the start of the breakfast time, Jason and I stood, arms folded, surveying the empty breakfast room. The sound of footsteps on the stairs heralded the arrival of the first guests, who were followed by all eleven others within the next ten minutes.

"We should have got the girls to help us," Jason muttered.

While I dished the beans into the ramekins, he plated four breakfasts. We had another four to turn around once I'd taken these out.

"They would have been no use. I heard Emily's door go at three this morning."

We'd just sunk onto the sofa with our cups of tea when the bell dinged. The conveyor belt had started. Everyone would be leaving today, with just three couples arriving. In the hallway the first of our guests waited to check out. The woman dropped the room keys into my hand and thanked us for a lovely first stay. As we said goodbye to her husband, Jean and Bob appeared. Knowing he had a bad back, Jason had told them to leave their case in the room, so he went to collect it, leaving me to chat to them. He reappeared a few minutes later, his face flushed.

As he hefted the case into the boot of their car, I took in his tense expression and his knotted jawline. Something had happened between him going upstairs and coming back down. But what? Jean and Bob were a lovely couple and kept their room immaculate, so it couldn't be them.

They drove away with a toot and a wave. After we headed back inside, I said, "So, what's up?"

He gave an irritable shrug. "Don't tell me you don't know."

"*What?*" Talk about frustrating. Why didn't he just come out with it?

A thump alerted us to another guest coming down the stairs,

gritting his teeth and clutching the handle of his case with both hands. Jason rushed over to help.

As we said goodbye to the final guests, I spotted a familiar figure heading towards us. Sarah. Except she carried an unmistakeable lump strapped to her front.

"Did you know Sarah was bringing a baby?" I asked Jason.

"I'm the last to know anything around here." He shook his head and stomped back inside, leaving me on the driveway. While I waited for Sarah, I kept my back to the graffiti on the cottage opposite. I'd hoped the horrible message might spur the occupants to paint the cottage but, almost a week later, it seemed the artwork would last until it had been obliterated by grime or it peeled off like the paintwork on the door.

As Sarah drew closer, I ran through all the possible explanations for why she carried someone else's baby to her cleaning job, but I could only think of one: she'd been babysitting and the mother would arrive shortly to pick it up. She leaned forward to counter the weight of the bag she lugged on her back. I'd never forget the paraphernalia I'd had to drag around with Emily. Technology had reduced the size of everything, it seemed, except baby accessories.

She didn't make eye contact until she reached me. It had been twenty-odd years since I'd last held a baby, so I had no idea of its age. Tucked inside the front-facing carrier, the infant snuggled into her chest. Its golden-brown hair tufted over the lip of the grey fabric, while its legs splayed through the gaps on either side. The tiny jeans with white socks – one of which had slipped down to reveal a pink heel – gave no indication of gender.

Sarah gave me a lopsided smile and her gaze fell from mine to the baby. "I'm sorry. The babysitter let me down."

Why would a babysitter be letting *her* down? Puzzled, I gazed from the infant to Sarah. With the baby's head buried in her top, it was impossible to see any similarities between them but, although she'd never mentioned having a child, there was only one possible explanation.

"Is it yours?"

She ran her finger across the baby's head. "She is. Sorry for not telling you, but I thought you'd never need to know. But it's a busy day at the guesthouse and I didn't…" She bit her lip. "It sounds ridiculous now, but I assumed you'd rather she came than I left you stranded."

Thankfully, we didn't have any guests until our new arrivals later, so if the baby cried it wouldn't disturb anyone. But why hadn't Sarah phoned or texted to check? Then I felt guilty. She'd carried the baby all the way here, along with that heavy bag.

The dangling sock slid from the child's foot and I bent down to retrieve it. As I rolled it back over the baby's stubby toes with their tiny translucent nails, Sarah smiled at me.

"It's been one of those mornings."

Had she been up all night with this little one? The grey daubing the skin beneath her eyes suggested she had. Yet, instead of going back to bed, she'd gone out of her way to ensure she didn't leave us in the lurch, not realising that we could call upon the girls this weekend. They could help with the baby instead while Sarah and I got on with the rooms, I decided. That's if Sarah didn't mind.

"How old is she?"

"Four months." Sarah kissed her daughter's head. "Poppy is no

163

trouble. Unlike her father."

"Are you okay if Emily or Lucy look after her while we work?" I unhooked the bag from her shoulder, surprised by its weight. "What on earth have you got in here?"

She grinned. "Just the usual. You know what it's like."

A shadow appeared in the hallway, taller than Lucy or Emily and thinner than Jason. Lester must have woken up. But when the figure moved towards the front door, it didn't duck beneath the frame. The reason for Jason's earlier tetchiness became clear as Tom hitched his arms through his jacket and bent to give Emily a kiss. Turning to leave, he spotted Sarah and me on the drive.

His smile faltered and he flushed crimson. With a stuttered, "Good morning!" he dashed off in the direction of his parents' house.

Emily stood arms folded, her stance combative, willing me into a spat, but I didn't want that. While it was discomfiting to think their relationship had moved to this stage much earlier than I would have expected, she and Tom were adults. I'd speak to her later – about Tom – and explain that we should be asked before anyone stayed the night, especially with the fire regulations in a guesthouse.

"I don't suppose you and Lucy could look after Poppy for a few hours?" I asked.

Her mouth dropped open – in shock at being asked to look after a baby or because I hadn't mentioned Tom? – but she shrugged. "Yeah. Okay."

# Chapter 19

DOREEN AND BERT ARRIVED LATE TO PICK UP CALLUM, thanks to a huge traffic jam near Exeter Airport. Even after his long journey, Bert looked better than he had for a long time. Good food had plumped out his sagging jowls and he glowed bronze, although his tan hadn't reached the creases by his eyes, so his crows' feet were more like chicken's feet in colour. How he'd got such a good tan in Scotland, I had no idea. He perched on the edge of the sofa, sipping his tea and harrumphing to himself as Callum told him all about his week and how well he'd been doing at work.

"So, who's this lass then?"

Startled, Callum looked at each of us.

I held my hands up. "I haven't said a word."

Jason chuckled. "Nor me."

I hadn't been aware there was anything to report, but the flush creeping over Callum's face told me Bert had hit the target. If we'd missed spotting Callum's new love interest, what else had gone unnoticed during his week here?

Bert gave his familiar *he-he* laugh and coughed. Patting his chest, he said, "I knew there'd be someone."

They'd slipped into their usual family roles. Callum transformed back into a child, complete with jutting lip and a sulky tone. "There's such thing as friends, you know."

Where had I heard that one before? Oh yes. Emily, before she hooked up with Tom.

Doreen tapped Bert's leg. "Don't tease him. A lad needs to do his courting in peace."

The antiquated expression suited Doreen. She and Bert seemed to act more like grandparents than parents, in age and attitude. Today's tweed skirt, beige tights and Hush Puppies, coupled with her pearl necklace, wouldn't have gone amiss on a woman twenty years her senior.

"What else has he been up to then?" Doreen asked me.

I swallowed. "He's been great." I stopped myself from adding, 'I think.'

Her brow furrowed. "So, you're saying our Callum has been a model citizen?"

"Well, unless that was him out with the spray can the other night," Jason joked.

I'd not thought about how adults discussed their children before. It seemed odd that we spoke about Callum rather than to him when he sat beside us. Not that I could tell Callum's views on this; he leaned forward to scratch his leg, hiding his expression.

Confused by Jason's comment, Doreen frowned. "A spray can?"

"Some idiot graffitied the house across the road." Jason nudged Callum with his knee. "You didn't spot anyone getting up to no good then, or were you too busy '*courting*'?"

Hunched over, Callum shrugged and retied the laces on his trainers. He'd suffered enough embarrassment for one day, so I changed the subject.

"You enjoyed your time in Scotland then? It looks like you had great weather."

♦

After Bert, Doreen and Callum left, I sat in the lounge thinking about the graffiti. I'd seen Shona four times since it had been sprayed on the cottage nearly a week ago, but it hadn't cropped up in our conversation. Did I think Shona would do such a thing? On balance, it was unlikely, especially with the potential damage it could cause to their business. But the more I thought about it, the less I could discount it. Kim's brother, Jeremy, had found out what a hot head Shona could be when he'd tried to stitch her up with the wallpaper remnants. Perhaps the neighbour's blackmail had made her so angry, she hadn't thought about the impact the graffiti could have.

The door creaked open and Jason ducked into the room. Puzzled, he gazed around. "Why are you sitting in the dark?"

Startled, I glanced at him. Even on the brightest day the sunshine barely filtered down the steps and through the lounge window, but I hadn't realised I was sitting in a murky gloom. He switched on the ceiling light but it did little to cut into the shadows. If I didn't know Jason had changed into a red polo shirt after his shower this afternoon, I'd swear it was maroon.

I sighed. "You wouldn't believe it's May."

He sat down. "Did you get the message that Emily is planning another visit in a fortnight?"

"That's good." With my thoughts absorbed by the graffiti across the road, I didn't register his words. "I think I'll go and see Shona."

He glanced at his watch. "What's the hurry?"

"She got four packets of veggie sausages in the sale and she's letting me buy one of them from her. It'll save me running down to the Co-op to get them for that new guest, Mandy."

167

A white lie. We had two vegetarian sausages in the freezer for Mandy, which meant I could pick up the other packet tomorrow. But it gave me an excuse to see Shona tonight and ask her outright about the graffiti. The answer wouldn't arrive by talking to myself. I gave her a quick call, to check she wasn't eating, and headed next door.

Shona opened the door and ushered me through. Kim lounged on their corner sofa, one leg dangling over the edge, so her pink-varnished toenails touched the carpet. Seeing me, she smiled and shifted around to make room.

"To what do we owe the pleasure?"

"Shaped sawdust," Shona said. "Are you gonna have a cup of tea first?"

Without waiting for a response, she disappeared into the kitchen, where she set about slamming cupboard doors and banging cups on the countertop.

"What's this about sawdust?" Kim said.

"I think Shona's referring to the veggie sausages."

"They're not bad, actually," she said. "But Shona managed to burn them the other day, so those were a bit rough."

Shona came back through, tongue poking out as she balanced three cups on a tray. She kicked the kitchen door shut behind her.

"What are you saying about me?" She put the tray down on the coffee table and handed me a mug. "Is she telling you about my sailing lesson?"

"Have you had one?"

"It got cancelled cos it was too rough, but Pete's taking me out next week. You'll have to join us."

"Can I come when you've finished learning?"

She tutted. "He's very experienced, you know." She took a sip of coffee. "You'd enjoy it. I know you would."

I gave a non-committal smile and picked up my cup of tea. I'd come to talk about the graffiti but how could I draw the conversation around so the mention of graffiti slotted in naturally? But there was no way. I took a deep breath. In for a penny, in for a pound!

"Have you heard anything about who did the graffiti?"

Shona gasped. "Not you too!"

She couldn't see Kim sitting behind her, hand across her eyes, shaking her head. But I could.

Shona leapt to her feet and held out three fingers. "Three flaming people have asked me the same sodding thing today. Why is everyone asking me? Do they think I did it?"

"I-I-I'm just asking. I mean does anyone know why someone wrote that? It's so awful. You'd have thought he'd have painted over it by now."

She dropped back onto the sofa. "Sorry Katie. I know you wouldn't think it's me. But why would anyone think I'd do such a thing? For a start, our guests have to see it at every breakfast time." Her wide eyes met mine, pleading for understanding. "And your Callum saw me that night when I took the bin out before bed and the graffiti wasn't there then. Plus, Kim can vouch for me too."

Kim nodded. "Your Honour, I can confirm she snored all night long."

"I had a cold," Shona protested.

"Aww, I know." Kim patted her shoulder but, keeping out of

169

Shona's view, she shook her head and mouthed, 'She snores. All the time.'

Shona looked at both of us. "I haven't seen him since that graffiti was sprayed on his place. But I just hope that idiot bloke across the road doesn't think I did it, or things could become a right nightmare."

# Chapter 20

I PICKED UP THE NOTE and skimmed through it, touched by its contents and the smiley face at the bottom. Mandy had arrived on her own over a week before, after booking for just three days, but then she'd decided to stay longer. That reminded me – Shona's second pack of vegetarian sausages had run out, so I'd need to buy more and replace hers.

I folded the letter into the pocket of my jeans and, picking up a bundle of used towels, headed downstairs to the utility room, where I found Jason stuffing a load of bedding into the tumble drier.

"How lovely. Mandy's written us another note saying how happy she is here."

Jason shut the drier door and took the towels from me. "Don't you think this letter-writing business is a bit odd?"

I shrugged. "She just seems to like writing. She says she's not felt at home like this in ages."

"She's here until tomorrow?"

"Unless she extends her stay again."

"Make sure she books through us this time. Why on earth would she talk to you at breakfast then go back to her room to book through that company again? Did you tell her it's cheaper to book with us?"

"Even if she does rebook, she can only stay a few more days. We're full this weekend. But I'll try to catch her later."

As I left, Jason muttered, "Write her a letter. She'd like that."

I threw him a smile, so he knew I appreciated his wit, and went in search of the hoover. Mandy's room needed a quick vacuum and so did the breakfast room and kitchen. Then I'd have a brief lunch, before tackling the ironing mountain while Jason went shopping.

A Mills & Boon book lay on Mandy's bedside table, a woman swooning into the arms of a dashing man on its cover. Not my thing at all but Mandy had told me she liked to read stories about love and happiness. Her eyes had filled with tears as she told me it kept the loneliness at bay. I felt for her. We'd had other people stay on their own, but they'd had friends in the area or enjoyed their own company. Mandy wore an air of isolation. She didn't talk about family – or anyone else, for that matter, apart from a brief mention of a long-time ex.

A couple of times she'd puzzled me. When I'd told her a joke two days ago, she'd laughed so much that I wanted to ask what was so funny. If she'd been six I could have understood, but she was nearer sixty. And yesterday I'd seen her running out of the guesthouse in tears but, when I caught up with her in the evening, not only did she say that she was as 'happy as Larry', but she denied having been anywhere near the guesthouse. Maybe she thought she wasn't allowed in during the afternoon. Not everyone realised that B&Bs had moved on from the days when people had to go out first thing and couldn't come back until evening. If Mandy asked to stay an extra day or so, I'd let her know she was welcome to come and go whenever she chose.

I switched off the hoover and closed the door. When I headed downstairs, a blast of wind whipped into the hallway and Mandy stepped through the front door. She paused when she saw me.

"Are you okay?" I said.

"I'm just getting something from my room, if that's fine with you."

"Feel free. It's your room."

I stepped aside to let her pass but she didn't move. At this rate the door would be wrenched off its hinges by the wind. Outside, cars and buses rattled past, wafting fumes into the guesthouse.

"I-I wanted to book for a bit longer but it said you were full."

"If you're trying on that booking site, it won't show our availability," I said. "We don't always use it. But you can have your room until Friday."

"I-I wanted to stay until next week."

She gripped the door handle so tightly that her knuckles turned to bone. Eyes welling, she stood mute, lips compressed, until – to my horror – she gave a sob. What on earth had happened? I coaxed her through to the day room, where she crumpled into one of the comfortable chairs by the window. As tears coursed down her cheeks, I patted my pockets hoping to find tissues before remembering the napkins in the drawer. I stuffed a bunch into her hand.

She couldn't stay. We had no room. A thought flickered – we would have space if Emily couldn't come this weekend – but I put it aside. The room Emily used was in our private area. Did I want a guest staying there? And no way would I turn down a visit from Emily so we could accommodate Mandy for an extra few nights, especially when there were other guesthouses nearby.

"I'm sorry," I stuttered, unable to think of anything better to say. "But we're full. You know we'd love you to stay if we had space."

She fell quiet. Hunched over in the seat I couldn't see her face, but her shoulders shook, telling me she was still crying. Sighing, I gave her shoulder a gentle squeeze. Something splattered the windowpane and I glanced up, to find the threatened shower had materialised into a downpour. A couple with jackets held above their heads sprinted down the road, while others hurried past under umbrellas. The gloom seeped inside. If the weather stayed like this we'd have cancellations which would be good for Mandy, except the forecast had predicted sun for this weekend.

"Would you like to stay until Friday? I'll see if anyone else has availability."

She nodded but didn't look up. I patted her arm.

"I'll make a few calls. I won't be long."

Selfish, I know, but when I walked away, I cursed myself. I had the dishwasher to empty and refill and the breakfast room to finish, along with a mound of ironing. Now I'd added another job to my list and Mandy wasn't going anywhere until I'd sorted it. My feet ached, I needed a coffee, and I hadn't eaten anything yet.

I thought about sending a message on the WhatsApp group the local B&Bers used, but I needed a quick response. Not all would check their messages if busy, so I opened the computer spreadsheet with their names and numbers. I started with the ones I knew well – Shona and Kim, Mike and Josie – then moved onto the others. The answer was the same for all the rooms in Torringham this weekend: fully booked. The weather forecast must have encouraged people to book. The next town, Berrinton, might suit Mandy. Some of the hotels there offered evening entertainment, which might make her feel more included.

I didn't bother phoning places in Berrinton – there were

hundreds of hotels and B&Bs – so I checked the online listings, relieved to find a good number had availability. After jotting a few names on a sheet, I went through to the day room to give her the news.

"They've got—"

Apart from a bum-shaped indentation on the tub chair seat, there was no sight of Mandy. Guessing she'd gone upstairs, I knocked on her door but she didn't answer and no sound came from the room. Either she'd gone out or she didn't want to talk. I stood for a moment, wondering if I should get the key and check she was okay, but that would be a step too far. If she wanted to speak to me, she could ring the bell.

I grabbed the abandoned hoover and dragged it through to the kitchen, where Jason pushed a plate into my hand.

"Ham," he said, when I lifted the edge of the sandwich. "Nothing else in the fridge. Before you tuck in, check the shopping list."

"I haven't finished."

He shrugged. "I need to get on. I've got to pick up that shower part too."

I didn't bother going through to our lounge, but stood in the kitchen holding my sarnie in one hand and typing a phone message to Mandy with the other.

Jason pushed the last of his sandwich into his mouth and slapped his hands together, apparently not noticing the crumbs he dropped. "What's up?"

"Mandy," I said. "She can't stay here after Friday. I'm just letting her know that she'll have to book a room in Berrinton soon in case they all get booked up."

◆

Mandy didn't respond to my text. By the time Jason got back from shopping to drag me up to room five to help him mend the shower, I'd forgotten about her. But I couldn't calm my feeling of unease when she didn't appear at breakfast the next morning. After taking a second pot of tea to Frances and Alf, I checked the box in the hallway where guests could deposit keys if they left before we got up for breakfast. Empty. She hadn't gone home. She hadn't rebooked either, even though I'd said she could stay until Friday.

The clanging pots and pans reverberated through the hallway. Jason wouldn't thank me for abandoning him.

In the kitchen I voiced my fears to Jason. "Mandy didn't make it to breakfast. I'm a bit worried about her."

He shrugged. "Probably wanted a lie-in."

No doubt he was right. I started to clear the tables. On the neighbouring table Frances sipped her tea. I'd removed all the plates, but she and Alf liked to sit for at least half an hour after everyone had left and peruse the papers. I'd learned to clear up around them and leave them to it.

As I turned to take the laden tray to the kitchen, Frances beckoned me over. "You were asking about your guest. The lady in the room opposite us."

How did they know? I'd mentioned Mandy to Jason but no one else. Then I flushed. If Frances could hear me murmuring to Jason in the kitchen, what else had she heard me say? Hopefully, she hadn't heard me moaning about how long they sat in the breakfast room each day.

"I'm sure I saw her going into her room when we came down to breakfast." Frances got to her feet, using the back of the chair to pull herself up. "We're off to Plymouth today, so we must make a move."

"Thanks for letting me know. I hope you have a lovely day."

Alf followed her out of the breakfast room, giving me a little wave when he reached the door.

I lingered in the hallway on the pretext of rearranging a vase of flowers until their room door closed and they were out of ear shot, unless Frances had bionic ear implants which, knowing her, seemed possible. I shot through to the kitchen to accost Jason at the sink.

"Please, please tell me that I haven't said a single word out loud about Frances and Alf's long breakfasts when they've been in the breakfast room."

"How should I know?" He tossed me the tea towel. "Give me a hand."

"Well, I've had good news. Mandy's okay."

He chuckled. "A guest misses breakfast and you want an all-ports alert?"

♦

Either Mandy had fallen asleep or else she'd gone out. I hovered outside the door, straining to hear the slightest noise. Nothing. If she'd gone out, she'd expect to come back to a clean room but if she was asleep, she wouldn't thank me for waking her. Not for the first time, I wished I'd remembered to buy some 'Do not disturb' signs. My stomach rumbled and I longed for the bacon sarnie Jason had promised me for lunch. I wouldn't be getting that until all the rooms were cleaned. I just had hers to finish.

I tapped on the door. Silence.

This time I called out, "Mandy!" and knocked. When she didn't respond I eased the door ajar to check she wasn't in bed. The covers were rumpled but not over a Mandy-sized mound. Her belongings were still in the room, so she must have decided to stay on.

People bring their own smells into a room. Sometimes it's the fusty odour of a rarely used suitcase or the stale stench of alcohol or tobacco. Other times it's the lingering scent of perfume or aftershave. The other day, I opened a guest room door to be hit by the acrid smell of mouldy boots. I had to take them downstairs and tell the boots' owner they'd (the boots, not the guests) have to stay in our outhouse. If I learned anything from that experience, it was that room fresheners do not get rid of all odours, no matter what the adverts say.

The smell of Mandy's room reminded me of opening an old-fashioned wardrobe in which lavender pouches were tucked between clothes that hadn't seen daylight for years. Except her clothes were stuffed inside a holdall, which she kept zipped tight. She didn't wear a noticeable scent either and, apart from a toothbrush and toothpaste, she didn't have any bathroom products on display, instead using our complimentary toiletries.

I opened the window and got on with cleaning the bathroom, grateful to see that the shower hadn't been used. One less job to do.

As I wiped the sink, the floorboards creaked. Had Mandy come back? But the familiar clinking of cups and glasses told me that Jason had made a start on the room.

"Another note for you." He appeared at the ensuite door, duster in one hand, a sheet of paper in the other.

He could see I was cleaning the loo. "I'm a bit tied up. Put it in the lounge and I'll read it later."

The doorbell rang and Jason disappeared. After giving the lid a final swipe, I headed to our bedroom to wash my hands before going back to finish Mandy's room. Voices filtered upstairs. I recognised Mike's deep guffaw. What was he doing here before lunch?

Jason popped his head into the room. "Mike's got car trouble again. He needs me to give him a hand."

Spotting my downcast expression, he came over and gave me a cuddle. "I'll be as quick as possible."

♦

After eating a cheese sandwich – I couldn't be bothered to mess up the kitchen by cooking myself the promised bacon sarnie – while I checked Facebook, followed by hours of ironing, I wasn't in the mood to listen to Jason's tale of woe about Mike's car and the chaos they'd caused trying to bump-start it down Howe Hill.

"And that took you three hours?" I said, for the second time.

Jason looked wounded. "You should have been there. Talk about a nightmare. We ended up having to go to the scrapyard. That reminds me – Mike has got me the details of a new plumber now you won't have Kris here."

I went to argue, but he was right. I didn't want Kris around. Even if he hadn't done much wrong. Sarah was more important to us.

Jason stuffed his hand in his pocket and pulled out a crumpled card, followed by a sheet, crushed by a day in his trouser pocket. "Oh, I forgot I had this."

I had to flatten it with my hand to iron the creases. Mandy's usually neat handwriting was an illegible scrawl, worsened by the mountain-range effect of the paper. I read the letter twice – the first time to decipher the handwriting, the second to check I hadn't been mistaken. It couldn't be possible. Surely not. As my eyes flew across the page, the words blurred through my tears. Why had I forgotten about her letter? What on earth should we do?

I pushed the letter into Jason's hands.

In a trembling voice, I said, "Do you think we should call the police?"

# Chapter 21

SHAKING HIS HEAD, JASON HANDED the note back to me. "Why would you call the police? She's just gone for a walk."

"You don't get it!" I jabbed the sheet. "She says she's sorry for being so upset and she's gone to Shadwell Point to sort her head out."

It must be serious if Mandy was attempting the walk to Shadwell Point. Only the other day, she'd taken the bus into town after explaining that her hips were playing up. Yet, it was a good forty-minute walk to Shadwell Point, a local landmark renowned for its beauty. On all but the calmest summer day, the wind whipped along the open plateau, but shelter could be found behind the misshapen bushes that huddled along the edge, while delicate wildflowers dotted the sloping rocky sides. On a clear day you could see for almost twenty miles to the horizon. Even on the drabbest day you could watch the waves crashing against rocky outcrops, the trawlers making their way in and out of Torringham and the infrequent but awesome sight of dolphin or porpoise pods arcing through the water below.

But at the end of the headland, there was a two-hundred-foot drop. No fence, no warning. No second chance.

Jason gave me a cuddle. "This isn't like you, Katie. Is there something else going on?"

Pushing him away, I said, "I saw this on Facebook earlier."

I tapped the laptop screen and scrolled through endless memes and photos until I found the post I'd seen on Torringham News &

Gossip earlier.

*'Does anyone know wots happening? The police have been speaking to people by the park and these guys are at Shadwell Point.'*

The photograph showed the coastguard team in hi-vis gear alongside a red helicopter. Earlier, I'd found the banal exchanges and spelling errors amusing but now they irritated me.

*'That's not the police helicopter, you div.'*

*'Your the div. I didn't say it was the police helicopter.'*

I opened more posts in the thread, but most of them were tagging people to alert them to the post.

Then I spotted the one I'd been looking for. *'Someone said they're looking for a missing person.'*

A chill ran through me and I read on. Since I'd looked, the post had been updated with more speculation: *'They've moved onto Helwall Head. Kelly said she saw someone looking upset heading that way too.'*

Helwall Head? That lay two miles in the opposite direction, towards Berrinton. I couldn't imagine Mandy walking that far. In fact, I knew she couldn't. Not with the steps near Penfold Cove and her hip problems. I'd been surprised she'd wanted to go as far as Shadwell Point.

The breath I'd been holding hissed through my teeth. I felt terrible for whoever was missing, but I couldn't help but be thankful it wasn't Mandy. As my tension seeped away, I smiled weakly at Jason.

"It isn't her."

"Well, we knew that." He squeezed my shoulder. "Stop

worrying about her. She's a guest, not your responsibility."

I sighed. He might be right, but that didn't help. I felt sorry for Mandy and wished she could be happy, rather than always having to explain herself in the long letters she wrote. The way she laughed and cried in the same sentence unnerved me too.

"We haven't got any check-ins later. How about we ask Mike and Josie if they want to go out for a drink?"

I smiled at him. "Why not? That's if Josie's back is better."

The doorbell rang. Probably Shona wanting to discuss a trip on her boat. She'd texted last night to ask if I had thought anymore about it, but I hadn't responded.

"I'll get it," I said.

The bell rang again. Through the opaque door pane, I made out two shapes – in white shirts, black ties and with chequered strips on their hats.

My fingers trembled on the door handle and it took all my strength to pull it open. I'd been wrong about Mandy. Maybe she *was* the person spotted at Helwall Head. Unless… what if the police were calling about Lucy or Emily?

The men dwarfed me, forcing me to look up to greet them. The one standing closest had a thick beard shaved in a severe line below his jaw.

My voice shook. "How can I help you?"

The bearded policeman swivelled around to face the cottages. "We've had a complaint about the graffiti."

For the second time in minutes, my anxiety evaporated. Until it took a different tack: they might think we had something to do with it. Just the thought of being accused made me feel guilty.

"Do you want to come in?"

As they stepped over the threshold, Jason ducked out from the lounge. His face blanched when he spotted the policemen.

"It's about the graffiti."

Jason frowned. "What graffiti?"

I rolled my eyes. How could he have forgotten? It was the first thing we saw each time we left the guesthouse.

"Across the road." It took effort not to add 'silly' to the sentence.

"Well, it's nothing to do with us."

The policemen glanced at one another. A tinny voice sounded from the radio strapped to the bearded man's chest and he turned the volume down.

"We've had a complaint from Mr…" He glanced at his pad. "Smith across the road about the graffiti. He's been away and says it was done—"

I butted in. "Almost a fortnight ago. Sometime on the Sunday night, I think. We had guests who saw it and insisted they move room."

The policeman raised his weary gaze to mine. No doubt he was wondering when I'd give him a chance to speak. He glanced at his pad. "Your neighbours have corroborated the time."

"Shona and Kim?" I couldn't help myself. "They're not happy about it. Their breakfast room looks directly at cottage and the graffiti."

The phone shrilled and I muttered my apologies and went off to answer it, leaving Jason to field the police's questions. A voice told me that I'd had an accident and their claims team would help me

184

win my rightful compensation. Sighing, I hung up and headed back to the hallway, where I found Jason saying goodbye to the policemen.

"All done?" I asked.

"Unless you know anything more," the bearded policeman said.

I shook my head. "There is one thing though. I heard there was a problem at Shadwell Point. Is everything okay?"

The policeman frowned and glanced at his colleague. Unspoken words passed between them and the one who'd done all the talking so far stepped back to let the other take the lead.

"Someone had reported a missing person but he's been found." He cleared his throat. "An elderly man with dementia."

"I was just a bit worried about our…" My voice trailed off as Mandy walked across the drive. An uncertain look flickered across her face when she spotted the policemen.

"They've come about the graffiti." She hesitated, so I signalled for her to come inside. Once in the hallway, I drew her into the day room and away from everyone. "We missed you at breakfast. Is everything okay?"

Her eyes sparkled and tiny spider veins webbed her flushed cheeks as she grinned. "You won't believe it. I'm leaving tomorrow. I'm going to stop with a friend in Berrinton, just like you said."

"A friend?" While I was pleased for her, I couldn't help feeling disconcerted by her sudden revelation.

"It's all so amazing. We bumped into each other at Shadwell Point café and I said about the trouble I was having. Well, she's only got a place in Berrinton, so she said I could stay in her spare room."

Mandy had met someone a few hours ago and now planned to stay at theirs? Like being on a ship during a hurricane and celebrating reaching the apparent calm of the eye of the storm, this felt like good news that could have foreseen problems ahead.

She giggled. "Why are you looking so worried? I've known her for years. We went to school together."

A school friend? That changed things. I'd assumed she'd met the person for the first time today. "That's great. I'm really pleased for you."

The front door clicked shut, casting the hallway into gloom. When Jason sauntered past, Mandy grabbed his sleeve. Surprised, he glanced at her.

"I'll be out of your hair tomorrow. I've met an old friend and I'm moving in with her."

While he smiled politely, I gulped. "Moving in or stopping for a bit?"

She clapped her hands. "Well, she said a few weeks, but we just clicked. She's like the sister I never had."

◆

Even after Mandy had left, the hint of lavender still hung in her room. Once we had stripped the bedding and given the room a good clean, it would smell of fabric conditioner, polish and bathroom spray. The latter seared my nostrils each day, especially after cleaning eight shower cubicles. I'd often thought about ordering a set of masks but I'd not got around to it. Now, as I scrubbed the

186

grout in Mandy's shower, I made a mental note to put them on the list.

Jason came into the ensuite, waving a sheet of paper at me.

"A bit shorter than usual," he said. "She must have been in a hurry to leave."

Jason had been helping carry another guest's bags to the car park across the road, so he'd missed saying goodbye to Mandy. She'd clutched my hand, after pressing the keys into my palm, gazed into my eyes and said thank you a dozen times before heading off to catch the bus, leaving me watching in bemusement as she hobbled up the road.

"Put the note downstairs and I'll read it later."

"No need." He pressed it against the shower screen glass.

A big love heart filled the page, enclosing the words: '*Thank you so much for looking after me. You have been incredible*' followed by an inverted pyramid of kisses which tapered into the point of the heart.

"That's it? Nothing on the other side?" She'd definitely moved on – in more ways than one.

Jason chuckled. "She'll be saving her ink for her new friend. Let's hope it doesn't run out."

# Chapter 22

I'D DONE EVERYTHING I COULD to avoid a trip on Shona's yacht until she found my Achilles heel. Emily. When I'd told Shona that I was going out with Emily on the Saturday afternoon so I couldn't come sailing, she'd texted Emily and sold her a package deal – a sailing trip and a stop-off at the pub afterwards, with the lovely Tom invited too. How could I compete? An excited Emily fired off a text pleading with me to switch shopping for yachting. Lucy would be staying with Lester in Plymouth and Jason and Kim excused themselves by saying they had guesthouses to run. While I hoped it would be a short trip – I hadn't been outside the shelter of the bay on a boat before, so I might get seasick – I knew that if it came down to votes on where to sail and what time to come back, Emily was bound to side with Shona.

Laden with rucksacks crammed with borrowed lifejackets, refreshments and extra jumpers in case it got cold away from the shelter of the bay, Shona and I took the lead. With Tom and Emily behind us, I didn't like to turn around too often in case it looked as if I was spying on them. But, every now and then, Shona would glance back, nudge me and grin.

"They're holding hands," she hissed.

We strolled past a harbourside stall, where the smell of cooked shellfish hung in the air. Customers stood to one side examining the menu while a seagull sat on the stall's roof, its beady gaze focused on a young child leaving a nearby ice cream parlour, her tongue stained the same vibrant blue as the ice cream on the cone she clutched.

We moved onwards, cringing when we heard a child's piercing cry, followed by a man's angry shout.

"One-nil to the seagull," Shona muttered.

Conscious of Emily and Tom behind, I didn't turn around, but kept a steady pace, until we had to stand aside by the railings to let a van crawl past. Below us, on the otherwise calm water, a myriad of rings spread out as darting fish touched the surface. A green, white and black Devon flag hung limply from a boat's mast. Would we find a breeze beyond the harbour? When we set off again, I gazed further out to the rippling channel of water near the inner harbour entrance. Would the tide be going in or out? I hadn't checked the tide times.

In the distance, I could make out Shona's yacht beside the town pontoon. Pete had moved *Jazzed Up* from its mooring in the middle of the marina after explaining that it would be easier to navigate away.

"Where are we meeting Pete?"

"We're not."

I glanced at her. "Who's that on your boat then?"

"Barry, a friend of Pete's. He used to be in the Navy."

"So he sails?"

Shona shrugged. "Pete phoned me after bringing the boat round and said he had to help a fishing mate with a problem at the fish quay, but Barry could step in." Even with her sunglasses on, she put her hand up to shield her eyes. "I think I can see him."

I squinted in the direction she faced, only to glance down when a dog dabbed its wet nose against my bare ankle. It padded back to its owner who sat on a nearby bench absorbed by the view.

"As long as he knows what he's doing."

"Pete wouldn't send us out with just anybody."

Hands tucked in her pockets, Shona set off again, strolling past families who leaned over the harbour wall, crabbing buckets at their feet, while clumps of people sauntered in either direction. When we neared the town pontoon, the buzz of chatter increased, interspersed by the sound of laughter and people calling out. As usual, the seats outside the Lord Mountfield pub were filled with people enjoying stunning views of the marina and the outer harbour. This was where Jason and Kim would join us later for drinks and food – if we made it back in time.

We turned onto the town pontoon, the wooden planks clonking beneath our feet, coming to a halt beside Shona's yacht. Shona's chest visibly puffed with pride.

"Do you like it?" she asked Emily and Tom.

"You took us to see it a fortnight ago," Emily reminded her.

"It's incredible, isn't it? I can't believe it's mine."

I smiled at Shona. She had every reason to be happy. It wasn't every day someone bequeathed you a boat.

As we clambered over the railings, Barry bobbed up from inside the cabin. He gave us a wave and a cheery "Hello!"

I put his age around sixty, although it was hard to tell with his weather-beaten features. If it wasn't for his dark tan – a testament to a life spent outdoors, I guessed – he could have been compared to Dracula, thanks to his long, pointed canine teeth and slicked-back hair which accentuated his widow's peak. He'd rolled up his sleeves to show wiry arms covered in a mat of dark hair.

190

"Don't trip on the guard rails," he said, as I straddled the yacht's wire railing. "You don't want a soaking."

My independent streak made me want to ignore his outstretched hand, but it seemed churlish to do so. His hand enclosed mine and he guided me over.

"This next one will be a bit more work." His piercing blue eyes crinkled with laughter and he winked.

"Cheeky!" Shona said. "I don't need your sodding help."

Beside me, Emily allowed Tom to help her. I grinned. Usually, she would have been first on board to prove a point, but this love-struck Emily played the dating game and made Tom feel useful.

"You lot take a seat and I'll go through a few bits with Shona," Barry said.

We clambered down into an open cockpit area, planting ourselves on the hard seats beside the rudder, while he and Shona disappeared into the cabin below. The last time I'd been on board the yacht, it had smelled of diesel and damp. If I didn't want to be seasick, I wouldn't be volunteering to go below deck once we set sail.

Emily and Tom sat on the seat opposite, murmuring to each other, so I closed my eyes and leaned back to let the sun warm my face. Gulls cawed overhead, mingling with the voices of people from the Lord Mountfield pub, the drone of a passing motorboat and the intermittent reverberation of hammer against metal, most likely from the fish quay.

A shadow fell over me.

"Right!" Barry clasped his hands. "We're ready. Shona, cast off the ropes." He pointed at Tom and Emily. "When I say, give her a hand to get the fenders in."

The engine chugged into life, its vibrations pulsating through the boat. The waft of fumes billowed in the air as Barry turned to me and winked again.

"You can sit there and look pretty."

I rolled my eyes. "Yeah, cos I always do that."

Behind him, Emily pulled a face and stuck her finger into her mouth. "That's my mum!"

In all honesty, I'd been planning to sit and watch them do all the work but, after his comment, I felt obliged to do something. I took the rope from Shona, wound it into a neat pile (not quite sure if that was the correct thing to do). She jumped back down into the cockpit.

Barry pushed a lever forward and swore under his breath. "Where's the damn gear?"

The boat headed backwards. Barry cursed and pushed the lever again.

"Problem?" Shona glanced from him to the outer harbour wall, just twenty yards behind us.

As the boat reversed, Emily, Tom and I threw each other a triangle of worried looks. The gap narrowed. Fifteen yards, now ten... Barry swore and wrenched the gear lever in the opposite direction. Too late! The boat shuddered. In a panic, I grabbed a metal pole to stop myself falling, while Emily clutched Tom.

Barry cut the engine. "Shit!"

"What?" From where she'd fallen backwards, Shona gazed up at the harbour wall that loomed above us.

"We've grounded. Hold on."

He fired up the engine and pushed the lever again. The engine roared and the boat shook but we didn't move. Surely, if we'd hit the rocks we'd have heard a noise? I'd seen the rocks appear at low tide by the outer harbour wall. Brown, craggy lumps covered in weed and debris. Were we on those? Barry turned off the engine. I gazed over the side of the boat but couldn't see below the water.

"The boat draws 1.7 metres," a white-faced Shona said. She looked at my blank expression. "We need that clearance for the boat and keel. Or else we're in trouble."

I didn't work in metres. After a quick calculation, I realised that the rocks must be less than six feet below us.

Barry tried again, this time sticking his thumb up. "I've found first gear!" But the churning engine couldn't move us from the rock. When the engine died for a third time, Barry faced the four of us.

"If the tide's going out, we're in trouble. I'll call the harbour master."

"Pete said you were in the Navy," Shona said. "How come you don't know the tide times?"

"I was. Thirty years ago."

"He said you could sail."

"I've got a motorboat but it's a bit different to this. It's forty years younger for a start. And it doesn't have a whacking big keel like this one."

"If you've only got a motorboat, how could you sail a yacht?"

"No one said anything about sailing it. I was just asked to take you out in the bay."

When Shona opened her mouth, Barry cut in. "Using its engine.

Anyhow, I need to make that call."

When he disappeared into the cabin, I gazed at the outer harbour wall stretching alongside us. The quaint inner harbour had been built using Devonian limestone rubble which could be seen as the wall curved within the natural bowl of the hillside. This straight newer section which ran towards the marina was made of concrete. Until now, I hadn't realised the blocks were hexagonal. I didn't take pleasure in my new-found knowledge.

Faces peered over the marina wall. Families enjoying the view of the Bay or watching their crabbing nets, unaware of our predicament. But if the tide was going out, they'd soon find out. The inner harbour emptied in a spring tide. In this section the rocks would jut alongside the marina wall. We could be left like Noah on Mount Sinai – except Noah could sit there gently rocking while the waters subsided, whereas our huge keel meant we would tip over. I prayed the tide was coming back in.

"Mum," Emily touched my shoulder. "Do you think we should get off this boat?"

If *Jazzed Up* had a tender, it was nowhere in sight. "How?"

She shrugged. "Ask someone to get us."

Barry stepped from the cabin. He pursed his lips. "The harbour master is sending help."

"No need to worry," I told Emily. "It's all sorted."

♦

When the harbour master's team arrived, the crowd swelled as people realised something was amiss with the yacht stuck near the harbour wall. Emily wanted to stay with us on board – at least, until she heard we would be waiting several hours for the boat to be freed from the rocks. Her decision was compounded by not wanting to be outed on a local Facebook site for being grounded in the harbour. Neither did I, but I couldn't leave Shona.

My heart sank as the harbour master's team motored away. I'd put my mobile phone and snacks in Emily's bag, which was with Emily and Tom heading to the pontoon after the men had agreed to drop them there. Shona, Barry and I had been left to the mercy of the neap tide. When I said 'mercy', I meant it in a good way. I'd not heard of a neap tide before but, according to the men, this was the best possible outcome. The opposite to a spring tide, it gave us the lowest possible difference between a high and low tide. The men had tied the bow rope to the pontoon and the aft rope to the railings – they'd done all they could to secure us as the tide went out. We'd been given instructions to keep tightening the ropes, but there was nothing else to do but sit it out until the boat floated off the rocks when the tide came in. Or that was the theory.

The gawping mass around the harbour wall seemed to have an unflagging appetite for boredom. Or perhaps it was worth standing there for two hours in the hope we'd capsize. That would make a good photograph.

Shona glowered at Barry. "The Navy, my arse."

He didn't respond but busied himself by checking one of the ropes.

Shona turned to me. "I wouldn't mind, but I've paid him sixty quid to ground us."

A familiar voice called out and I glanced up. Emily stood beside the harbour wall, her mobile phone at eye level. She gave me a cheery wave and disappeared.

I wished I'd brought a book to read. Not only would that make the wait more bearable, but it would also give me an excuse to keep my head down.

Like a mob of meerkats, it seemed the pub-goers kept one spy in place beside the wall. Each time I looked up, there always appeared to be someone bobbing up and down, pointing at us and reporting back to the others.

In need of respite, I headed into the cabin, but the sickly tang of mildew and diesel made me reconsider. I snatched an abandoned baseball cap from the table and planted it on my head, making sure to pull the peak forward to obscure my face. When I headed up the ladder onto the deck, Barry looked curiously at my head. Was it his cap? I slumped onto the bench, refusing to catch his eye. If I had to stay on board, I needed protection from Emily and the Facebook mafia.

A while later, I woke to find Shona and Barry retying the ropes. Most of the onlookers had dispersed.

I yawned and stretched. "How long have we been here?"

"Just over an hour," Shona said. "The tide should be turning soon."

"It hasn't done so yet?"

She shook her head. "But at least someone's having fun. Your Emily's still at the Lord Mountfield. Apparently, they've got some great pictures of you drooling in your sleep."

♦

The two men from the Harbour Master's Office had returned, along with the crowd of people. But now it included many familiar faces: half a dozen Torringham B&Bers stood by the harbour wall, with pints of beer and glasses of wine, chatting and calling encouragement to us.

I hoped one of the B&Bers had spotted us and sent a WhatsApp message out. While this wasn't ideal, especially if we wanted to save face, the alternative made me shudder. Shona, Barry and I could be starring in the latest post on the Torringham News & Gossip Facebook page. When I got my mobile phone back it would be the first thing I'd check. Pulling my cap lower, I skulked in the corner of the boat, leaving Barry and Shona to talk to the men.

The deck shuddered and Shona's trainers appeared as she dropped into the cockpit. She tapped the peak of my cap.

"They reckon we'll be free in the next few minutes. Barry's checked the depth gauge and it says we'll have clearance soon." She raised her voice. "It's a shame he didn't check it before grounding us."

"I told you, it wasn't working," Barry called out.

Ignoring him, she plonked herself down beside me. "I need a drink. Your flaming daughter has been waving her gin at me for the past hour."

With Shona being a barrier to the crowd's view of me, I felt comfortable sneaking a look at Emily and her friends. "She'll have a sore head tomorrow. She doesn't do daytime drinking."

"She seems like a pro," Shona muttered.

Then the harbour master's men set off. They'd given Barry instructions on what to do next. Now we had to wait for the tide to free us. The sea glittered beneath the late afternoon sun. Although we were just twenty feet from land, it might as well have been twenty miles. Laughter echoed from the Lord Mountfield. Within the next hour, I'd be sitting there too, no doubt the butt of B&B friends' jokes. But I wouldn't care. At least I wouldn't be stuck here.

"Are you sure you know where forward is?" Shona shielded her eyes to gaze at Barry. "Or do we need to call those men back to tow us?"

I'd forgotten that once we were freed from the rocks, we had to motor the yacht back to the pontoon. My stomach lurched, along with the boat which suddenly rose and dipped.

"Shona!" Barry signalled for her to join him. "Grab the rope."

"Do you need help?" I asked, but they ignored me.

Again, I felt the yacht lift as the tide hoisted it free. Barry and Shona's renewed activity seemed to have stimulated the crowd. Increasing numbers lined the harbour. Then I spotted a familiar face – the man from the cottage across the road – who stood by the harbour wall, roll-up dangling from his mouth, squinting at us. If he stood up straight, he'd be much taller than the people around him, but he hunched over so his lanky hair curled into his neck. His eyes met mine and I glanced away. I decided not to mention him to Shona.

The yacht heaved. Barry shouted something to Shona and climbed down into the cockpit. He grinned at me.

"Ready?"

When he turned the ignition, I crossed my fingers. The engine rumbled. Barry smiled, licked his lips and gave me a thumbs up.

"Set us free!" he called to Shona.

To cheers from the onlookers, the yacht motored forward. My relief was tempered by the realisation that we would soon be among the multitude. The cap couldn't save my embarrassment then, but it would be better than nothing. From the corner of my eye, I spotted Emily hugging Tom, while Jason stood beside Kim, shaking his head. Whether this was due to Emily's drunkenness or mine and Shona's humiliation, I didn't know. It wouldn't be long until I found out. The pontoon loomed closer.

"You can buy the first round," Shona told Barry, checking the position of the fenders.

As the boat bumped against the pontoon and Barry reversed into position, another ripple of cheers rang through the crowd. I tugged the peak of the cap down to touch my nose.

"If I'm going to face that bunch, I'm keeping this. Sorry, Barry, but you can have it back when that lot have gone."

# Chapter 23

A FORTNIGHT LATER, EMILY GRACED us with another weekend stay. So far, we hadn't seen much of her – within thirty minutes of Lucy dropping her off, Tom had arrived to take her out. Not that I minded. With a full guesthouse and a busy breakfast ahead, I'd fancied an early night. We didn't get to see her much on Saturday either, other than a brief appearance to change her clothes in the morning and another breathless 'hello' as she rushed upstairs to get ready for a night clubbing in Berrinton.

So her appearance at the back door during Sunday morning's breakfast service was a bit of a surprise – not least because she'd showered and changed into a white shirt and jeans. Shadows smeared the skin beneath her eyes. Or had her mascara run? From where I stood, I couldn't tell.

"Where's Tom?" I flicked on the kettle and shook the dregs from the tea pot. The sodden tea bag splatted into the bowl and I tossed it into the food bin. Carl, a single guest, was proving to have a massive appetite. He'd asked for refills of tea and toast within minutes of being handed the first lot.

She shrugged. "Probably at home."

"You didn't stay at his then?"

"His mate got into a fight at the Royale, so he had to take him to casualty."

"A fight? Is he okay?" I took in Emily's wan complexion. Why had she got up so early? She clearly needed more sleep.

Jason spun around, jabbing the spatula at me. "We won't have enough toast if you keep burning it."

Toast! I'd forgotten about it again. When Jason turned back to the hob, I gave Emily a wry smile and dumped Carl's charred slices into the toast graveyard our food bin had become. Yesterday, two of the compartments in our four-slice toaster had died, leaving us with the other half which seemed to have one setting: burn mode. Not that I needed an excuse for killing the toast, since I was the charcoal queen. I twisted the dial down to one, hoping this round would live to see the rack.

Emily stepped beside me. "I'll sort the toast and you do the tea."

I opened my mouth to argue – she needed to go back to bed – but decided against it. She could sleep while we cleaned the rooms. Sarah would be coming to help at ten o'clock. We had five couples leaving and the same number arriving later. I tipped hot water into the teapot and headed back into the breakfast room.

"I 'eard you talking about that fight," Carl chewed while he spoke, his food churning like a loaded washing machine in his mouth. He came from Hemel Hempstead, which he pronounced as 'emel 'empstead. It seemed his aitches were expendable in all words.

"You've got good hearing!" The door through to the kitchen might be open but Emily and I had been standing near the back door.

As he grinned, yolk spilled over his lip. Fork in fist, he swiped his arm across his mouth, smearing orange across his checked sleeve. Was it the same shirt he'd worn the previous night? A sour smell wafted in the air. Stale vodka.

"They don't call me Ear Wig for nothing."

Not knowing how to respond, I got to the point. "What about this fight?"

"So, I met my mate in Berrinton."

Within minutes of his arrival the night before, he'd thrown his bags in the room and headed straight out, saying something about meeting a friend, but I hadn't heard him mention where he'd been heading.

He swigged his tea. "Well, we decided to have a nightcap at the Royale. We'd been there for, like, five minutes when there was this right racket. This bloke's missus thought 'e was away working, so she'd gone out for the night with her mates, only to find 'im there with this girl. Well, she lumped him good an' proper and then decided to have a go at 'er. A little thing, she was. Wouldn't have stood a chance 'ad these geezers not stood in front of her. Well, 'is missus didn't like that much and gave one of them a proper smack in the chops."

"Poor man," I said.

He shovelled a load of beans into his mouth and swallowed them without chewing. Gesturing towards the kitchen door, where Emily held a tray with a rack of perfectly cooked toast, he said, "I think someone wants you."

"Oh, your toast is ready." I took the tray from my exhausted daughter and headed back to the table.

"She was there." He jabbed his fork to where Emily had been standing by the door. "With the lads that tried to save that girl."

My heart pounded. Had someone died? "Tried to save her?"

He took another gulp of tea, rounding it off with a gasped, "Ahh" before continuing, "That woman was a right vicious thing.

She gave them both a lamping and then landed one on the girl before the bouncers dragged 'er away."

"Horrible." I rushed back to the kitchen to interrogate Emily, only to find Jason had served up the Andersons' breakfasts. Plates in hand, I went back out to the breakfast room, avoiding Carl's gaze in case he wanted more tea.

When I returned to the kitchen with another order, Emily was resting against the worktop examining her nails. "I forgot to tell you, your cleaner Sarah can't come in this morning, so I'll help with the rooms."

I'd been planning to ask her about the incident at the nightclub, but this was more pressing. "I didn't hear the phone. Is she ill?"

When I leaned past Emily to pop two slices of white bread into the toaster, she took over, twisting the dial round.

"She and that guy, Kris – I think you know him – were at the nightclub last night. They're the reason Tom's friend got hurt."

"What? Sarah was with Kris the plumber?"

Emily shrugged. "Dunno. He wasn't in work gear."

"They were at a nightclub? But Sarah's got a baby. And Kris's wife has just had a baby too."

"There are such things as babysitters, Mum."

In the corner, Jason sliced the tomatoes, ready to add them to the frying pan when the timer beeped. He often had several timers on the go, depending on the order – one for sausages, one for poached eggs, another for omelettes – whereas I was more slapdash. Even if I had a timer to hand, I'd forget to use it. Which explained our breakfast roles.

"How did you know it was our Sarah?"

"I looked after her baby for you, remember. Saying that, we didn't recognise each other until we were sitting in casualty. That's when she asked me to tell you she wouldn't be in today, which is why I'm here now."

She lifted the toast out between pincered fingers and popped the slices in a rack.

As I headed back into the breakfast room, I said, "I'll phone Sarah after breakfast to see how she is. Maybe we should go and see her."

"She won't like that," Emily called after me. "She didn't want you to know about that Kris guy being there."

♦

The sound of Emily's heels tapping on concrete echoed through the stairwell. We could have been in a council car park with the two-tone walls – painted slate grey on the bottom, white on the top – and the dank smell of urine. But this block of flats was home to a dozen families, including Sarah and her baby. I grasped the plastic handrail then wished I hadn't. Thankfully, whatever the stickiness comprised hadn't transferred to my hand – at least not that I could see – but I smeared my palm down the leg of my jeans, just in case.

We reached the third floor and the end of the stairwell, where two identical white doors stood in front of us, each had a window with wire safety glass. I checked for number eleven and pressed the buzzer.

"Hold on," a voice called.

Through the glass a shadow headed towards the door. It dropped down and the letterbox flicked open and clanged shut. The shape stood up again and pulled the door open.

I stifled a gasp. If I'd masked half of Sarah's face with a sheet of paper, she would have looked like her usual self, other than a bit tired. But move the sheet to the other side… I gulped at the sight of her eye, a bloodshot slit enclosed within a purple and crimson bulge. A gash jutted above her eyebrow, laced with butterfly stitches, while a raw patch marked her cheek like she'd scraped it alongside a wall.

From inside the flat came the sound of a baby crying. After ushering us inside, Sarah stole a glance into the stairwell then shut the door. The wailing intensified as we moved along the dim hallway and into her lounge where little Poppy lay, legs flailing, on a changing mat on the carpet. The aroma of poop hung in the air. Thankfully, the tied nappy sack told us that the cleaning operation had been completed moments before our arrival.

Emily knelt beside Poppy and popped her dummy back into her mouth.

"Can I pick her up?" she asked Sarah.

Sarah nodded. "Just let me sort her babygro." She joined Emily on the carpet before taking away the used nappy. She returned moments later, wiping her hands on a towel.

"Coffee? Tea?"

Orders taken, she left Emily rocking Poppy in her arms, while I took a seat in the single armchair.

The room was brighter than I'd expected, thanks to the large window which gave a view over the rooftops and a glimpse of the bay between the buildings. Not having a fireplace or a mantelpiece,

Sarah had placed a few ornaments on the long, squat radiator that stretched below the window. Where would she put them in winter when she needed to turn the heating on? In the corner sat a baby's bouncy chair and a plastic box filled with nappies and other bits. On two sides of the room the carpet didn't reach to the skirting boards, but a sofa had been planted in the missing section on one side. Its rear castors sat on lino, while the ones at the front perched on the carpet. Oddly, the rectangle-shaped centre section of carpet had a deeper pile and a brighter colour, whereas the outer area had been flattened and dulled by age. I scratched my head. Then it came to me. This must have once been a bedroom carpet.

Sarah returned clutching two mugs in one hand and a third in her other, which she handed me. After placing Emily's coffee on the radiator, she sat on the sofa and raised her tea to her mouth. I took in her swollen eye and injured face; dumbfounded that someone had hurt her so badly.

Emily, who stood by the window cuddling Poppy, threw her a sympathetic smile. "Does it hurt?"

Sarah raised a tentative hand to her face. "A bit. I've taken some painkillers."

"Is there anything we can do or get you?" I asked.

She grimaced. "A brain. I can't believe I fell for Kris. He said their marriage was over but he was living there until he found another place. He even asked about staying here."

"They've just had a baby," I blurted.

As Sarah's face crumpled, Emily glared at me.

"I know!" Sarah wiped a tear from the side of her uninjured cheek. "Three children according to that woman. She reckons she's

206

going to come after me."

"Hardly," Emily said. "I doubt she'll be out of the police station yet. Tom texted me. His friend, Josh, is pressing charges."

Through her tears, Sarah gave us a lopsided smile. "You've got a lovely boyfriend and his friend was amazing. I can't believe he stepped in like that."

"They weren't the best barricade. Neither of them would punch her back." Emily's eyes opened wide. "Talk about crazy! I've never seen anyone flip out like that. That Kris's face was a picture. At least you know what he's like now."

A tear rolled from Sarah's swollen eye and splashed onto her top. Wincing, she patted her cheek dry with the back of her hand.

"Just for once, it would be lovely to meet someone nice. I do get a bit lonely here. That's why I like my cleaning jobs. They get me out of the house." She turned to me. "I'm sorry about this morning."

Still rocking Poppy, who had fallen asleep with one tiny fist in the air, Emily wandered over to Sarah.

"You could come out with Tom and me sometime. Maybe I'll ask Josh to come too. He's single and nice."

"There's no way he'd want to be anywhere near me. Not after he got a black eye for his troubles." But her expression became hopeful. "Would he?"

Emily smiled. "I'm not coming back down again for three weeks now, so we've got plenty of time to find out."

# Chapter 24

I WANDERED THROUGH TO THE KITCHEN humming the same six bars of a tune I'd heard on the radio earlier. Then I came to a stop in front of the open kitchen door, and frowned, mentally going over my movements that morning. I'd closed the door while cooking a bacon sandwich, as I hadn't wanted the smell to percolate through the guesthouse. Afterwards, I'd gone out the back door to eat my lunch outside on our patio until the phone rang, which meant going into the lounge via the utility room.

It had been Jason phoning from the supermarket, asking me to check and see if we needed napkins. We did. After I hung up, I'd headed to the kitchen to put my plate away, making a full circle of the ground floor of the guesthouse. I hadn't gone back through the kitchen door. So if I hadn't opened it, who had?

A shadow moved across the kitchen wall. No mistake. Someone was there. My heart thumped. Should I go next door and get Shona and Kim or deal with the intruder myself? As I stood there, undecided, a figure stepped into view. I screeched and leapt into the air.

Startled the man backed away. I knew him! The lank hair, the beard, the jeans with their loose threads dangling over his sandalled feet. And those socks! Red and green stripes. Who on earth wore socks with sandals? But that wasn't the point.

"What are you doing in our kitchen?" I demanded. My voice shook.

"Looking for you."

"We have a bell." I pointed to the door. "And this sign clearly says *Private*."

"I didn't see that."

"Or the bell?"

He stood his ground by the kitchen door, scratching his beard. It sprouted in tufts on reddened skin like a fox with mange.

"What do you need?" I said.

"Need?" He looked puzzled. "Oh, of course. Ice."

"Go back to your room and I'll bring you some."

He hesitated. "I can wait."

"Fine. Go and wait in the hallway, but this area is private."

I'd spoken to him harshly, but I didn't care. He had no right traipsing around our kitchen. After handing him a glass filled with ice cubes, I watched him head back to his room. Something about the way he kept glancing back set me on edge, so I locked the breakfast room door before going into the lounge to start the ironing.

An irate Jason appeared an hour later. "Where's the key to the breakfast room? I've got a stack of shopping to bring in and I can't get into the kitchen."

"Sorry." I picked up the set from the coffee table and tossed them to him. "I forgot to put them back. I'll give you a hand."

I switched off the iron and followed him outside. He hefted four carrier bags from the boot, while I took the lighter multipack boxes of cereals. When I stashed the boxes in the cupboard and started unpacking the fridge and freezer items, Jason headed back outside to fetch more bags.

He returned, frowning. "That guest's a bit nosey."

"Which one?" Then I guessed who he meant. "Long hair, tall, beard?"

Jason nodded. "I found him sticking his head through our lounge door."

I pulled the half-used box of eggs forward and slotted the new boxes into a gap at the back of the fridge. "I caught him in here earlier. That's why I locked the door."

"How long is he here for?"

"Three days," I said. "We'll just have to keep everything locked."

But I'd forgotten one thing. The rooms! We left them open when we were waiting for new guests to arrive as there was no need to lock those doors. Luckily, we only had one arrival today. I went upstairs. Room two's door was still on the catch, but footprints on the floor and the bum-shaped indent in the duvet at the bottom of the bed told me our creepy guest had been inside. I counted the towels in the rack, opened the drawers, checked the hairdryer, the guestbook, the cups, milk in the fridge and finally the ensuite. Everything seemed to be in place, but I fetched the vacuum cleaner and duster and gave the room a quick spruce up anyway.

Since all the other guest rooms were locked, I didn't bother to check them. Instead, I gazed around room two, trying to see if I'd missed something. Why had he wandered into an empty room and then sat on the bed doing nothing?

Back in the kitchen, I spoke to Jason. "He didn't seem that odd when I checked him in last night and he was fine at breakfast."

"It's strange that he's not out, though. It's a lovely day."

"I wanted to go for a walk once these people arrive, but I don't want to leave him alone in the guesthouse."

Jason handed me a cup of tea. "If we lock all the private areas, there's not much he can do."

♦

We didn't go out that day. Our new arrivals – who'd anticipated getting to us between three and four o'clock – ended up stuck on the M5 due to a serious accident and didn't reach the guesthouse until the early evening. While I'd checked them in, I'd noticed Creepy Carl hanging around near their luggage. When I showed the guests upstairs, I emphasised they should keep their door locked at all times. I might have got a bit carried away. Isobel's eyes widened, and I had to reassure her that we weren't anticipating the arrival of an axe murderer – or even the common-garden variety. At least, I hoped not.

But in the early hours of the following morning, the sound of floorboards creaking roused me from my sleep. Someone skulked outside our door. Emily's vacant room was next door to ours, while the guest rooms were on the other side of the landing. Another creak. Jason snored beside me, his mouth pressed into the pillow. He'd been known to sleep through doorbells and guests making a racket, so a squeaking floorboard wouldn't wake him. I clambered out of bed and tugged on my jeans, tucking my T-shirt 'nightie' into the waistband. Taking care to open the latch so it didn't click, I drew the door open. I held my breath as the door brushed against the carpet and gazed out to the landing.

The light in the hallway below pierced the gloom but didn't

touch the furthest corners of the landing or the staircase leading upstairs. But the shadowed areas didn't offer enough darkness to allow someone to hide there. Either the intruder had returned to one of the rooms or they had gone upstairs.

I debated whether to get Jason. What if a stranger had managed to get in the building, like they had a few months before? We'd changed the lock since and all keys were accounted for, but a guest could have accidentally let someone in. But my heart told me the culprit lay closer to home.

Taking care to skirt the edge of the carpet, I crept onto the landing. I knew this old building and the areas where the floorboards creaked: outside our door and a stair on the second run, which we'd tried and failed to silence. Above a door shut, confirming my suspicions. Several doors made a definite sound, including Carl's on the second floor, which clunked even when closed with care. Adding a strip of foam seal to the frame was on our list of jobs. I padded up the stairs, hesitating when I reached the landing where the stairs branched in two. The area by the front-facing rooms was in darkness but moonlight bathed the rear-facing section, projecting a spotlight beam through the window to illuminate the path to Carl's room.

No tell-tale strip of light could be seen beneath his door. Even when standing next to it, I couldn't hear a sound. Perhaps he'd been eavesdropping, like me, when he'd been outside our door and I'd woken as he'd walked away. I'd have a lot of explaining to do if he found me here with my ear planted against his door – especially with no evidence to prove he'd done anything wrong. Guests could come and go when they pleased – if they didn't disturb anyone.

Back in our bedroom, I got undressed and slipped beneath the covers. Jason's body enticed me with its warmth, but he grunted and shook me off. I gazed into the darkness as the shapes begin to form and make sense. The doorframe, the lampshade and my coat hanging on the wardrobe, no longer a ghostly figure. All the while my mind churned over the mystery of the strange man who rarely strayed from the guesthouse but, it seemed, spent little time in his room.

♦

The next morning, my eyes stung with tiredness. It took all my willpower to smile at Carl, although his raised eyebrows told me I'd barely managed a grimace. Usually, I'd bother more with a lone guest, but I took Carl's order and handed him his breakfast without asking what he'd done the previous day. There seemed little point. I couldn't imagine he'd done much during the two hours or so when he'd left the guesthouse.

He looked rested for a man who'd been wandering around in the dead of night. As he sawed at his sausage, he gazed at a print of Torringham harbour on the wall, which showed the old fish quay and the colourful cottages steeped behind. When I next passed, he signalled for me to come over.

"Do you know what time Torringham Museum opens?"

I shrugged. "I think about ten o'clock, but I can find out for you."

"No need. I'll go for a walk until it is."

I went into the kitchen, prodded Jason and hissed, "Carl's

actually venturing out today."

True to his word, as I took two breakfasts to a nearby table, Carl gulped down his coffee and murmuring, "Thanks" he slid from his seat. Moments later the front door slammed.

"Crikey," a nearby guest exclaimed. "I don't think he likes your door."

With the kitchen cleaned and our coffee break over, Jason and I headed upstairs to make a start on the rooms. I decided to do Carl's first. Who knew when he'd reappear? Although I was certain he hadn't come back, I knocked and called his name, before cracking the door open. His room lay in a dank half-light and smelled musty. Wrinkling my nose, I stepped over the damp towels and balled socks littering the floor. I tugged the curtains open and unlatched the window to let the fresh air in. The duvet hung from the end of the bed and crumpled into a heap on the floor. Perhaps he'd pushed it there to make room for the pile of paperwork strewn across the bed. Photocopies of old birth certificates and other historic documents, by the look of it, with black and white photographs showing buildings and people in Edwardian clothing. I picked up a print showing a building that resembled our guesthouse. Squinting, I looked closer. There was no mistaking it – it *was* our guesthouse with its elegant sash windows and the cornerstones distinct against the render. A wall topped with iron railings ran around the front garden, with a little gate in the centre. What had once been a garden filled with flowers was now our paved driveway. Just two squat stone walls remained on either side. According to local people, Flotsam and Jetsam Cottage had been built as private homes by the same trawler owner, one for him and the other for his son. Why they'd been given those names, I didn't know. It seemed odd for a fisherman to name his home after debris.

"Snooping?"

I jumped when Jason walked into the room. "Look. This is our guesthouse when it was first built."

He took a disinterested glance. "Nice." Pointing to the mass of paperwork, he said, "What are we going to do about that lot?"

"Just leave it and fold the duvet at the bottom of the bed."

"How about we do that now? Unless you plan to spend all day in here."

I stuck my tongue out at him but – point taken – I took his advice. But as I moved through the rooms cleaning the ensuites, while Jason made a start on the bedrooms, my thoughts stayed with the wonderful image of Flotsam a century ago. When we finished cleaning and Carl hadn't returned, I took my phone into his room to take a picture of his photo of Flotsam. I wanted to capture its fresh facade when the paint on the render – I had no idea what colour it would have been – had not been layered with a dozen or more coats. And the floorboards probably wouldn't have creaked either.

But thank goodness they now did. That gave me the opportunity to tuck the photograph back where I'd found it and leave the room when I heard Carl heading up the stairs.

I waved the duster at him. "Just finished. Your room is ready now."

# Chapter 25

LATER THAT AFTERNOON, A MAN'S SHOUT alerted me to a commotion outside. I put down the cutlery I was holding and hurried over to the breakfast room window. Our new neighbour stood opposite, his fist raised, a paintbrush in his other hand, bawling at someone. I didn't need to guess who. Chin jutting, teeth clenched, Shona danced along the opposite pavement, mirroring his raised fist. Kim stood to one side, arms folded, a smile on her face as she surveyed them both.

"You should be painting this. Not me!" the neighbour yelled.

"I'll paint you all right."

Our front door clicked open and Carl shuffled out onto the driveway, shoulders hunched, hands stuffed into his trouser pockets, so the rear of his trousers slid further down his backside to reveal underpants patterned with love hearts.

"I'm gonna tell everyone about your dad." The neighbour jabbed his finger at Shona, but he didn't look so confident when Shona checked the road in either direction as if about to cross over to him.

A passing van seemed to make her rethink. She bellowed, "Do what you like. I don't care."

"You will care."

"Won't."

Kim touched Shona's arm and muttered something to her.

"Leave us alone," Kim called. "I don't know what you've done to make someone write that on your house, but it wasn't us. And

216

stop blackmailing Shona – or you'll have me to deal with."

She linked arms with Shona, who allowed herself to be drawn inside.

"Ooh, I'm scared." The man called to their backs. "Go off with your lover and leave me to clean up your mess."

Grumbling to himself, he dipped his paintbrush in the pot and daubed a line of magnolia paint across the 'A' graffitied on the wall.

I'd forgotten about Carl standing on the driveway but, when he turned around, our eyes met. We'd caught each other being nosey. I went back into the kitchen to finish emptying the dishwasher, leaving him to do goodness knows what.

As I tossed the cutlery into the tray, I thought about what I'd seen. Kim knew Shona's secret. It made sense that she'd finally get it out of her. But what had Shona's dad done that she could be blackmailed over? Once I'd refilled the dishwasher, I went through to the lounge where Jason stood ironing in a fug of steam. Spotting the condensation dripping down the windows, I tutted. Shamefaced, he set the iron down and opened the door

"Did you hear the argument outside?"

He shook his head. "Some of us are working, darling."

I gazed at the TV and the action film he'd paused. On the screen, a man clutched his chest while blood trickled through his fingers.

"You know that issue Shona has with the neighbour across the road." Jason shrugged, so I continued, "Well, it's something to do with her father."

"You shouldn't keep sticking your nose into other people's business. You moan about that strange man wandering about, yet you're in his room looking at his stuff."

"He had a photo of *this* house! Anyhow, Shona's my friend."

"And she'll tell you if she wants you to know."

He was right, but my curiosity had been piqued. I'd try to wangle more from Shona but not today. That would be too obvious. Anyhow, we had a million and one jobs to do. But tomorrow was a different story; we didn't have any check-ins until the evening. I'd pop around for a coffee and mention hearing the row. The rest would be up to her.

♦

I don't know what made me forget about Carl. I'd seen him come into his room, spotted him watching the argument outside, yet when Jason went to fetch the sausages from the butcher, I decided to join him. I needed a bit of fresh air. On a busy day, the shrieking gulls were our only reminder that we lived by the sea.

We wandered down to the harbour, pausing to watch the pigeons nestling in the drainage pipes of a tall stone wall. Then we moved to stand beside the railings by the harbour wall and look out across the water to the steeped cottages beyond. The tide was in and the rows of boats gently bobbed on the calm sea, their flags flapping in the breeze. The sun warmed my back and glinted on the water. Spotting movement beside a yacht's hull, I leaned forward to take a closer look. A small jellyfish glided from the shadows. A compass jellyfish? I'd seen a few in the sea around Torringham before, but none in the inner harbour. Unlike some of the others, this one was almost translucent but for the faint V shapes on its pulsating head surrounded by a rim of dark markings. Its tentacles streamed behind it like seaweed fronds.

I tugged Jason's sleeve and pointed. Once he'd seen it, I retrieved my mobile from my pocket and took a picture to send to Emily and Lucy. Their 'shocked face' emojis made me chuckle, especially when Emily swore she wouldn't be going into the sea again.

Jason turned to leave. We weaved through the throngs of families, couples and dogs – often Torringham seemed to have more dogs than people – to make our way back to the shops. Sausages purchased, we were strolling back to the guesthouse when we spied Mike and Josie standing outside the greengrocers with Bessie, a friend's dog. When I knelt to fuss Bessie, she pushed a wet nuzzle into my face and I recoiled from her meaty-smelling breath.

"Is Laura not around?"

Josie jerked her head towards the greengrocer. "She's in there."

"It's been ages since I saw her." I hadn't been to book club in a while and missed chatting with Laura over a glass of wine afterwards.

Mike and Jason had stepped to one side to talk. I heard Jason mutter something about engines and switched off from their conversation.

As Laura stepped out of the shop, Bessie strained at her lead desperate to be reunited with her owner. Seeing me, Laura beamed, but she didn't forget to welcome Bessie with a gentle scratch of her head. She didn't coo or speak to her, which would have been pointless, since Bessie was deaf.

"Katie! Sorry I didn't join the welcoming committee the other day, but I'd promised to take Mum out."

I frowned. Welcoming committee? Then it dawned on me. I blushed. "You saw us stuck on the boat? That was so embarrassing."

"Who am I to talk? I still cringe about Bessie and I having to be rescued last year. At least you got to shore under your own steam." She laid a hand on my arm. "You must come back to book club, though. And you, Josie. I notice you've been slacking with your reading."

Josie laughed. "No flies on you. My to-be-read pile can't cope with more, especially with Grace choosing the last book. Why she thinks she has to pick weighty tomes to prove her intelligence, I don't know!"

The nearby church bell donged three times. Our guests would be arriving. I waved to attract Jason's attention and pointed to my watch.

"Can you give me half an hour?" he said. "I won't be any longer, but Mike's got a problem. It's a quick fix."

I shot him a look that told him I meant my words. "Half an hour, max. No longer."

"Would I?" he joked. But he had the grace to blush when everyone nodded.

Goodbyes said – with a promise that I would make the next book club – I walked briskly back to the guesthouse. The space on the driveway told me the guests hadn't arrived yet, thankfully. I slipped the key into the lock and went inside, to hear an odd scratching noise coming from the day room. Silently, I shut the door and tiptoed across the hallway. In the day room, Carl was heaving the sideboard back against the wall.

"What on earth are you doing?"

He spun around, his mouth falling open when he saw me.

"I d-d-dropped something down the back."

I looked from him to the sideboard. Something didn't add up. And he'd scratched the laminate where he'd dragged the heavy sideboard forward! A metal object protruded from an open rucksack leaning against a nearby chair. I peered inside. Carl flushed as I pulled out a chisel.

"What are you really doing? Jason's a few minutes behind me, so if you don't tell me, you'll be explaining yourself to him."

"Please don't be angry." He took a step backwards holding out his hands. "It's not what it seems."

He'd been snooping around our property and damaging our floor. What did he expect? "Well?"

"My great-grandfather was born here when it was a private house. In his diary it mentions a cubby hole in one of the rooms. It doesn't say which one. But in his mid-twenties he put a box in there – a sort of time capsule – before he boarded up the hole and wallpapered over it."

Usually, I'd be excited to learn about the previous occupants of this house, but the thought of Carl wandering around trying to enter our rooms made me prickle with unease. Did I believe his story? But what other reason could he have for pulling out the sideboard? No one would do that unless they were looking for something behind it, which could only be the wall.

"What were you planning to do if you found it? Destroy our

wallpaper? Pull our guesthouse walls apart? You've damaged our floorboards as it is."

His gaze strayed to the cream gouge in the beige laminate. "Sorry. I know you won't believe me, but I was going to come to you if I found it."

"You should have approached us at the start and not gone sneaking around in our private areas."

Just then the doorbell rang. I pointed at him. "If I didn't have to check these people in, you'd be going this minute, not tomorrow. But don't think this is the end of it. If I find you anywhere in the guesthouse other than your room, you'll be out immediately."

The bell sounded for a second time. I stomped off to answer it and Carl ran up the stairs, his rucksack jangling as it bounced against his back. I frowned. He'd mentioned a time capsule, but I hadn't thought to ask him about the contents. But I might never get to know. When I told Jason what Carl had been doing, he'd be furious and would no doubt say that Carl should leave that minute.

On the other side of the opaque glass, the figure moved, drawing me back to the present. I fixed a smile to my face.

"Mr and Mrs Kawa? Welcome to Flotsam Guesthouse."

# Chapter 26

IN THE END, WE DID NOTHING ABOUT CARL. A guest had come downstairs half an hour later to say that his shower wouldn't work. We'd only just replaced the part the month or so before too. Jason, who'd kept to his word and come back within the promised thirty minutes, followed him up, returning to give me the bad news. The shower would need to be replaced and we'd have to move the guests to another room. Thankfully, we had a similar-sized vacant room next door to theirs, but it gave us little time to mend the shower. We were full the next day.

The electrician agreed to come out the next morning. In the meantime, we had to sort the new room out for the guests and make an urgent trip to the DIY shop to buy a replacement. Carl slipped from my mental to-do list until I found myself awake at three o'clock that morning. It wasn't due to him creeping around, but a strange dream that faded from my memory within seconds of waking. While I lay there, staring into the darkness, hoping to succumb to sleep, I remembered Carl. I spent the next hour awake, puzzling over his actions.

He approached me in the breakfast room after everyone had left. At first, I thought he'd come to check out, but he cleared his throat.

"Can I speak with you for a moment?" He signalled for me to go through to the day room, the scene of yesterday's misdemeanour, and out of Jason's earshot.

I placed the laden tray back onto the table and followed him through. He glanced at the scraped floor and flushed.

"I'll pay for that. I didn't think there would be a nail or bit of grit underneath. But I shouldn't have lifted it."

He turned his watery blue eyes to mine. "I'm sorry. I've been up all night thinking. I have no idea why I didn't tell you when I first got here. You might already know about the box."

I didn't. But he'd said sorry and that was a start. The cubby hole had piqued my interest, along with all his documents and photographs.

"Come to me before you check out. I need to clear up the breakfast room and kitchen. I'll see if anything you know rings a bell and we can figure out where this cubby hole is."

The chances of the hidden cubby hole still being in existence were remote. The guesthouse had been remodelled over the years. Even if it was somewhere in the building, the chances of it containing the time capsule were even more unlikely. But it would be wonderful to stumble across it.

As Carl left to creep back to his room and pack, I realised I still hadn't asked him what he expected to find in the cubby hole.

♦

Jason hurried past the day room, tutting. I didn't blame him. We had six rooms to refresh and two changeovers, including Carl's room and the one currently being worked on by the electrician. Wistfully, I surveyed the papers piled on the table. If only I could spend the day looking through them. We'd had a history-loving guest stay the year before, but he'd bored me to death when he pored over maps and told us detailed stories about Torringham's past. These documents were different. They brought the past to life. I'd seen the old photograph of Flotsam Guesthouse on Carl's bed but not the others. I gazed at a photograph of an Edwardian couple, its edges rippled and torn. According to Carl the picture had been taken before they lived at Flotsam. The husband sat upright in a high-backed chair, his hands clasped in his lap, while his wife stood beside him, her collar high, her dress cinched at the waist by a corset. Her attire appeared black, but it could have been dark blue. Their glassy eyes reminded me of Carl's.

"My great-great grandparents," he said. "They had five children. Three were born in this house, and one of those died here."

"I wish you had come to me earlier. It would have been lovely to look through everything." I made myself put the photograph down. "I really must get on though. Email me with what you know, and I'll have a look."

He gathered all the papers and photographs together and shuffled them into a neat stack before sliding them back into the folder.

As he picked up his bags, I remembered what I'd been meaning to ask. "What are you hoping to find?"

He shrugged and grinned. "I have no idea. My family are known for their eccentricities so it could be a cake for all I know, although that was done later."

He noticed my puzzled gaze and elaborated. "My grandmother was known for her terrible cooking, so my granddad hid one of her cakes in a tin at the back of the wardrobe. When he got it out, he told everyone she'd made a rock cake. It's now a family heirloom."

"I don't know that I fancy a mouldy cake being hidden somewhere."

"It doesn't go mouldy if it's stored at the right temperature."

Impossible at Flotsam, especially with the various water leaks we'd suffered since moving in. No doubt other owners would have suffered similar issues with the mangle of old lead pipes and various botches undertaken in the last century.

"I'll let you know if I find anything." I opened the front door. "And, if you come back in winter when we're quieter, I'll show you around."

I closed the door on him and rushed upstairs to get changed, fetch the cleaning utensils and get started on an ensuite. If Jason found me cleaning there would be less chance of him moaning about my tardiness this morning. But as I came out of the bedroom after getting changed into my bleach-stained work clothes, he accosted me.

"Fancy joining me at work any time soon?"

"I have been working, darling," I told him tartly. "Just dealing with a guest's queries."

♦

When Jason left to go shopping, I went around to Jetsam Cottage on the pretext of needing a spot of milk. Usually I wouldn't need an excuse, but I didn't want Shona asking why I had come around in case I flushed and alerted her to my ulterior motive.

Kim answered the door wearing an apron, her braids tucked into a pink and green silk turban. Spotting the small jug in my hand, she ushered me inside. Baking aromas wafted from the kitchen, where a dozen muffins sat in rows on a tray.

She pointed to the cakes. "Do you fancy one with a cup of tea? They're chocolate chip."

Even though I'd just eaten a tuna sandwich, my mouth watered.

"Please! They smell incredible."

While she bustled around, pulling two cups from the cupboard, and settling a cake onto each plate, I wandered into the lounge and sat on the settee. It seemed my 'plot device' was not required, so I tucked the empty jug by my side.

"Where's Shona?"

Kim carried the tray through and set it on the coffee table. She couldn't have caught my question. She handed me my mug of tea and slid one of the plates to my side of the coffee table. The delicious smell of still-warm cake made my stomach rumble, so I wasted no time in breaking off a chunk and stuffing it in my mouth.

"Shona?" she asked, as if collecting her thoughts. "She won't be long. Did you hear the argument yesterday?"

I hadn't expected her to raise the subject. Keen to keep the conversation heading down this track, I nodded.

"The cottage looks better now he's painted it, although I noticed he's used the same paint on the door and window frames."

She chuckled but then her mouth set in a grim line. "Shona's worried that everyone will have heard what he said. She's gone through so much worry over that man this year, that's all she needs."

"About her dad?" I blurted.

She frowned. "So she's told you about her dad being in prison?

227

I've only just learned about it all."

I flushed. "Oh no, I meant that I'd heard that man shouting that he would tell everyone about her dad."

Kim's eyes widened and she clamped her hand to her mouth. "Shona is going to kill me. I promised not to say a word."

"Don't worry. I won't say anything."

She gave me a rueful smile then sighed. For a moment, we sat in silence, her gaze on the gorgeous cast iron fireplace – the centrepiece of the room – with its blue and green tiles. Was she looking at the damaged tile in the hearth? I'd been here when Shona had smashed it and knew it had been a sore point.

"You know, Shona's lost so much…" Her words trailed off. Looking lost in thought, she picked at a loose thread on her sleeve. Her teeth worried her bottom lip.

She got to her feet and made her way over to the mantelpiece to pick up a strange glass fragment. Reverently, she brought it to me in her cupped hand, then took it between her finger and thumb to place it in my hand. With the blue strand running through the glass, it reminded me of a marble.

"Take care. It's sharp. Shona's dad bought her this paperweight before he got put away."

Was this part of the paperweight Shona had accidentally smashed the year before? When that had happened, we'd been so worried about the antique hearth that the paperweight had been all but forgotten in the rush to hide the evidence of the damaged tile. I'd swept up the fragments and dumped them into the bin. But Shona had obviously salvaged this piece, for some reason. When I angled my palm the shard tumbled forward, revealing the core of what had once been the stem of a coral reef covered in anemones. I thought back to the events of the previous year and Shona's reaction after breaking her beautiful paperweight. She hadn't seemed upset at losing it. Or had I simply not noticed?

"He died in prison," Kim said as if to emphasise Shona's double loss.

If my memory served me right, she'd seemed more concerned about Kim's upset over her beloved hearth, with its original tiles, than her paperweight. But that was her all over. Shona had always been a complex character. She could be a stubborn, pain in the backside but was extremely loyal to family and close friends.

"She didn't say much about the paperweight."

Kim chuckled. "The mourning period came later. Every time I mentioned the tile, she'd bring up the paperweight." She took the piece of glass from me and carried it back to the mantelpiece. "Even though he'd been a useless father, never turning up when promised, missing every milestone in her life, mostly due to being in prison, she was gutted about the paperweight."

"What did he do?" I asked out of sympathy, rather than the blatant nosiness I'd displayed earlier.

"He was a swindler. He preyed on vulnerable, lonely people and persuaded them to part with their savings. Which he then spent. At least he got his comeuppance. But only after one poor woman took her own life after he stole her life savings."

Kim pursed her lips. "He was horrible. But he was her father."

I couldn't imagine plain-speaking Shona having a sly, nasty relative. She was usually an open book in thoughts and behaviour, but she'd kept this quiet. No wonder! But a child wasn't to blame for their parent's actions.

"Why is she allowing this man to blackmail her?"

"Stinky Smith?" Kim spat his name. "He knew her dad. They were friends in prison but they had a massive falling out. Stinky reckons that one of the relatives of the woman who died lives in Torringham. She has a large family who would be *very* interested to know who Shona is."

Stinky? That suited the neighbour. "But she had nothing to do with what her father did."

Kim winced. "Shona was twelve or so at the time and had a gardening job at this woman's house. The woman used to give Shona little gifts. Trinkets, mostly, but a lovely necklace too. She told her dad. Innocently, of course, but when her dad was sentenced, the local press made out they were some sort of Fagin and daughter team."

"So what's made Shona fight back now?"

"That was me," Kim said. "Enough is enough. We can't go on with her being up and down all the time. She doesn't deserve the stress. I don't either. You have no idea of some of the things she's been getting up to because she's not thinking straight."

I did. But I let Kim's comment slip by.

She pursed her lips. "I'd rather we dealt with this Stinky bloke once and for all, so she doesn't have to live with the worry of it coming out."

# Chapter 27

I COULDN'T HELP WITH THE NEIGHBOUR, but I could do something to cheer Shona up. The opportunity didn't arise for another week but, when she next mentioned her boat, I told her how much I'd love to go on it again. I hoped I sounded sincere, as I didn't feel it. Shona narrowed her eyes.

"I thought you said 'never again'?"

"Heat of the moment. I don't think anyone would *choose* to go for a double grounding."

"Pete and Barry are gonna sail it around to Kentingbridge on Friday. There's a food festival on and their mates are playing in a band."

"That's a shame. I can't make Friday. Too many check-ins."

"Me neither. So I said they could borrow the boat if they let me sail it back on Saturday. Otherwise, I'll never learn."

"What time are you going?" I tried to sound buoyant but Kentingbridge was four miles away – probably further by sea. Would we be safe sailing all that way back? Many of our guests went there on the day cruiser, but that was a large vessel with a well-trained crew. Pete might be trained but I'd seen Barry at work and he didn't know first gear from reverse. But this was wind power, rather than an engine.

"We'll leave by three to get to Torringham around five."

"I've just remembered, Emily will be here this weekend."

"She can come too, along with Jason and Tom, if you want."

My smile faltered. I didn't like the idea of me being out on the

231

open sea on her boat, let alone Emily. But I wanted to do something nice for Shona. At least we'd have life jackets and Pete was more experienced than Barry.

"She'd love that!"

It wasn't a lie. Emily would. But I wouldn't.

♦

Three couples had left that morning, so I went into these rooms with Sarah and pulled out the beds, bedside tables and chest of drawers. Thankfully, we'd replaced all but one of the wardrobes with hanging rails, so there wasn't anything too heavy to move. While she hoovered behind the furniture, I tapped on the walls to see if I could find this boarded-up cubby hole. Not that I would be able to do much if I found it. We could hardly shut down a room so I could tear off the wallpaper to locate a hidden box, but I was intrigued to see which of the rooms, if any, could be the possible location.

Sarah giggled when I bent down to tap the wall near the skirting board. "You're taking this very seriously."

If it hadn't been for the cut above her eye which she – or a nurse – had covered with a plaster, I wouldn't have been able to tell she'd been in a fight a few weeks before. Just the faint traces of a yellow bruise could be seen around her eye, while the graze on her cheek healed.

I shrugged. "He's sent me a copy of the page from his great-grandfather's diary that talks about the cubby hole. It'd be nice to see if we could find anything."

Either way, I'd email Carl later to update him. He'd sent me some wonderful copies of old photographs and documents relating to his family and Flotsam Guesthouse. It would be interesting to see what else he'd found.

The search of the three rooms proved fruitless, so I got on with cleaning the ensuites and left Sarah to the rooms. Below us, Jason slaved over the ironing board, pressing the pillowcases, duvets and sheets. I preferred the days I worked with Sarah in the rooms. She had a methodical approach, which meant we finished an hour earlier than when Jason and I worked together. It also meant that Jason could launder the bedding and towels as we stripped the beds, so we didn't have a big pile to tackle that afternoon. Best of all, Jason had made lunch.

I'd just taken the first bite of my sandwich when the phone rang.

"Typical," Jason muttered.

I gulped down the sandwich, wincing as a jag of crust rasped in my throat.

"Flotsam Guesthouse. How can I help you?"

"Katie!" a female voice sobbed. "Thank goodness."

I tried to place the voice but couldn't. It felt rude to ask, especially when they seemed to know me well, but I had no choice.

"Who is this, please?"

"Mandy."

"Hi Mandy. Are you…" I nearly said 'okay' but stopped myself in time. What could I say? While I searched for the right words, she blubbered down the line. If history was anything to go by, she'd soon be howling.

"Do you need help?"

"Y-y-yes." Jerky sobs punctuated her words. "I-I-I've be-e-e-en th-thrown out. Sh-sh-she's g-got my th-things."

Why was Mandy calling me? I wasn't her friend or relative. Just the owner of a B&B she'd stayed in for a week or so. Then I recalled how vulnerable she'd seemed during her stay and how helpless I'd felt when she'd disappeared. She had no one down here. I should help.

"Hold on. Is this your number? I'll call you back."

Jason frowned. "Who was that?"

"Mandy." I stuffed the sandwich into my mouth.

"Mandy?" Then his eyes widened. "Not *the* Mandy! What does she want?"

I held up my finger to tell him to wait while I chewed. When I could speak, I said, "Are you going out shopping or anything this afternoon?"

"I wasn't planning to."

"Good. I need the car."

His expression told me he hadn't seen that coming.

"You're not getting yourself involved, are you? We haven't got time for this."

"Just give me a couple of hours," I said.

Not waiting for an answer, I picked up the other half of my sandwich and left. While heading across the road to the car park, I phoned Mandy.

"Where are you? I'll be there in twenty minutes."

♦

As I followed the sat-nav instructions through Berrinton and turned into the road Mandy had told me, I gasped. Mandy's friend must be loaded. Large houses and opulent apartments with underground parking lined one side of the street. On the other side cars edged the road beside a tall stone wall, twice the height of ours at Flotsam Guesthouse. Between the gaps in the properties I could see the bay below, the beautiful sandy beach and rust-coloured headland. The water glittered in the early afternoon sun. I drove on, slowing at each name plate, even though the sat-nav hadn't given me permission to stop yet.

Then the road veered around a sharp bend marked by double yellow lines. I swerved around a huddle of wheelie bins that littered the roadside. Several detached properties lay on my right, their rear windows overlooking Berrinton harbour, while to my left the wall – now just six feet high – abutted a row of terraced cottages, not unlike the ones opposite Flotsam Guesthouse, but these stretched down the length of the road. Some were in good order, with revamped frontages and pristine net curtains, while the rest were in various stages of decay, with peeling paintwork and gutter pipes choked with grass and weeds. Sheets and other oddities had been utilised as window blinds.

The sat-nav led me further down the road where *Room to let* signs were nailed to the facades of what must be houses of multiple occupation – where people lived in one room but shared a kitchen and bathroom. In other towns, many of these houses would be occupied by students who had homes to return to at the end of each term. But not in Berrinton. While many rooms would be filled with younger people who could hope for a better life, for others this world was their past, present and future.

The sat-nav chirped, "You have reached your destination." But I didn't need to be told this. Through the windscreen I could see two people. One leaned against the window ledge of a house, roll-up in one hand, a plastic water bottle in the other, filled with an amber liquid. Cider? The other sat on the kerb, her head burrowed in her knees, her shoulders jerking. The road was too narrow for me to park, so I indicated and bumped the car up onto the path between two green wheelie bins. There seemed to be more of those than houses.

Jason's words echoed in my mind. *This isn't your problem.*

But I'd made it mine.

With a heavy heart I stepped from the car. The man raised his bottle to me and gave me a cheery hello.

"D'you know her?" He jerked his head towards the hunched figure.

I nodded, then knelt beside Mandy and placed my hand on her shoulder. The familiar scent of dried lavender surrounded her. After she'd vacated her room at the guesthouse, the smell had lingered for days.

"They had a right ding-dong. Her and that nutter in there. Mad as a box of frogs, she is."

I gave him a brief smile of acknowledgement and turned back to Mandy. "What happened?"

"She flipped." Mandy lifted her head to reveal red eyes and blotchy cheeks. She swiped her arm across her face, daubing a trail of snot along her sleeve, the remainder clinging to her cheek.

"Flipped?"

"Ripped my letter into shreds. Said I had to get out."

I felt oddly betrayed that Mandy wrote letters to her new friend as well, but I shrugged away the niggle. Why wouldn't she? I hadn't been special, just her landlady. I didn't want to be special either. Once we'd sorted out this mess, I'd be happy to close this chapter.

I debated asking about the contents of the letter but decided against it.

"Has she done this before?"

"No!" She curled into a sobbing ball, her words muffled. "But I can't go back in there. She scared me. I want to leave but I need my stuff."

"She's inside? Do you want me to ask her for your things?"

She nodded. Sighing, I got to my feet. A stack of black plastic boxes jumbled with tins, plastics and card, leaned against yet another wheelie bin and cigarette butts littered the pavement by the door.

The doorbell clicked when I pressed it but I couldn't hear it ring, so I used the knocker. It dropped with a satisfying clang onto the metal knob. Again, I bashed it.

"Hold on to your blooming horses," called a female voice.

The door juddered open and a woman appeared. She wiped damp hands down her thighs, darkening the fabric of her jeans. Frowning, she gazed at me, but her face contorted when she spotted Mandy.

"You still 'ere?"

She must have guessed that I had something to do with Mandy. She grasped the door as if she was going to slam it.

"Please…" I put my hand out to stop her. "I just need Mandy's things."

My voice wavered. I had to do something. If she shut the door, I couldn't see how we'd leave with Mandy's possessions. Unless we called the police. But forcing the door open might get me into trouble too.

"Then we'll go." I stepped back, holding my hands out in a conciliatory gesture. "I promise."

The woman glowered at me. Her gaze stole to Mandy and her mouth rose in a sneer. "I'll get her stuff."

This time the door banged shut, leaving me standing there, trembling. I detested confrontation. A curtain twitched in a nearby window and the man leaning against the window ledge grinned and gave me a thumbs up.

This time the woman pulled the door wide open and tossed Mandy's holdall out to me. When it thumped into my chest, my arms curled around as if it were a rugby ball.

Placing it on the path beside Mandy, I said, "Is this everything?"

She unzipped it, peered inside and nodded. A good thing too. Behind us the door slammed shut. I didn't want to have to knock again.

"Come on, then. Let's go."

She didn't take my hand but pushed herself up from the pavement and brushed the grit from her palms. In the car she buckled her seat belt and stared straight ahead.

"Mandy." I kept my tone soft. "I can't take you back to the guesthouse. We're full."

Although she nodded, her bottom lip quivered and tears spilled down her cheeks. She brushed them away and sniffed. I winced when she swallowed but tried not to show my disgust. Like a frayed rope being over-tightened, today had been too much for her. Any moment she would snap, but I needed her to talk. We had to find her somewhere to stay, at least for tonight.

"Did she own the whole house?" I started the car and headed down the road.

She shook her head. "Rented it." She sniffed. "I thought we were friends. We've both got similar issues."

Now it was my turn to look puzzled. "Issues?"

"I don't tell many people. It's not like me telling you is going to change things." Then she shrugged. "I've got borderline personality disorder, if you must know. I thought..." Her voice caught and she swallowed. "My friend understood. But no one does."

Poor Mandy. I didn't know what borderline personality disorder was, but I could see how it affected her. I squeezed her shoulder. Ahead of us stood a café. We could do with a cup of tea. "Do you want a coffee and something to eat?"

Shaking her head, she said, "I want to go home."

She picked up her holdall, unzipped it and rummaged through, pulling out a slip of paper. I thought it might show a phone number or something, but it was blank. Then she stuffed her hand back inside and pulled out a pen, popping it in her mouth to wrench off the lid. In her familiar scrawl – with a few errant squiggles as the car bumped along the road – she jotted down the name Alan and a mobile phone number.

"Can you call my son? I would but..." She buried her head in her hands. "What is he going to say? He said I shouldn't go. That I needed help. And he was right."

"I think he'll be glad to know you're safe and coming home." At least, that's what I hoped he'd say.

To the sound of her sobs, I pulled the car to the side of the road and dialled his number.

When a man answered, I cleared my throat. "Is that Alan? I've got your mum here."

"Mum?" he said. "Thank goodness. We've been so worried."

# Chapter 28

SHONA SAT IN THE FRONT SEAT next to Jason, while I squished into the back with Emily and Tom. We were on the way to Kentingbridge, where we would join Barry and Pete on Shona's yacht. How Kentingbridge got its name, I had no idea. It didn't have a bridge but a ferry running back and forth between it and Kentsmouth, the larger of the two towns. Perhaps there had been a bridge centuries ago which wasn't replaced after it fell into disrepair.

Jason wouldn't be able to join us – we had guests arriving in the late afternoon – and Kim had remembered a hair appointment that couldn't possibly be cancelled. Thanks to Shona we were already running an hour late, as she had taken longer than expected to service her rooms. I'd debated whether or not to cancel our trip, since Lucy and Lester were staying the night. Our new departure time meant I'd only see them for an hour or so before they went out for a meal with Emily, Tom, Sarah and Josh. How much arm-twisting did Tom have to do to convince Josh to go out with Sarah for a meal? Especially after their first introduction had been in casualty after the fight.

Emily tapped my leg. "Mum, Mum!"

"What?"

"I was telling Tom that you'd had to take that woman home. Did she pay for the train or did you?"

"She did. I just had to take her to the station."

"Dad wasn't pleased." Emily turned back to Tom. "Mum

disappeared all afternoon because this woman had been kicked out of her mate's house."

"I was gone just three hours and her name is Mandy."

Realising I was talking to myself as neither Emily or Tom took any notice, I turned back to the window to find us heading through a tunnel of trees. Around the next bend would be the sign welcoming us to Kentingbridge, where we'd get our first glimpse of the river – or, more accurately, one of the tidal inlets. Sure enough, through a break in the trees I spotted the muddy basin below. The tide had gone out, leaving a few boats scattered by the riverbank. Shona's yacht would be moored downstream, in the deeper channel of the river, not impacted by the tide.

Colourful terraced cottages with hanging baskets and jaunty names lined the street, one of many tiers rising above the river. We headed down the road then Jason indicated to turn into the marina. In winter it became a storage facility, but in summer it offered parking for visitors. When Jason pulled up near the river, I peeled myself from the stuffy car, welcoming the gentle breeze. While Emily and Tom sorted out their bags, I gave Jason a kiss on the cheek. Shona checked her watch and instructed us to shift our backsides into gear.

"Wish us luck," I whispered to Jason. He raised his eyebrows.

Shona strode ahead, taking us down a path beside the riverbank that led to a pontoon. After a short wait, we boarded a river taxi to the berth where Shona assured us Barry and Pete would be waiting. The river taxi chugged past lines of yachts moored to pontoons in the centre of the river. Unlike the moorings at the marina, these pontoons had no direct access to dry land. Tom whistled as we passed a huge, sleek yacht with blacked-out windows and an upper deck that could fit a helipad.

On the other side of the river lay Kentsmouth, with its array of riverside eateries, art galleries and hotels. The promenade teemed with tourists queuing for ferries or sea and river cruises. The thump of a drumbeat and the tinny sound of a tannoy filtered across the water. The festival was in full swing.

The river taxi stopped by Shona's yacht. After paying our fare, we stepped onto the wooden pontoon. Dismayed, I noticed that the slatted door to her cabin remained shut, with no Pete or Barry in sight.

"Where are they?" Shona hissed. She tapped out a number and swore. "Anyone got a signal?"

I handed her my phone and she tried again. "Pete! Is that you? Where are you? What're you doing there? You should be here." I could hear a man's voice down the line. Not good news if her expression was anything to go by.

"One hour? Are you taking the p…" She glanced at a man on the adjacent boat. "…mick?"

She jabbed the phone and handed it to me. "We're in for a wait. Barry's gone walkabout and Pete's watching his friends finish their set and then he's coming. I'm sure he told me they were playing last night."

Emily shrugged. "We'll sit on your boat and watch the world go by." She slipped her hand through the crook of Tom's arm. "Want to sit by the bow?"

While Shona grumbled, I stepped into the cockpit, giving her a smug grin. Knowing that nothing ever went to plan with Shona, I'd come prepared. I'd brought a jacket as it would be cold out at sea later, but for now it would be a good cushion. I dragged a book from my bag and, to the sound of Shona moaning, seagulls screeching and the hubbub from the distant festival, I found my bookmark and settled back ready to be transported to another world.

♦

For the past hour Shona had been muttering and pacing the pontoon. It had been a job to screen out her grumbles and concentrate on my book – I kept having to stop to reread the same paragraph. Finally, she decided to go and bother the man working on the neighbouring yacht.

"Mum!" Emily called for the tenth time since we'd boarded the boat.

If she wanted me, she could come over. I forced my attention on the page, determined I would reach the next one at some point.

"How long before we leave?"

Much as I loved Emily, she made me realise why there wasn't a different name for children once they reached adulthood. When it came to their parents, they reverted to well-rehearsed roles.

I ignored her, but regretted it when she shouted, "Shonnnnaaaaa! When're your friends getting here?"

Shona finished her conversation with the man and trotted back over. She didn't come on board but clutched the rail.

"Your guess is as good as mine. I can't believe it's half past four and we haven't left yet. It'll be dark before we get there at this rate."

With the book shielding my face and my back to her, I could safely roll my eyes. Talk about exaggeration. It wouldn't be dark for another four or five hours. But I hoped Pete would show up soon. My acting skills had been proven when I'd told her that a trip from Kentingbridge to Torringham would be lovely. On a larger vessel with different crew it probably would be. But I had a niggling feeling about this trip. I didn't think we'd die or anything. Just that it wouldn't go to plan. Perhaps Pete and Barry wouldn't turn up, so we'd have to get Jason to pick us up.

Then the din of an engine cut through the air and the water taxi came into view, carrying a man I recognised – Shona's friend, Pete.

"Thank flaming goodness. I thought we'd never flipping leave."

She clambered over the guard rail and jumped down beside me with a thump, where she unlocked the cabin door and lifted out the slats. A musty smell wafted from the cabin. Pete stepped on board with a cheery, "Hello!" and Emily and Tom made their way down the gangway to the cockpit.

"Here! Put these on." Shona tossed life jackets to us. She cackled at Emily. "Hope you won't need them. There'll be no disappearing off to the pub this time."

"Talking about that, where's Barry?" Emily said.

"He's feeling a bit dodgy." Pete patted his stomach. "Best he didn't come."

Pete didn't bear any resemblance to Barry in looks or demeanour. He shrugged off his jacket and handed it and a small holdall to Shona to put in the cabin. Then he shook our hands and introduced himself, reaching me last.

He wore his grey hair in a crew cut, which suited the casual look he sported – a navy polo shirt, cotton slacks and deck shoes. Perfect for a boat, but not the type of gear I'd expect him to wear when watching his friends in a band. Although I hadn't been able to block out Shona's moaning and Emily's questions, the heavy bass beat had faded into the background, but now it reverberated again across the water.

"I'm sorry, Shona, but I don't think the wind is right for sailing back. We'll check when we get past the mouth but I think we'll have to stick with the engine for now."

Shona's smile faded but she shrugged. "You're the skipper."

After a quick check of the controls and equipment, we followed Pete's orders and untied the mooring ropes. When we set off, Pete directed us to pull in the fenders, which were tucked under my seat.

Relieved to be moving, I settled back to enjoy the view. Last year I'd walked a four-mile stretch of the South West Coast Path, stunned by the awe-inspiring scenery, but we'd not gone this far. Many of our guests had been on the cruise to Kentsmouth and had come back with wonderful stories of dolphin sightings and the incredible coastline. Fingers-crossed we'd get to see some sea life on our trip.

The pastel-coloured towns of Kentingbridge and Kentsmouth rose on either side of us, giving us lots to see while we motored down the river. Pete slowed as we neared the two car ferries that criss-crossed each other, then let out the throttle to move into the channel they'd vacated. The townscape became greener, with buildings – old and modern – dotted along the river edge and between trees, while houses with huge windows nestled along the hilltops. When people in passing boats greeted us, Emily waved back enthusiastically.

When we moved past an ancient church perched on the cliff edge and reached the river mouth, the water became choppier.

"Sit down now," Pete instructed. I hadn't realised I'd got to my feet.

"He's a bit grumpy," Emily mouthed.

Shona whispered into Emily's ear, but she could be heard over the engine. "He takes it very seriously."

"I don't want you to drown." Pete didn't look at us as he pulled the tiller to the port side – or was it the starboard side? He'd told us the technical terms for parts of the boat when we were pulling up the fenders but I'd forgotten them.

We sat in silence until we got past the row of buoys marking the channel, when Pete said, "Right, Shona. Are you ready?"

"Aye-aye." Shona saluted him.

"I'm not joking, Shona. If you want to learn you have to listen and do precisely what I say."

Opposite me, Emily pulled a face. I chuckled to myself. This would be interesting – Shona doing exactly as she was told.

"Who's going to keep an eye out for buoys?" Pete wasn't letting us off the hook. "I don't want us to get caught in the lines."

"For the lobster and crab pots," Shona explained.

Emily stuck up her hand. "Can we go up front again?"

Pete frowned. "For now, but if I call you back, you come immediately. And keep your eyes peeled."

As Emily and Tom scarpered off, I wondered if I should ask for a job to do, but I didn't want to interrupt Pete who stood with Shona showing her how to use a piece of equipment he held in his hand.

247

It looked like a mobile phone, but he pointed to it and said something about it being much deeper here. The boat rolled with the waves and the depth gauge by the cabin door registered 42.6, then 42.8. It would be showing metres, but I'd wished it was feet. I hated the idea of the water being so deep below us. What if something happened? We were no longer surrounded by boats and people. If we got into trouble we could sink before help reached us. A passing cloud dimmed the sun and the water became gloomy, almost menacing. Out on the horizon sat a tanker while, behind it, the sea melded with the sky in an obscure haze.

I turned to face the coastline which rose in verdant peaks and troughs. It looked incredible from here, but I'd walked those hills and knew the deceptive curves were muscle-aching inclines and hard-fought climbs. Behind jagged outcrops stood limestone cliffs, some an upright impenetrable barrier, others tumbling heaps of boulders. A reddish patch scarred the rock face – a recent cliff fall. We moved onwards to where lush greenery rolled down to almost kiss the sea.

Then Marsham Beach came into view. A good hour's walk from Torringham it was where last year Laura's dog, Bessie, had got caught in a rip tide and had to be rescued. I gazed at the depth gauge which registered just 16.2. I shivered. It looked a long way back to land. I couldn't see the small lake behind the strip that was Marsham Beach, but I knew it lay there, surrounded by sweeping hills.

"Buoys," Tom shouted. "There and there."

"Just woken up, have you? What about the other half dozen you've missed?" Pete barked.

I could imagine Emily's face and the glare that would pass between her and Tom. Pete wasn't here to make friends – he'd been a skipper of a tall ship at one point and had years of experience sailing all kinds of boats– but I wished he wouldn't work so hard to drain all pleasure from the trip.

We fell into silence, apart from the occasional command from Pete to Shona, or a bored call of "Buoy" from Tom or Emily. A familiar headland came into view, growing closer, and my spirits rose. Shadwell Point. Thank goodness! Once we'd passed it, we'd be in the bay and minutes from home.

Pete pointed to a trawler chugging towards Torringham. "Take it wide. You need to keep well out at this point. Go around that buoy."

The digital figures on the depth gauge started to move upwards: 25.7, 26.2. Watching it became a weird form of masochism, as I didn't really want to think about how deep the water was. The gauge rose until it touched 30 metres and I turned away.

Shadwell Point's impressive limestone cliff rose beside us. At its edge tiny figures gazed down. We'd stood in that spot more than a dozen times, captivated by the incredible view and the drop below. One of the bystanders pointed towards us.

"Dolphins!" Emily shouted.

To our left, a sleek grey body arced from the water, followed by another. When I stood up to watch, Pete snapped, "Shona! You should be going that way. See those buoys?"

Shona moved the tiller and the boat swung to the right, as if heading out to sea. Once we were back on course, she moved the tiller into position and the boat nosed into the bay.

For the first time since we'd left Kentsbridge, Pete grinned. "Let's see what this girl can do."

He pushed the throttle and the engine roared as the yacht ploughed forward. We were back in line with the tip of Shadwell Point, but now on the familiar section of the austere headland.

Berrinton stretched along the other side of the bay and I squinted to see the landmarks: the big wheel by the promenade, the masts rising from the harbour, and lovely Victorian hotels beside the modern buildings housing cafés and restaurants. I didn't need to strain to see the apartments on top of the hill. The trio of concrete blocks seemed as out of place here as they did from every other angle.

Emily and Tom shuffled along the gangway and into the cockpit. The beautiful Georgian building that was now Shadwell House Hotel came into view. From this distance, I couldn't make out people sitting on the terrace, although I knew they would be there. Who wouldn't want to enjoy the glorious views while sipping a glass of wine? Ahead lay Torringham with its colourful harbour cottages. In ten minutes we would be on dry land and within fifteen minutes I'd be raising a glass of delicious Prosecco to celebrate Shona's first voyage.

"Can anyone else smell that?" Emily said.

I sniffed. "What?"

"A burning smell."

A puzzled look passed between Shona and Pete, but then Shona's frown deepened. "Flipping 'eck! I can smell smoke."

Pete shoved the throttle back and the engine died. As silence fell, we looked at each other. Then our attention focused on Pete, who crouched beside the ignition. What would he do now? The sounds we hadn't been able to hear above the engine began to filter around us. Waves lapped against the boat, while a seagull's cry echoed.

Cursing, Pete got to his feet. As he disappeared into the cabin, Shona gazed at me in dismay. "This boat is jinxed."

For some reason her words brought to mind the elderly woman with the black beady eyes in the portrait at the solicitor's office. Perhaps, when Shona had ruined her grandson's books, she'd cursed this boat. I chuckled at the ridiculousness of my thoughts. But it seemed that the boat only had problems when Shona was on board. After all, Pete and Barry had managed to sail it to Kentsmouth without a hitch.

A good ten minutes later, Pete popped up from the cabin, his face beaded with sweat. "Have you got a spare impeller on board?"

Shona shrugged. "What's a spear impaler when it's at home?"

# Chapter 29

WE'D BEEN TACKING ACROSS THE BAY for two hours now. I'd never heard this term before and I wished with every fibre in my body that it had remained unlearned. It meant going back and forth under sail to try to get the wind to draw us into the harbour. But we didn't seem to be moving any closer to our target.

Huddled on one side of the cockpit with Tom, Emily had fallen into a morose silence. Their phone batteries were low and needed to be saved. Emily had done her best to make the most of our floating prison, playing I-spy and rock, paper, scissors but as the grey light of dusk wrapped itself around us, I wished I could transport her back to land. Her promised night out with Lucy, Lester, Sarah and Josh was no longer a meal followed by drinks. Now she and Tom would be meeting up with the others for a few cocktails. That's if we ever made it back.

Lucy hadn't met Sarah or Josh before, so I wondered how they were getting on at the Lord Mountfield pub while they waited for us.

Sighing, I rested my head against the hard panel. Pete's obstinacy had gone beyond a joke. While the sun cast its swansong rays across the horizon, the moon hung nearby, waiting its turn.

"Can't we call someone to help us? *Please*."

Even Shona, who'd been thrilled to get the sails up and had been playing the role of obedient pupil, found her voice. "I'm fricking hungry. If you'd called for a tow, we would have been back ages ago."

Each time we'd spotted a passing boat, we'd begged Pete to call out for a tow, but he'd insisted we'd be okay. He'd phoned Barry several times and left a message asking for help. But now his eyes tracked towards Torringham and uncertainty flickered across his face.

"Let's try the engine one more time."

He hit the ignition. Nothing.

"If we don't get help soon, we'll be stuck out here," Shona said.

'And die of hypothermia,' I nearly added. I hugged my fleece around me. I'd buckled the life jacket around it and the bulky weight dug into my shoulders.

It would be warmer in the cabin below but, so far, I'd manage to stave off the intermittent feelings of seasickness. I didn't dare go below and risk feeling worse.

Pete held his hands up. "Okay. I'll give them a call."

"Who?" Shona gazed around. There wasn't a boat in sight.

Pete sighed, his earlier vigour seeping from him, and slumped onto the seat. "I really don't need this."

"We do!" Shona jerked her thumb towards Tom and Emily. "They need to get back to see their friends, and Katie and I need to eat."

We'd finished the crisps and drinks shortly after we'd started tacking. Pete had promised us that under sail we'd be back within an hour, so we hadn't thought to ration supplies. Neither did I fancy having to use the loo again, which was little more than a hole surrounded by a bit of ceramic, a plunging flusher and a curtain. The latter was there for modesty, but it displayed most of your legs.

*Jazzed Up* had downed Pete. He shuffled past me to the cabin,

253

where he radioed for assistance. I caught the odd words.

"We tried that… I've checked… the impeller… No, we haven't… Sorry, Kev, I wouldn't do this, but…"

I hadn't realised the sun had set until he stepped from the cabin. His features were shaded, except for the whites of his eyes and his teeth.

"They're coming. Let's get the sails down."

We got to work, taking care not to trip in the darkness as we followed Pete's instructions. Then we headed back to the cockpit to await rescue. The lights of Berrinton shone reds, yellows and greens. Torringham's harbour was hidden from view, but we could see the flood lights in the fish quay, the crimson flash of the lighthouse, and the boat heading towards us. We shielded our eyes from its dazzling beams.

"Bloody hell," Shona gasped. "It's only the sodding lifeboat. I thought we were getting a tow."

"What did you expect? I wanted to wait for Barry to get back to help, but it's a bit late now," Pete said.

So that's why he'd been so keen to keep us out in the bay. He wanted to save face and have his friend come out to tow us in, but now we'd have the ignominy of being rescued by the lifeboat.

"How embarrassing!" Emily echoed all our thoughts.

♦

Once again Jason and Kim met us on the town pontoon. The last time I'd been here, the harbour master's team had helped us after we'd grounded the yacht. Now we'd gone one step further and called out the lifeboat. They'd been lovely about it and understood that we'd done all we could and had no option than to call for help. None of us mentioned the boats Pete had watched slip past before darkness had fallen. I cringed at the lifeboat crew's kindness. They had enough to do without rescuing us.

The lifeboat crew waved goodbye and headed back to the station, leaving Pete to tie the ropes to the mooring posts, while Shona checked the boat.

My legs were stiff after hours spent sitting and I struggled to clamber over the guard rails. Although the pontoon gently rocked, it was nothing compared to the swell of the sea in the open bay. It felt strange to be on land once again. Chilled by the wind and a long day I shivered with fatigue.

Jason drew me to him. "The rest are in the pub. Fancy joining them? I think food is still being served."

I longed for my bed. But that involved a walk, whereas the cosy pub sat just yards away. When Emily and Tom drifted ahead, Kim urged me to go with them, saying she'd follow with Shona. I shouted goodbye and thanks to Pete and snuggled into Jason's chest, welcoming the familiar scent of his aftershave. Even though he wore a simple cotton shirt, heat radiated from him. A gentle hubbub rose from the people seated outside The Lord Mountfield. Its south-facing aspect meant it was popular for evening drinkers and, even though night had drawn in, people clustered outside.

We followed Emily and Tom over to a bench where Lucy and Lester sat with Sarah and another lad, who must be Josh. He stood to shake my hand, while Lucy rushed over to give me a welcoming kiss. She'd draped her cardi over her bare shoulders.

She wrapped her arms around me. "You're freezing. We'll go inside."

Emily had already sat down next to Sarah. I didn't want to force them inside when it was just me feeling the effects of a long day at sea.

"Us oldies can go in, while you stay out here and enjoy yourselves. We've got a busy morning, so we won't be stopping long."

Jason stroked my hair. "While you're inside you might want to find a mirror. You're looking a bit windswept."

Pretending to be affronted, I shrugged his arm away – but when the cool air filled the gap between our bodies, I tucked myself close to him again. Lucy nudged me and pointed to Kim and Shona, who were heading towards us. Shona's mouth was set in a grim line.

"She looks happy. Should I ask what her next party trick will be?"

"Probably sinking the boat for the grand finale hat-trick." Lester sniggered.

"What hat-trick?" Shona asked.

We gazed at her, innocently, hoping someone would say something. Lucy took the mantle. "The boat race in the bay next weekend. Do you think they'll win for a third time?"

Shona didn't ask who she meant by 'they'. I doubted Lucy had any idea either.

Instead, she sighed. "Well, it won't be me. I'm giving sailing a rest for now. At least until I find a better teacher."

# Chapter 30

"I HEARD YOU GOT BROUGHT IN BY THE LIFEBOAT." Laura's jubilance rang down the phone line.

I winced. Our engine breakdown hadn't been in quite the same league as her and Bessie's rescue the previous year. But I knew how embarrassed she'd been, especially when photographs of their rescue made it onto Facebook. At least now she had others to share the ribbing she still occasionally endured.

Tartly, I said, "We got towed in. We didn't go on board."

She shrugged off my correction. "But still, you had to be saved. And Shona too."

The last part delighted her, I could tell. While she and Shona were friends, there was an undercurrent of friction between them, which was not helped by Shona's behaviour at previous book club sessions. I was under strict instructions not to let Shona know when these were held.

"Shona wasn't impressed." The least said about that, the better. "How are you though?"

"Good. Just calling to check if you're still coming on Thursday night?"

She meant to book club. I'd forgotten to check with Jason but I couldn't see why there'd be an issue. By the time book club started at 7pm, any check-ins should have arrived. People tended to arrive earlier at this time of year to make the most of the sunnier days and warm evenings.

After chatting for a bit longer, I finished the call and went through to the laundry room, where I found Jason frowning and holding up a towel.

"Why do people do this?"

He turned the towel to me. It could have been the Shroud of Turin: it had the perfect outline of a face smeared over the white cotton, except this was in colour: black for the mascara, orange-ish foundation and crimson lipstick.

He tossed it into the washing machine, followed by a shovel-load of Vanish.

"Is that the person who got ring marks all over the wood?"

"Yup. The amount she's cost us, I think we've paid her to stay." I needed to lighten the conversation. "Well, she's gone now. By the way, I'm going to book club on Thursday night."

He frowned. "It's beginning to feel like I'm running this place on my own."

"Aww, don't be like that." I gave him a cuddle. "I'll be nice and let you go out on Shona's boat next time."

He chuckled. "Trying to get rid of me?"

♦

Emily phoned as I headed out of the guesthouse on Thursday evening to go to book club. Her call was unexpected, being as she'd left on Sunday. I managed to say, "Hello," until cut off by one of Torringham's many mobile blackspots. In frustration, I tapped the redial button but it wasn't until I reached the shops that I got a clear signal.

"Hi. It's me again!"

She sighed. "You don't need to tell me it's you all the time. It shows on my phone."

Sometimes she made me feel old.

"Tom's coming to see me this weekend," she continued, "but I wondered about staying at yours the following weekend."

"Your room's free then, if that's what you're asking."

"Great." She hesitated. "What if I came down for longer? Would that be a problem?"

"You're always welcome. How long are you talking about?" A man bumped into my elbow and I mouthed an apology.

"I don't know. It depends on Lucy, I guess."

This was becoming more cryptic by the moment. I glanced at my watch. Five to seven. I didn't want to be late, but my curiosity had been piqued. As I headed into the harbour, the smell of fried fish wafted through the air, making my mouth water. A queue straggled from the chip shop onto the pavement. Checking for cars before I stepped into the road, I lost my train of thought.

"Where were we? Lucy. What's this got to do with her?"

"Let her tell you, Mum. I've already said too much. She…"

I didn't catch her words. People milled outside the pubs or sat on benches, cartons of chips balanced in their laps, while seagulls stalked the pavement. Outside the ice-cream parlour a screaming child tugged his father's arm trying to drag him inside. Nearby, the Torringham brass band set out chairs in preparation for their performance, while someone blasted a few notes on a trumpet. I pressed the phone to my ear and hurried towards The Anchor's Rest.

"Is she okay, though?"

"She's good."

"And you. Are you all right?"

"Absolutely fine."

It didn't seem as if she was hiding anything from me. She sounded happy. I'd have to trust her.

"Okay," I lied. While the hulking elephant in our conversation would have to wait for another day, I knew I'd brood about it in the middle of the night. "I've got to go now. It's book club tonight. But I'll call you soon."

"Make it Sunday," she said. "Tom'll be with me straight after work."

We closed the conversation with a 'love you'. Something was up but I couldn't tell whether it was good or bad. Should I speak to Jason about it, to see if he could talk to Lucy to find out more? No. Lucy would call him when she had something to say. I'd promised Emily to leave it until then. *But leave what?*

As usual, the punters at The Anchor's Rest had chosen to stand on the pavement to enjoy the warmth of the evening, even though this part of the harbour was cast in shade. Turning sideways, I edged between two groups who clutched glasses as they chatted. Clouds of smoke hung in the air, sweetened by vapers. When I pushed the pub door open and stepped inside, the tang of beer filled my nostrils. A queue thronged the bar but I headed past them and through the door marked *Toilets*. In the alleyway, I took the door on the right into the familiar room, which was filled with the usual faces – and one new one. She was about my age, with frizzy hair, high cheekbones and wrinkles around her lips that suggested a lifetime spent smoking cigarettes.

Josie patted the empty chair beside her. Bessie's tail thumped on the tiled floor. I stooped to stroke the dog before taking my place at the oval table. The new woman, who sat on the other side of my chair, gave me a friendly smile, which made me feel bad for judging her looks on her cigarette intake.

Josie took a sip of coffee and leaned over to whisper to me, her hot breath patting my ear. "I see the lovebirds are doing well."

I hesitated, wondering if I should ask her if she knew anything about what was going on with Emily, before deciding against it. If she didn't know, my questioning might encourage her to snoop further.

"It's lovely to see them looking so happy." A book sat on the table in front of her, but not the one I thought we'd been asked to read. "What's this?"

"My suggestion for next time." She grinned at me. "Did you think you'd read the wrong one?"

I smiled, not wanting to confess I hadn't read the set book. To change the subject, I shuffled through my bag to locate my book and a bottle of water. Although the book club was held in The Anchor's Rest, experience had taught me to expect a ten-minute wait at the bar during the summer season. Even if I found the bar empty, I wouldn't succumb. One time, Josie and I had bought a bottle of wine to save going back to the bar. A few glasses in, we'd giggled each time one of the women mentioned cod pieces when discussing a book set in Tudor England – except they'd accidentally called them cock pieces and we wouldn't let it drop. Ever since, we'd had an unspoken rule to save the wine until later.

Not wanting the discussion to return to the book or Emily –

Josie's innocent comment had reignited the anxiety I'd barely quelled after the phone call – I took longer than usual to arrange my belongings on the table, pulling out a pen and notepad too, although I didn't usually make any notes. It worked. By the time I looked up, Josie had turned to chat to her neighbour.

The woman beside me fingered the pages of her book. "What did you think of it?"

I grimaced, wishing she hadn't asked.

"I didn't like it either," she said. "A load of overblown claptrap. The author talks about being in prison but it's nothing like she said."

My eyebrows hit my fringe, but I masked my shock with a smile and a bland response. "That's often the way."

Laura cleared her throat and held up her book. "What are our views on this one, ladies?"

As the conversation flowed, I waited with trepidation for Gemma – we learned her name when Laura finally introduced her to the group – to mention her stint in prison to the others. Would they be shocked? Although Gemma nodded in agreement when someone raised a point about the prison scenes, she didn't mention her actual experience. I stole a glance at her. She didn't look the type to have been in prison. But was there a type? Not everyone in prison would have done something terrible. She could have evaded paying her council tax or something. Unlikely, I knew, but what business of mine was it?

"So, we're in agreement. We read Josie's choice for next time and Clara's choice the time after that." Laura brought the meeting to a close. My misdemeanour in not reading the book had gone undetected.

Usually most of us would decamp to the bar across the road, while some would excuse themselves by pointing out it was a 'school night'.

"Drink?" I asked. When several people nodded, I turned to Gemma. "Will you join us?"

After a moment's hesitation, she shrugged. "Why not?"

◆

Somehow we managed to find seating for seven. We bunched onto the corner benches, sipping our drinks and shouting above the din of the pop music blasting overhead. Instead of my usual white wine or Prosecco, I'd chosen a strawberry daiquiri, which was slipping down too smoothly. A hazy glow embraced me, not helped by Gemma who had squished into a sliver-sized gap between Laura and me, while on the other side Josie stuck her elbow into my rib cage each time she slurped her drink.

When a table became free opposite, we nabbed it. Again, Gemma sat next to me, almost spilling her drink in her haste to bag a chair.

"Whoops!" She steadied her glass on the table. "By the way…" She covered her mouth and leaned towards me conspiratorially. No longer sited beneath the speaker, she didn't need to shout to be heard. "Just in case you're wondering, when I said about prison at the book club, I've not done a stint there myself. I worked there."

She must have spent the whole book club kicking herself about what she'd mentioned and looking for an opportunity to correct it.

"That's interesting. Were you a prison officer?"

She shook her head. "One of the medical team. Saying that…" She glanced around to check who might be listening. "There's the odd one or two bad eggs in my family. We've got a bit of a reputation around these parts."

With the lines between empathy and confidentiality blurred by alcohol, I wanted her to feel I wasn't judging her, that I understood – even though no one in my family had even stolen so much as a fiver – so I said, "My friend's father went to prison and she has a hard time talking about it. Especially because of what he did."

"It's hard for the families," she murmured.

I nodded. It was worse for Shona. An innocent remark had got her mixed up in her father's actions. I bent to sip my drink, disappointed to find little but air funnelling through my straw.

"She was only a child but she got blamed for what her father did."

Frowning, she assessed me. "Laura said you ran Flotsam B&B. You're talking about your neighbour, aren't you?"

My hands shot to my mouth and a shiver coursed down my back. I hadn't said anything to give away Shona's secret. Or had I? But how had Gemma known from what I'd said? It couldn't have been a guess on her part. She must know Shona, know her secret. But how? Shona had only just told Kim.

My expression must have given away my thoughts, as Gemma touched my shoulder and gave me a sympathetic smile."

"Don't worry. You haven't said anything out of turn. We blame her father for what he did to our aunt, not Shona."

I swallowed. Kim would kill me for giving away Shona's secret.

But— hold on… Gemma had mentioned her aunt! She must be the woman the man across the road had been threatening Shona about.

"You know about Shona?"

She chuckled. "Torringham's too small for secrets. How many Shona Albrights are there in this town?"

It felt strange hearing Shona's full name. I never thought of her as anything but Shona and wouldn't be able to remember Kim's surname even if fifty pounds was placed on the table.

"You're not angry with her? None of your family is going after her?"

Gemma shot back in her seat, affronted. "Of course not! Why would we?"

"The man across the road said you would. He's been blackmailing her about it."

Confused, Gemma shook her head. "We might have a few bad 'uns in the family. Who doesn't? But Shona's never done anything to us." She paused. "That man. Is he Stinky Smith?"

"Yes! You know him?"

"I know of him."

"He's been terrible to Shona – abusing her in the street, threatening to tell your family who she is. I don't know why he hates her so much."

Gemma sighed. "He's a Neanderthal and he's probably got an issue with Shona being with Kim. He's also a bully. His family got that house but not long after he moved in uninvited, they moved out."

Now I thought about it, I hadn't seen the woman or the two teenagers for ages. They could have died for all I knew.

"Why did they leave?"

"Mo – his ex – didn't want him back, but he wouldn't go." She downed the dregs from her glass. "He spent all their money on beer, betting and weed. He's always short of money. I heard on the grapevine that he's been back to his old stomping ground to get cash to set up a new sideline."

"What sort of sideline?"

"I dunno. I just overheard my brother Johnnie talking about it. He was saying Stinky needs to take care he doesn't get the police called on him, in case he ends up back in prison."

"But he can't be that worried about the police. He called them about the graffiti."

"Stinky doesn't mind stitching other people up. Just not himself. Anyhow, he wouldn't be stupid enough to run his sideline from his house."

For someone who didn't know what Stinky's sideline was, it seemed an odd remark to make.

She looked me in the eye. "He drinks in the same pubs as my brothers. Not that he'll be going anywhere when our Johnnie gets hold of him. He can't be treating women like that."

She stood up and tugged her skirt down. "Fancy another?"

"No one's going to hurt him on Shona's account, are they?"

"Don't be daft! Johnnie's started dating Mo, Stinky's ex – you know, the woman who left him – and found out how he used to treat her. We thought Johnnie'd sprayed that graffiti on Stinky's place, but he says it wasn't him."

I could barely keep up, but I got the gist. Johnnie didn't like how Stinky had behaved with Mo, so he wanted to teach him a lesson by thumping him. I also understood why Gemma had found the book we'd discussed a bit tame. In comparison to her world, the characters had lived such simple lives.

"But you won't mention Shona to anyone."

Chuckling, she said, "There's plenty more ways to skin a Stinky Smith. Shona won't be involved." She held up my glass. "Another strawberry daiquiri, or are you going to try something else?"

As she walked away, Josie nudged me and jerked her head in Gemma's direction. "Gemma's lovely but, just so you know, she's one of the Harringtons."

"The Harringtons?" I hadn't heard of them.

Laura leaned across the table and hissed, "Shh! Don't say it so loud. She'll hear you."

"Dodgy family," Josie whispered. "Gemma's apple might appear shiny and bright, but the Harringtons never fall far from the tree."

Laura burst into laughter. "Have you had too much cider, Josie?"

Josie looked indignant. "No! I'm just telling Katie to take care what she says."

# Chapter 31

With our bedroom sited at the rear of the guesthouse, I'd missed the early-morning commotion. But our guests hadn't. I stood incredulous in the breakfast room as they took it in turns to tell me what had happened. How the police pulled up, blue lights flashing at six o'clock, and dragged Stinky Smith from his house.

"Screaming at the top of his voice, he was. I can't believe you didn't hear it." Nancy plucked the hearing aid from her ear. "I had to take this out to get back to sleep."

"You're telling me you could sleep with your face planted to the window," Alfred said.

Nancy ignored him. "The man wouldn't stop screeching about a stick up."

Ross cut in. "You mean stitch up."

Across from him, William nibbled on a slice of toast. He looked a bit peaky this morning and had refused the offer of a cooked breakfast. Most of our guests were holidaymakers, but he was here for business. He'd put his suit on but had pulled the notch of his tie loose and undone the collar button on his shirt. A heavy night down the pub? I didn't like to exclude lone guests, so I turned to him.

"Did you see anything?"

"Not a word. Excuse me." He got up.

Nancy tutted and held out her hearing aid. "You lot need this more than me."

As William headed out of the breakfast room, I glanced outside the window to where a solitary white trainer lay in the gutter. Stinky

Smith must have lost it in all the commotion. Or, perhaps it was the companion to the trainer that had been dangling from the telephone wires for the past few months. I shrugged and went into the kitchen to tell Jason what had happened.

◆

An hour later, while I waved goodbye to a pair of regular guests someone tooted behind me. I leapt from the pavement into our driveway to find Mrs Hollacombe trundling by. Like a Roman road, she didn't believe in going around unless absolutely necessary. Nor did she apparently realise that her mobility scooter came with brakes. A teddy bear sat in the shopping basket in the front, sporting a natty sweater. I couldn't make out the words, but a banner in the same colours was draped over the back of her chair. It gave a boat's number and the name *Our Boys*. Her scooter had been decked in Union Flag bunting. She must be heading down to watch the trawlers racing each other.

"I didn't realise she had fishermen in the family." Shona walked over with Kim, who watched Mrs Hollacombe's journey down the street.

"She's a menace."

Shona chuckled. "It's my ambition to be like her one day."

"Aiming high then?" Kim rolled her eyes.

Her gaze turned to the cottage across the road. With the render, door and window frames all covered with the same sickly magnolia, it reminded me of a woman who'd plastered on foundation, but hadn't got around to adding mascara or lipstick.

From what I could tell, Stinky Smith had even covered the door knocker too. But he'd failed to obliterate the graffiti. The black spray seeped through the paint, so *Abuser* crept back into view.

"Did you see him hit that policeman?" Shona mimicked a fist swinging out.

"We slept through it."

She narrowed her eyes. "So, you never heard *anything*?"

"Nothing. I wish I had. It would have been interesting to see."

"I got bored once they took him away, but Shona stayed up," Kim said.

"Drugs," Shona said. "I heard he had a stash of them."

"Are you sure they were his?" I asked.

She turned to me, her expression incredulous. "They were found in his house. Who else would they belong to?"

I didn't respond. But I recalled Gemma's words. She'd said he had a sideline but he wouldn't run it from his house. I hadn't expected his sideline to be drugs though. How dreadful.

"The drugs alone will put him back behind bars," Kim said.

When Shona smiled, I noticed the pinched line between her eyes had vanished. I promised myself I'd tell Kim what Gemma had said – even if it meant she'd be furious with me for being indiscreet – so she could somehow let Shona know that she didn't need to worry about being blackmailed in the future.

Then I remembered that I hadn't finished cleaning the guesthouse yet. In fact, we'd barely started.

"I need to get on."

As I spoke, Jason stormed out of the guesthouse. "You won't believe what I've just found!"

He clenched his fists. "If he was still here. I'd kill him."

I rushed inside – not thinking to say goodbye to Shona and Kim – and followed Jason up to room eight.

"Don't touch anything," Jason said. He bent down to retrieve a pair of Marigolds from the cleaning basket.

The bedroom seemed in order. Confused, I stared at Jason, who flipped the duvet aside. One corner of the sheet, mattress topper and protector had been pulled out of the way – presumably by Jason after he'd made his grim discovery. He lifted a sodden pillow between his gloved finger and thumb.

"He's wet the bed. Soaked it! It's gone through the mattress protector and the topper. The mattress is wrecked."

I gasped. "But he seemed such a nice professional man." Would we find anything else? I hoped not.

Then I shuddered. "We've got guests arriving for this room later. What will we do?"

♦

After a morning spent scrubbing room eight until I was sure every speck of the man had been eradicated from the room, followed by an early afternoon drive to the tip with the mattress and bedding once all the other rooms had been serviced, I was ready for lunch when we finally stopped at three o'clock.

"When is the new mattress arriving?" I asked.

"Next week."

"Great. A whole week of sleeping on the floor."

He shrugged. "That, or the slats on the bed."

"The floor. We'll have to move the bedframe though."

Jason had rung William that morning and he'd immediately agreed to pay rather than us get in contact with his company. How much had he drunk the previous night not to notice he'd wet the bed? But, more to the point, why hadn't he told us what had happened? We'd donated our own mattress to room eight until the new one arrived, and we had enough spare bedding without buying more, but I shook with anger at his disgusting, selfish behaviour.

Jason folded the crust of his sandwich into his mouth and took a swig of tea to wash it down. He slapped his hands together to rid himself of crumbs but, unlike every other day, he did so over his plate.

"Come on then. We've got time before the guests arrive."

We headed upstairs to our bedroom. In the rush to move our mattress to room eight, we'd piled our bedding onto the slats. Jason bundled the duvet and sheet into the bottom of the wardrobe for now, leaving me to stack the pillows on my stool. We each took an end of the bedframe and turned it onto its side, tucking it against the wall. For people who took pride in our guesthouse being spotless, we'd failed with our own room. A sweet wrapper, receipt and a few coins littered the bed-shaped rectangle of dust that speckled the carpet.

While Jason left to get the vacuum cleaner, I started to pick the bits from the floor. When he returned, the doorbell rang.

Handing me the vacuum cleaner, he said, "Looks like the guests are early. I'll leave the room to you."

I set about hoovering the carpet. A layer of dust lined the skirting board. Rather than going downstairs to fetch the nozzle attachment, I knelt to dust the edge. Close up the woodchip wallpaper appeared to bulge over something, so I ran my hand down the wall, finding the rim of something hard beneath the wallpaper. As I traced the outline – about one foot by three foot in size – excitement burbled inside me. Was this what Carl had been searching for? I knew I should check with Jason before destroying the wallpaper but, not wanting him to tell me to stop, I took my nail scissors from the bathroom cabinet and began to score a line around the shape.

It took ages to peel several layers of wallpaper from what appeared to be a cream wooden board. Once I'd managed to do so, the panel refused to come away from the wall, even though two small gold hinges at its base suggested it could be opened. Surrounded by curls of paper and slivers of woodchip, I gazed at it. A hole near the top and an arc of scraped paintwork suggested there'd once been a latch holding it in place.

The bedroom door opened and Jason appeared. "They're in." Then he frowned. "What are you doing?"

I didn't give him the courtesy of blushing or apologising for the mess. Instead, I waved him over. "Give me a hand. I need to get this off."

He shook his head but came over to examine the panel. When he got to his feet, he told me to give him a minute. He returned with his toolbox, which he settled on top of the mess and took out a chisel, which he tucked into the gap.

"It looks like someone's glued it. You don't think there'll be anything in there do you? Someone must have come across it in all the years since Carl's relative lived here."

I shrugged. "It'd be nice to know. We didn't spot it when we painted this room, did we? There's so many humps and ridges in the walls."

"Fetch the dustpan and brush. I'm getting covered here." He flicked a strip of wallpaper off his trousers.

When I came back, Jason gritted his teeth as he pushed hard against the chisel handle. A crack told me something had given way. Hopefully, not the chisel. He levered the blade along the gap. When the wood began to jut out, he gave a swift jerk of the chisel. The wood popped clear and I dropped to my knees, grinning. I'd not come across a time capsule before. What would be inside it? I peered into the gloomy cubby hole before Jason had even lowered the board. It smelled musty but not damp. He delved into the space and drew out a brown paper bag stuffed with papers, then another bag, which he passed to me.

I stifled a giggle. It was an old pick 'n' mix bag. "Woolworths? That's hardly a 1920s time capsule." I pulled out a handful of postcards and leaflets and a handwritten letter. "There couldn't have been sweets in the bag, or else these would be coated with sugar."

Jason brought out a small tin and dusted his hands down his trousers. "That's it. We've destroyed the wall for this lot."

The tin piqued my interest. Rust spotted the lid but an oval picture on the front, depicting a horse pulling a card laden with straw, could clearly be seen. The tin had once contained biscuits, but I didn't recognise the company name. What did it now hold?

"Open the tin, then!"

Grimacing, Jason tucked his nails under the lid and tugged. It opened with a ping. He gazed inside. Frowning, he turned the tin on its side so a few objects toppled onto the carpet. I picked up a small metal box dulled by time and turned it round. It had been engraved with people in Victorian costume. The lid opened upwards. The inside was silver in colour but marred by a brown stain. I had no idea what kind of metal it was, but there were no hallmarks to denote a precious metal.

"Snuff box?" I handed it to Jason.

He pointed to the sloping wooden interior of the box, which was separated into two compartments by a piece of wood. "For stamps, most likely. They used to cut them up before they got serrated edges. Even then, people often kept them in these."

When I gazed at him, he added, "My uncle collected stamps."

We placed the objects on a nearby section of clean carpet and sifted through them: cufflinks, a pair of dice, a wooden peg with a painted face, and a beautiful diamante brooch shaped like a fern leaf and inlaid with, what looked like, jade.

"These are nice." Jason chinked the cuff links in his cupped hand. "There's a note too. What does it say?"

I scanned the sheet. "It's definitely from Carl's great-grandfather. He says he's put some information about the house in the bag. He hopes future owners will do the same. The cufflinks are his father's, the brooch his mother's, the dice and the peg were donated by his siblings."

I turned to the brown paper bag, taking care as I took out the photographs and papers. All the photographs were in black and white. One showed a field dotted with trees, fronted by a dusty road off which led a little track. It ran alongside a hedgerow before meandering up the hillside. The faded looped handwriting on the back told me it was the land on which Flotsam had been built. Had Carl's family built the guesthouse? He hadn't mentioned this. Nor had he said his great-grandfather was a trawler owner. But it seemed fitting that his family would give the two houses such odd names. Carl had said his family were eccentric.

The next image showed Flotsam and Jetsam Cottage shortly after they'd been built. I'd seen a similar photograph in Carl's folder. I flipped through the papers. Several sheets showed bills for various purchases and I put these to one side to examine later.

Jason had been scrutinising the contents of the Woolworths bag, so we swapped packages. A postcard caught my attention – from the 1970s or early 1980s, I guessed. The words *A warm welcome awaits at Flotsam Guesthouse* were in the centre in a jaunty font, surrounded by four images. One showed the guesthouse, its render glowing white in the sun. The lintels and cornerstones had been painted red. I'd come across that layer last year, when we were prepping the house for it to be painted sage and white. The postcard showed parking for two cars. What was now our third space had been a grassed area covered with patio tables and chairs back then. The next picture showed the dining area, with round tables covered in frilly tablecloths, while the third showed a bedroom with a row of three beds and tasselled lampshades. The final photo was of the guest lounge with an old-fashioned chunky TV the centrepiece of the room.

A leaflet had also been added to the collection. In the days before the internet, enquirers would have been sent a brochure on the guesthouse. Now, if anyone asked to see information, we directed them to our website.

The leaflet mirrored the postcard's promise of a warm welcome, but this went one stage further, with the offer of comfortable rooms and a colour TV. I chuckled. They didn't promise a TV in the bedrooms, nor was there mention of ensuite facilities, because there would have been none then. We had the old fire plans for the building, which showed the loos and bathrooms in a row on each floor. The pick 'n' mix bag contained other photos and pieces of paper, all with four-digit phone numbers. Strange that I'd been alive back then, but knew nothing of this guesthouse or the part it would play in my life. Lives running in parallel only to link in some small way in the future.

The owners of the guesthouse at this time had found the hidden cubby hole and had done as Carl's great-grandfather had requested – not taking anything but adding to it. We decided we would do the same.

"What shall we add?" I asked Jason. "I'll invite Carl to see the cubby hole when he next comes down."

"What about his family's belongings?" Jason asked.

I could see his point. They were personal to his family, rather than to the house.

"I'll ask him about those. But the rest belongs to this house." The word 'family' made me remember what I'd meant to ask Jason several days before. "By the way, have you heard from Lucy?"

"She's coming down this weekend with Emily, if that's what you mean."

"But has she said anything to you other than that?"

He shrugged. "The usual: boring job, lovely Lester." He

scrutinised me. "Should there be anything else?"

"Honestly, I don't know."

"I hope I'm not about to become a granddad or something."

I decided not to remind him about the previous year when Lucy had got pregnant with her previous boyfriend. She'd been devastated to lose the baby – and her relationship. It was wonderful to see her looking happy again, especially as Lester seemed to be a lovely man.

Pulling a face, Jason got to his feet and left me sitting cross-legged with the scraps of wallpaper around me. I'd clean up later – and make up our temporary bed – but thanks to Carl and our disgusting guest – I'd found a trove that would keep me occupied all evening.

# Chapter 32

WHEN THE LAST OF OUR GUESTS checked-in the following evening, Jason suggested going to the Lord Mountfield for a bite to eat and to soak up the last rays. Stir-crazy after an afternoon spent ironing, I had my sandals on within moments and hovered impatiently by the front door, begging him to hurry up.

I led the march down to the harbour, where I slowed to navigate the hordes of visitors still milling in the street. Even at seven o'clock, the sea glittered and the sun beamed from a cloudless sky. Across the road a busker strummed on his guitar, while music blared from a pub and people crammed beside the doorway, pints and cigarettes in hand. My stomach rumbled at the smell of fish and chips and I gazed enviously at the people leaving the chip shop with their take-away boxes.

We rounded the harbour, slaloming past people and dogs. Above us, pigeons cooed from the tall stone wall that ran alongside the walkway, while Jason's attention was taken by four swans gliding past a row of boats.

He pointed. "They're back."

As I paused to look, someone jostled my shoulder. I muttered an apology, but they'd passed without noticing, melting into the crowd.

"Do you think there'll be any seats left?"

He shrugged.

When we arrived at the Lord Mountfield, I tried to spot a free bench but could see none. I threw Jason a dejected look, but he grasped my arm.

"There's Josie and Mike. They've got spare seats too."

We headed over and gave each other a welcoming hug. After they had batted away our polite questions about invading their space, I sat down, while Jason got the drinks. When we'd started dating I'd been happy to get the drinks, but we'd found his height an advantage when getting served at bars. Now, I had to confess, it had become a habit and we took our roles without thinking.

"I saw Shona and Kim by the boat," Josie said. "They said they might pop by later."

"Are they going out in it?"

She chuckled and shook her head. "I think they just use it to sit in and have a drink in peace."

Jason leaned across me and placed a glass of white wine on the table. Condensation lined the cold glass. I took a sip and sighed in pleasure.

Someone gripped my shoulder. "Can't keep away now you've met me!"

Gemma swayed into view. When I say 'swayed', I mean literally. She patted her chest. "Happy birthday to me. I've had a few."

As she plonked herself onto the bench, beer splashed over the rim of Jason's glass. He and Mike gazed at Gemma with bemused expressions. She laid her hands flat on the tabletop, apparently not noticing the cigarette ash and sticky patches of liquid left by previous occupants. Her nails were a fetching cerise, rimmed with silver. A diamante stud decorated each ring finger.

"Like them? I could tell you where to get yours done."

I examined my work-horse hands, roughened by cleaning chemicals and washing liquid. Somehow Sarah managed to clean the guesthouse and keep her fashionable nails, but I couldn't imagine myself with them.

"They look great on you. Happy birthday."

"Here, let me get you a birthday drink," Josie said. "You look like you could do with another one."

Gemma threw her head back and laughed raucously. I glanced around, hoping none of our guests were nearby.

"You know me too well, Josie. Rhubarb gin and tonic, please. Tell them to go easy on the ice."

As Josie headed off, Gemma nudged me. "Stinky's Smith's gone then. Got caught good and proper."

"Were the drugs really his, do you think? Was that the sideline you mentioned?"

"Who else would they have belonged to?" She cupped her hands as if to tell me a secret, but Mike and Jason were too engrossed in their conversation to hear. "The police knew he'd started dealing. But I bet they couldn't believe he'd made their lives so easy – they found the drugs on the kitchen side rather than stashed away under the floorboards of his mate's allotment shed."

I eyed her suspiciously. Strange how much she knew about his 'sideline' now. Maybe the drink had loosened her tongue? Or, perhaps, she'd found out more after the raid? I'd heard about police raids in other parts of Torringham and Berrinton, but I'd never considered that a drug dealer could be so close to home. In all the time he'd lived across the road, I'd not even seen anyone go to his door, so he must have met his clients elsewhere.

"He didn't usually have them in the house?"

"Never!" She tapped her nose. "No one has any idea how they got there. Especially Stinky."

"Stinky?" Shona stood beside us, frowning. "He's not coming back, is he?"

Kim stood behind Shona, her mouth turned down in despair. Their expressions turned to consternation when Gemma burst into laughter.

"Hold on!" Gemma struggled to her feet, bashing her knee on the bench and splattering more beer onto the table. Jason picked up his glass and wiped its bottom on the edge of the bench before taking a sip. I noticed he didn't put his glass back down but clutched it to his chest like a treasured child.

Gemma planted a hand on Shona's shoulder. "Don't you worry," she slurred. "Stinky's going nowhere. You're Shona, aren't you?"

Puzzled, Shona gazed from Kim to me. Kim shrugged, while I tried to hide my alarm. Given Gemma's drunken state, she could say anything.

When Shona nodded, Gemma hugged her. "You poor thing! I heard what you were going through."

Kim turned an accusing glare on me. I stuttered, trying to think of an explanation, but I couldn't come up with one. Gemma waved her hand around, narrowly missing my eye.

"Someone told me about it, that's all. They spoke to me because I knew you."

"You know me?" Shona's face registered bewilderment. "We haven't met, have we?"

Gemma put her finger to her mouth and drew Shona aside. "I'll tell you – but no one else."

As Gemma peeled Shona from us – while leaning heavily on her – Kim perched herself on the edge of the bench seat. "What was that all about?"

"I'm not a hundred percent sure." Not a lie. While I was ninety-nine percent sure it related to Shona's father, there was a one percent chance it didn't. Actually, scratch that. I knew *exactly* what Gemma would tell Shona. I just prayed Gemma wouldn't drop me in it.

Either way, Kim accepted my response and settled down to watch Shona's myriad of expressions. While Gemma told Shona what she knew, her hand never left Shona's shoulder, most likely because she'd collapse without her support.

I had no idea how Shona would react, so I tried to quell my nerves by chatting with Josie. It looked like the lengthy wait she'd suffered at the bar had been in vain. The rhubarb gin she'd brought Gemma as a birthday gift sat unloved in the centre of the table.

"Talking of Stinky." Looking bored of watching the silent movie taking place by the harbour wall, Kim turned to Josie and me. "His landlord is getting the cottage painted next week. Pete knows the man doing it. I don't think the landlord had much choice though. Not if he wants to re-let it."

"Hopefully, he'll be a bit choosier with his next tenants," Josie said.

Shona headed back, while Gemma stumbled towards another bench. Giving us a little wave, she toppled into her seat. Josie shrugged and lined the rhubarb gin up behind her glass of wine.

"Looks like I'm on the gin then," she said.

Shona slumped on the seat next to Mike. Her eyes sparkled. She shook her head, more to herself than anyone.

"So?" Kim said.

"What?" Shona grinned and tapped her nose.

Kim sighed. "You can't not say anything. Tell me!"

Shona gave us a mysterious smile. "Let's just say that not only will we not be hearing from a certain man for a long time, but he'll never have anything on me again." She glanced from me to Josie. "Sorry if that's a bit cryptic but that's all I'll say."

Thank goodness, Shona had no idea that I knew what she meant. The breath hissed from between my lips, releasing my tension with it. Somehow, even in her inebriated state, Gemma had managed not to implicate me. Not only that, but even though she'd lost her aunt, she had taken time to reassure Shona that the only person to blame for her father's actions was him – certainly not the child Shona had been or the adult she'd become.

# Chapter 33

WHEN THE DOORBELL RANG THE FOLLOWING EVENING, Jason and I turned to each other frowning. I'd answered the door earlier to someone enquiring about a room, so it was his turn. Sighing, he pushed himself to his feet. Moments later, his cheery voice echoed, welcoming someone inside. I heard him say, "Go through to the lounge," so the caller wasn't related to business. A pair of balled socks sat beside me on the sofa – I'd taken them off when my feet got too hot – so I shoved them behind a cushion and stuffed the sweet wrappers I'd tossed onto the coffee table into the pocket of my jeans.

The lounge door creaked open and a sullen-faced Callum appeared, followed by Bert and Doreen. Jason brought up the rear.

Callum stood to one side, ignoring me. I kissed Bert and Doreen and invited them to take a seat. When Jason shot me a puzzled glance, obviously wondering if I had a clue what was going on, I shrugged. I had no idea.

"Callum, sit down!" Doreen pointed to the sofa.

Not looking at any of us, he slouched over to the sofa, hands in his pockets, and slumped onto it. Bert had removed his cap and sat beside Doreen twisting it nervously.

As the atmosphere thickened, Doreen cleared her throat. "We might as well get this over with. Callum has something to tell you. In his favour, he came to tell us or else we wouldn't have known. But that's the only thing he's done right in this matter."

A flush crept over Callum's face. I thought he'd refuse to speak

285

until Doreen prodded him. He hunched forward, head down, palms outstretched, as if pleading for understanding from the carpet.

"I was trying to be nice to the woman next door. The one he was being mean to. You know, that man across the road." He raised his head and our eyes locked for the briefest moment before he glanced away. "A friend got the can and it seemed like a good idea to let everyone know what that man was like. It might have even stopped him too."

My mind had whirred through everything he might have done to help Shona – until he'd mentioned the can. That meant one thing. He'd graffitied the cottage opposite. While I wondered what to say, Jason struggled to compute the basics.

"So you helped Shona by letting people know what that man was like?"

I rolled my eyes at Jason. "Callum's telling us he graffitied Stinky's cottage."

Jason scratched his head. "Who's—"

Callum cut in, "No! I only did it to the man's place across the road. Not anyone else."

I'd started thinking of our ex-neighbour as Stinky Smith after hearing Kim, then Gemma calling him that. With other people I usually referred to him as 'the man across the road' or 'the new neighbour'. Or just 'that man'.

"That's his name," I said.

Their mouths fell open. Callum spoke first. "Couldn't have chosen better myself."

"But why?" Jason asked Callum.

"I'm sorry. I wasn't thinking. But I'll sort it."

Doreen had been sitting straight-backed, her hands in her lap, her calm demeanour at odds with Bert's agitation. "He's going to apologise to the man and paint the cottage."

Although it would be good for Callum to make amends, we had the perfect outcome. A professional painter had already been booked to paint the cottage, starting Monday.

"There's no need," I said. "Stinky's moved out."

Doreen smoothed her skirt. "Nevertheless, we can't have your guests looking at that each day. You can see the writing through the paint. What on earth made you think to write that, Callum, I'll never know. You'll have to speak to the new owner."

Callum sagged into himself. His posture was mirrored by Bert, who sat shamefaced on the settee. I hated to see him looking so dejected. The graffiti hadn't caused us that much trouble – apart from the guest who'd insisted on being moved to another room and the odd grumble from others. But it had all worked out in the end. We'd get to look at a freshly painted cottage – done professionally – which wouldn't have happened if Callum hadn't graffitied it. Also, if Callum painted the cottage to make amends, he might not do it right.

I perched on the arm rest. "Callum knows what he did was stupid. But there's no need for him to paint it. The landlord rented it out in a shocking condition. Now he's paying someone to decorate it, so he can let it again. Hopefully, if it looks good, he might get better tenants. Then it'll be a win all round."

Doreen appraised Callum coolly. "It looks like you've got off this time. But…" Pursing her lips, she left the rest unsaid.

"I know, I know," Callum said. "Honestly, I won't be doing

anything like that again. I fessed up because I felt bad about it."

"Right." Jason slapped his thighs. "Cup of tea, anyone? Or a beer? I know what I could do with."

Bert released his cap from its stranglehold and settled back into the settee with a sigh. "A brew, you say? That'd be grand."

♦

The air lay thick with anticipation. Across from me, Emily and Lucy sat on the settee, knees together, hands in their laps. It felt as if the lounge had become our interrogation chamber. First Callum a few days ago and now the girls. Emily looked smart in her work clothes – a jacket, skirt and blouse. Usually, she changed into casual clothing but she couldn't have had time before leaving for Torringham. Her professional attire made what they came to tell us feel even more significant.

Within minutes of their arrival, Lester had gone up to his and Lucy's room upstairs, which had made me more concerned about the girls' request to have a word with us. He and Lucy were staying the night in one of the guestrooms before heading to Plymouth the following evening, while Emily would be in her old room for the weekend – ostensibly to see us, but we all knew she'd spend more time with Tom. I didn't mind. I'd seen more of her since she'd met him than I had in the months after she'd moved away.

Jason mirrored the girls and perched on the edge of his seat. His forehead furrowed and lines scored the skin between his eyebrows. Determined to appear calm, I sat back and crossed my legs. Thoughts churned in my mind. Was Jason really about to become a granddad? I hoped not. Or, at least, not for many years. I wanted Lucy and Emily to have freedom from the constraints Sarah faced each day with her little one. Although, Sarah's date with Josh had gone well, according to Emily, she'd never be able to go out for the night on a whim.

Strangely, Lucy appeared more composed than Emily, whose hand clamped down on her jittery knee. As a child, she'd distracted herself in stressful situations by humming a beat or tapping a rhythm with her pencil. She must be nervous for her knee to be bouncing up and down like that.

"We've got something to tell you." Lucy pulled at a loose thread on her trouser leg. It ruched the fabric and she pulled the material nearby in an attempt to undo the damage.

Emily elbowed her, bringing Lucy's attention back to us.

"As I was saying…" Lucy's mouth moved like a goldfish as she floundered for words. "I don't know why I'm finding this so difficult to tell you. It's good news really. I hope you'll think so too."

"Lucy's moving to Kingsmouth," Emily broke in.

In normal circumstances, Lucy living less than five miles away should be wonderful news, but Emily's statement left too many unanswered questions. How did she feel about it for a start? After all, Emily had moved from Torringham to be with her half-sister in the town we used to live in. And it wasn't that long since Emily had been annoyed when Lucy mentioned Torringham being a possible location for Lester's future venture. I'd all but forgotten their spat in the restaurant. Emily had shown her true feelings then, by shooting furious barbs at Lucy. I searched Emily's face for signs of upset, but she gave nothing away.

Lucy took a deep breath. "Lester's taking on the lease on a pub there. It's renowned for its food, so it's a great opportunity for him. I'll be joining him."

"What about your mum? Won't she be sad to see you go?" I felt for Marie. When Emily had left to move back to Normansby, I'd missed her so much, but I'd felt reassured knowing her older sister would look after her. "If you move out of your flat, where will Emily live?" I clamped my hand to my mouth. "Sorry. I'm pleased for you but it's a bit of a shock."

"Mum's really happy for us. She's got this new guy." For some reason, Lucy flashed a look at her dad. Probably an instinctive reaction when talking about his ex-wife. "You haven't got any arrivals tomorrow. Why don't we give you a hand tomorrow morning and then we can take a trip out to Kingsmouth. You can see the pub and we can have lunch there."

"What about my news?" Emily said.

"Shhh!" Lucy glared at Emily. "I thought we'd agreed to tell them at the pub."

"News?" Jason frowned and my heart plummeted. Great! It would be Emily giving us the news that we'd become grandparents, I felt sure of it.

Lucy mimed zipping her mouth. "No more questions."

She yawned widely and stretched. "I'm off to bed. Emily..." She nudged her sister. "Aren't you going to see Tom?"

"Oh yes!" Emily leapt to her feet and kissed me and Jason. "See you in the morning."

◆

We wouldn't all be able to fit in Lucy's car, so Jason drove. How Lester managed to curl himself into the passenger seat of Lucy's car, I had no idea. Even with the seat all the way back, his knees touched the dashboard and his head brushed the roof. I'd let Lester sit in our front seat. I couldn't imagine him squeezing between the girls with his gangly legs.

Now we knew Lucy's plans, she and Lester were back to their usual selves, laughing and joking, while Emily didn't say much. She'd come back late after meeting up with Tom and each time I saw her and Lucy as we serviced the rooms, she'd yawned. I had no idea whether her quietness related to her news or exhaustion. I had no chance of finding out either. The girls had deployed well-rehearsed strategies since last night to ensure that Emily didn't tell us her news. Not once had I been given the opportunity to say anything other than what needed to be done in the rooms before Lucy butted in with a wag of her finger. Even in the car, the girls had arranged themselves with Lucy in the middle in the back seat, preventing me from quizzing Emily.

Were they keen to be in public when Emily told us, because Jason and I were less likely to be angry in front of other people? Especially a place where Lester would be in charge soon and needed to make a good impression on his staff. It might be a risky strategy, but they knew that Jason and I would never damage someone else's business.

Or would it be exciting news? I hoped so. But I couldn't imagine what.

We'd been queuing for the ferry for the past ten minutes, but the line of cars rumbling past in the other direction, told us it wouldn't be much longer. When a man signalled us forward, Jason steered the car down the slope and we bumped onto the ferry ramp. Soon, the rumble of the engine told us we were on our way and I gazed out of the window, enjoying the view. This would be my first trip to Kingsmouth this year – we hadn't made it to the other side of the river when we'd sailed Shona's yacht back – but no doubt we'd be making this journey more often when Lester and Lucy moved into the pub.

To our left lay the mouth of the river, while on our right the river bustled with pleasure cruisers, yachts and boats of all sizes, some berthed, some slicing through water that sparkled in the glorious sunshine. The ferry reached the other side and we waited in the shade of an old tiled building while the foot passengers disembarked. As Jason pulled away, my stomach lurched. I gazed across at Emily. *Please let it be good news.* To my surprise, Jason found a parking spot within minutes and we clambered out of the stuffy car to be welcomed by a warm breeze. Above the trees rustled, and I could hear a brass band playing faintly in the distance.

Jason popped the parking ticket on the dashboard. "Where now?"

Lester gave an elusive smile and loped ahead. I hoped the pub was a modern building, because he'd have a perpetual stoop otherwise.

We strolled behind him past art galleries displaying huge oil canvases and cafés advertising hog roasts or – a few doors along – quinoa salads. Sparsely laid-out shops for the fashion-conscious with a big bank balance nestled beside stores crammed with clothes rails, while jewellers with watches the price of artwork in the gallery stood next to gift shops selling amber, turquoise and shell trinkets.

We'd turned into a cobbled side street and Lester picked up his pace, taking two steps to every four of mine. He ducked beneath a low porch. I chuckled as Jason, Emily and Tom did the same. This didn't bode well for Lester's future posture.

The smell of food assailed us and a gentle hubbub filled the space. A well-trod parquet floor provided a solid base for the tables, armchairs, cushioned benches and high-backed mahogany seats littered throughout the room. There was not a free seat in sight. A row of bar stools sat on tiles surrounding the gleaming bar area, where people supped their drinks as they leaned against the bar. Paintings of all sizes covered the walls, while brasses had been nailed to the vertical timbers that abutted the gnarled ceiling beams. While old-fashioned, the bar wasn't dreary, thanks to the daylight streaming through the leaded windows.

A woman stood at the bar, drying a glass. Spotting Lester, she put the glass down. "Hello again! Your table is ready."

She led us through to the back of the bar area, where a black beam crossed another squat doorway. At this rate, Lester would have to become adept at limbo.

"What will you be doing here?" I murmured to Lucy.

"Managing everything but the cooking." She covered her mouth and whispered, "We don't want to kill the clientele."

When we sat down at a large round table, I smoothed my hand across the pristine cotton tablecloth. A single crimson rose sat in a small patterned bottle in the centre of the table – a step up from the candlesticks in wax-encrusted bottles of years ago.

After our drink orders were taken, an expectant hush fell over the table.

"Well?" I turned to Emily. I'd waited so long, my patience had to be rewarded soon. A waiter leaned over to put a jug of water on the table, reminding me this might not be the right time with all the people milling about. "Although you don't have to tell us this minute if it's not appropriate."

"We said we'd tell you when we got here. But let's order food first." When Lucy took control, Jason raised an eyebrow, but a smile touched the corners of his mouth.

"Getting into practice for your new management role, are you?"

Lucy frowned, missing his joke, and handed out the menus. Jason and I decided our orders within minutes – curiosity tends to speed up the decision-making process – while Emily ummed while perusing each page. Finally, she put her menu down and folded it shut.

When the waiter left having taken our orders, I turned to Emily. "Is it good or bad?"

She shrugged. "It depends on how you view it."

Lucy clapped her hands together. "I can't hold it in anymore. I'll burst. Emily, tell them!"

Emily's teeth worried her lip and her dark eyes flashed from mine to Jason's before she glanced down. Then she looked up, rewarding us with a sly smile.

"Well. I've got a job. Here in Kingsmouth. I had the interview yesterday afternoon. They phoned to tell me just before I arrived at yours. I'm going to be a hotel receptionist again, but it won't be like last time as Lucy'll be nearby. And Tom and Lester too."

Lucy squealed. "Isn't it amazing!" Blushing, she glanced around at the diners who'd turned to see who'd made the noise. "Sorry, sorry!"

She lowered her voice. "We'll all be near each other."

"But what about your other friends?" I recalled how desperate Emily had been to return to Normansby after our move to Torringham. She'd moved back to live with Lucy soon afterwards.

"When I went back I realised life wasn't better back home. Just different. I missed you and Dad, although it was lovely being with Lucy and my friends. Then, when Lucy kept coming down to see Lester, and I came with her, I found I was building a life for myself here. When I go in a pub now people know me. Tom's been introducing me to loads of people. It's much easier to make friends when you have a starting point."

"Where will you live?"

"Here!" Emily chuckled. "Don't worry. You and Dad won't have to put up with me full-time. Lucy and Lester have got upstairs accommodation."

Lucy clutched her shoulder. "We'd love to have you with us too."

I gazed around at our little family and a lump tightened in my throat. Jason looked dumbstruck, but pleased. He caught me looking at him and his hand searched out mine, giving it a gentle squeeze. Lucy and Emily giggled together, while Lester, his arm hanging over the back of his chair, looked rapt as he surveyed his new home and business. It would be hard work. I didn't need to tell

Lucy and Lester that, especially when they hadn't lived together, let alone worked together. But I had a feeling they'd do well. They had the energy to adapt.

Jason's eyes welled with tears and he swallowed. "I won't tell you what I thought your news might be. Having both of you living here is better than I could have imagined."

"What did you imagine?" Emily asked, then clamped her hand to her mouth. "Oh, you didn't! Why are you old people so hung up on sex?"

"Sex? How does that come into it?" Jason asked.

"Babies," Emily said, as if he was a child.

Their bickering went over my head. I didn't care. I couldn't wish for any more than to have my family with me. When Emily had moved out, I'd missed her so much, but now she'd be back and with Lucy too. My thoughts strayed to Lucy's mum, Marie. She must be feeling the opposite right now. But one day she might choose to move closer to Lucy. We could work around that.

"Waiter!" A man nearby clicked his fingers. "My soup is tepid."

With my gorgeous family living nearby, I could deal with anything. Even demanding guests. I gazed at the rose in the middle of the table. Among the roses of life, we'd always find the odd thorn, as the diner across from us was proving. But troubles were a lot easier to deal with when you had a garden of joy surrounding you.

# About B&Bers Behaving Madly

B&Bers Behaving Madly is the second novel in this series. Although it can be read as a stand-alone, it is the sequel to Bedlam & Breakfast at a Devon Seaside Guesthouse. This featured Katie and Jason's arrival at Flotsam Guesthouse and the issues they encountered with a dilapidated building alongside the stresses of a new business, not forgetting the quirky guests and interesting people they encountered too.

While I am a guesthouse owner, both of my Devon Seaside Guesthouse books are fictional. Thankfully, we have been blessed with lots of amazing and kind-hearted guests, who are nothing like some of the characters featured in this novel. Many of our guests return on a regular basis and I look forward to seeing them. While unusual events occur in a guesthouse – as they do anywhere – most of the stories featured are imagined or taken from snippets I've heard in passing.

Torringham is loosely based on Brixham, a seaside town in South Devon famed for its fishing industry. All the people and businesses featured are fictional, but if you do visit Brixham you will find some of the scenery familiar, including the stunning harbour bowl. South Devon is a gorgeous place to visit.

*A plea!* If you do stay in a hotel or B&B, please **book direct**. B&B owners are couples and families trying to get by, so please fund a small local business rather than giving a substantial percentage of the fee to a global corporate giant, as happens when booking via a third-party. *You'll often get better rates by booking direct too.*

Printed in Great Britain
by Amazon